RITTER'S GOLD

PALMETTO
PUBLISHING
Charleston, SC
www.PalmettoPublishing.com

Copyright © 2024 by Frank N. Hawkins, Jr.

All rights reserved

Excerpts by T. S. Eliot are reprinted by permission of Harcourt Brace Jovanovich, Inc.; copyright 1935, 1936 by Harcourt Brace Jovanovich, Inc.; copyright © 1963, 1964 by T. S. Eliot; also reprinted by permission of Faber and Faber Ltd.

No portion of this book may be reproduced, stored in a retrieval system, or transmitted in any form by any means–electronic, mechanical, photocopy, recording, or other–except for brief quotations in printed reviews, without prior permission of the author.

Hardcover ISBN: 9798822980136
Paperback ISBN: 9798822965928
eBook ISBN: 9798822965935

RITTER'S GOLD

A WINDING ROAD OF BREATHLESS ADVENTURE
PAVED WITH GOLD AND TREACHERY

FRANK N. HAWKINS, JR.

For Inge, of course, and TWB

PART I

APRIL 1941

April is the cruellest month.

—T.S. Eliot

Prologue

The main road was jammed. Greek refugees fleeing south clogged the muddy highway like drenched sheep, men and women of all ages shouldering tattered bundles bulging with as many possessions as they could carry. The fortunate ones trudged silently behind overloaded donkeys braying in protest. Others pulled crude wooden carts while still others wandered along in shocked bewilderment. The general disorder was heightened by fragments of the shattered Greek army bullying their way along the narrow two-lane road. Horse-drawn wagons and columns of men struggled in both directions, roughly pushing the refugees aside to get through. Some units were clearly in retreat, stumbling away from the rapidly advancing enemy. Others moved anxiously forward to retrieve kits and machine guns. Sprinkled among them were disheveled Yugoslav soldiers, dispirited remains of King Peter's former army.

The seething chaos was intensified by a growing sense of disaster that hung menacingly in the damp, gray dusk. It was April 7, 1941, one day into the German invasion of Greece and Yugoslavia.

Corporal James Waddell of His Majesty's First Armoured Brigade shared the chilly front of his truck's cab with Major Charles Coarde and Lieutenant Phillip J. Breckley. The two young officers had come with Waddell's cargo, five heavy, anonymous boxes that made up the entire load. For almost ten hours they'd been driving steadily, ever since they were ordered to move from Edessa to the relative safety of Athens in the wake of the overpowering assault by Von List's Twelfth army. At the temporary headquarters pickup point, Coarde and Breckley helped Waddell load the truck. There were two massive army strongboxes, painted in flat primer gray with coarse Manila hemp handles, so heavy all three men were needed to lift each box into the vehicle. The others were also strongboxes, but of a different type, each about the size of an old English tea chest; they were slightly smaller and lighter than the first two, but it still took all hands to load them. Waddell realized it was highly unusual for officers to get involved in such back-breaking labor, but he said nothing. The load was top priority, they said, and secret. He had been ordered not to discuss it with anyone without the direct permission of Major Coarde.

For miles at a time no one spoke. The rough drone of the six-cylinder engine and the rattle of a loose exhaust pipe was punctuated by the constant squeak of the seats as the truck bounced on the ruts and potholes furrowed into the road. The gray Greek countryside, shivering in the early April chill, steadily darkened as it slipped past. The men kept their eyes on the drab skies, expecting to see a pack of Stukas come blazing out of the skies to strike at any minute. They were thinking of the lightning advances of the German army since the invasion had begun. There was no panic yet, but they realized the cushion of space and time between them and Von List's divisions was narrowing rapidly.

With each wearying mile, the road woved higher into the wintry mountains. There were no road barriers or protective fences. The sheer drops over the side became increasingly threatening and precarious, made even more dangerous by the undisciplined Greek drivers. Driving for many of them was simply leaning on the horn and keeping the accelerator pedal crushed down onto the floorboard.

Eventually Waddell discovered his own horn. It was the only way they seemed to make any sort of progress. But in fact it accomplished little more than adding to the turmoil of frightened, exhausted horses; cursing, overtaxed men; doubtful, worried women; hungry, crying children; sputtering, overheated trucks and other vehicles.

The drawn-out columns of troops and refugees, easy targets from the air, drew repeated strafing runs from the Luftwaffe. Twice in the past hour, as the German planes screamed overhead, the already wet and nervous Britons were forced to steer their truck to the side, leap out, and take cover in muddy ditches. Machine-gun and cannon fire took a deadly toll on the narrow road, where there was virtually no room to hide and no place to run.

Angry bullets splattered indiscriminately, blasting pack animals, Greek troops and their vehicles, and the helpless civilians.

"Here come the bastards again, sir," screamed Waddell. He jerked the wheel of the truck to the left, maneuvering up against the hillside at the edge of the road, providing partial cover. Waddell, Coarde, and Breckley scrambled out into the drizzle and squatted under the side of the vehicle against the hill. The dreadful hammering of the plane's guns momentarily drowned out the pathetic screams and cries of panicked people trapped on the road unable to find shelter. The planes swished overhead only a few hundred feet above. Several of the braver Greeks fired their rifles at the planes in defiance and frustration. A string of bullets spat into two horse-drawn carts of the

Greek Army, slaughtering the horses, ripping the food supplies they carried, and killing two of the men. An old woman farther down the road was killed instantly. Shrieks of agony erupted from those traveling with her as they turned her over in the mud. Up the road a boy was hit in the leg, his thigh bone shattered. As the planes vanished, the three shaken men pulled themselves out of the mire.

"The rotten bastards …" Waddell kept saying over and over to no one in particular.

Coarde brushed off the fresh globs of mud from his wool trousers and his jacket as best he could. Like the others, he was wearing a gas cape over his uniform, a cotton cloak soaked in linseed oil intended as protection against a mustard gas attack. But even with that extra covering, he was drenched through. Never in his life had he felt more uncomfortable or miserable. He sloshed around the truck to see if he could help the Greeks nearest them. The bullets that tore through the cart had missed the truck by only inches. Two men were sprawled dead in the mud, a Greek officer poised over them gazed down helplessly.

"Not much can be done," said Breckley without thinking. Coarde shrugged helplessly and walked up the road to where the boy had been hit. Fifty yards behind, he could hear the wailing of the family of the old woman. A horse making an awful failing whimper went quiet after a single shot. The boy's leg was a mess. An old man, his face strained with anguish, and unmindful of the tears in his ancient eyes, was holding the boy's head in his lap, trying to comfort the youth. Coarde stopped to look at the wound.

"Need a tourniquet to stop the bleeding," he said. Breckley, who had followed Coarde up the road, pulled his gasmask holder off and removed the strap. "Been meaning to chuck this for some time anyhow, sir." He handed the strap to Coarde, who wrapped it around the boy's upper thigh. A Greek medical orderly arrived. Coarde turned the job over to him, and he and Breckley walked back to the truck. "Almost dark. Doubt if the Jerries'll come back tonight. But we're way behind schedule. We certainly aren't going to make Larissa tonight."

"Should be able to reach Ptolemais," said Breckley.

"That's what I was thinking. It can't be more than a mile or two from here. We'll pull in for the night. We could avoid the planes by driving in the dark, but these roads are too dangerous. We'd find ourselves on a one-way roller-coaster ride. Down only."

Breckley sneezed. His nose was starting to run. For the past hour his face had felt very warm. "You don't look so good," said Coarde. "We've all got to dry out a bit. Otherwise we might all die of pneumonia before we ever get to Larissa, much less Athens."

Waddell could not stop his hands from shaking. He had already had enough of war. The noise and violence produced by the planes had scared him badly. He had the growing feeling that he wasn't going to make it. If only the rain would stop. If only he could be warm and dry again. The lieutenant looked like he was coming down with something. A bottle of warm rum would help. Waddell rubbed the back of his hand across his running nose. His black boots were soaked through. It was not just from the mud and water outside. Water was leaking through the rusted metal floor of the unheated cab.

After a nervous bit of coaxing, the motor snorted and started and they lurched forward toward Ptolemais. It was almost nightfall. The planes did not return. The road remained packed with refugees and Greek military units, slowing their progress along the narrow, twisting road. At one point a group was clustered at the edge, where a vehicle of some sort had taken an unwanted and final detour. They didn't stop. Nothing could be done, and Coarde was becoming increasingly anxious about their lack of progress.

Around 2200 hours they crawled into Ptolemais. The village already showed the effects of the new war. The remains of a large building in the village center were still smoldering, and refugees and vehicles were scattered haphazardly throughout the area.

After a short search they found a stone house occupied by a New Zealand unit. The lieutenant in charge said they could bed down on a floor in one of the rooms. It wasn't the Ritz, he admitted, but it was dry. After a meal of stale biscuits, hard chocolate, and goat's cheese provided by the lieutenant, Coarde and Waddell settled down to sleep. Breckley had a light fever, but it was agreed he would take the first watch in the back of the truck with the boxes. He would be relieved after two hours by Waddell, who in turn would be replaced by Coarde for another two hours. Coarde wanted to get going before dawn to take advantage of darkness as well as a hoped-for lessening of the refugee flow at that hour of the morning. A wood fire glowed in the fireplace of the main room of the house, and Coarde and Waddell found themselves using much of their precious rest time to dry out their clothing, particularly their smelly socks. Waddell was already suffering from athlete's foot. The constant moisture in his boots during the past forty-eight hours had begun to painfully rot the skin between his toes.

By the time his watch period arrived, Coarde had napped only an hour. But at least his socks were dry. His once highly polished brown officer's boots were ruined. Even the brass eyelets at the bottom of his trousers, meant to tie the pants legs shut in the event of a gas attack, were caked with mud. But it all mattered little if they could just get the cargo to the warm safety of Athens.

At 0330 hours, only an hour into his watch, Coarde heard the fresh boom of artillery fire. The Germans were launching another predawn assault. The rain had stopped. They were obviously making another attempt to break through the pass. If the rain had stopped, it also meant the Luftwaffe would be in action as soon as it was light.

I'm not going to be too popular around here, Coarde thought as he walked into the house to wake Breckley and Waddell. Neither man was well. Breckley's fever had been high when he came off his watch. He hadn't complained, but he was clearly weakened. As for Waddell, the air attacks had badly unnerved him.

"What's up, guv'ner? I just got to sleep. It ain't the Jerries, is it?" Waddell said.

"They're moving again. We've got to keep ahead of the Germans. That means we've got to get out of here," Coarde said, trying to introduce a reassuring tone into his voice. He roused Breckley, who responded groggily. He was obviously weaker but pulled himself together to leave.

Dawn broke to find the truck inching its way along the slippery winding road out of Ptolemais. As Coarde had predicted, during the predawn and early dawn hours, traffic was considerably lighter. As he also predicted, as soon as it was light, the Luftwaffe reappeared. Two yellow-nosed ME-109s shrieked low over them on their way south but did not attack. Waddell's hands began to shake again. Coarde was not soothed by the fact that the planes didn't open up on them. The next ones probably would.

"They'll be back," he said. "But if we can get onto one of the back roads, maybe they'll leave us alone." Consulting his map, he could see several secondary roads and trails that could barely pass for roads running vaguely parallel to the highway. He directed Waddell toward one of the narrow paths.

When they turned off the main road, however, a fresh hazard presented itself. Ice. The way upward had reached the freezing line, and the rains of the past few days had left the passageways coated with a thin, slick layer. They nudged forward carefully for the next three hours, patiently slipping their way along. The Luftwaffe ignored them, as Coarde had hoped. The absence of the planes eased the strain, but they were all numb with cold. Their bones and fingers ached, particularly Waddell's, from gripping the icy metal steering wheel.

Nevertheless, they were feeling more relaxed as they passed through the village of Ardhassa, when it was suddenly obvious a dreadful miscalculation had been made. Ahead, two dozen vehicles, mostly trucks, had been stopped by a landslide that blocked the road through a small pass.

Coarde jumped out to confer with the driver of one of the British Army vehicles in the jam.

"Bombed it shut, sir," said a sergeant, hiding his hands under his armpits from the cold. He didn't bother to salute. Coarde pretended he didn't notice. "Jerries flew over about two hours ago and blasted the pass. The earth and rocks musta been loose from all the rain. One of the blokes up ahead said the sides of the pass caved in and spilled down onto the road. Luckily one bloke had just got through. Some of the men are trying to dig through, as you can see, sir. But it might take the rest of the day."

We don't even have the rest of the morning, thought Coarde.

He walked briskly back to the truck. "Back it up, Waddell," he snapped. "It's blocked. We can't afford to get stuck here."

Waddell slowly edged the truck down the narrow road for about four hundred yards, looking for a place to turn around.

"Up there. Turn up there," ordered Coarde. His voice had acquired a raspy tone.

"That ain't even a road, sir. It's only a streambed."

"I can see what it is. But it might take us over that rise, and perhaps from there we can get back onto the highway. Anyhow, it's our best chance. Now, get this damned thing moving. If we have to go all the way back we could end up greeting the Jerries."

Waddell dropped the truck into first gear and prodded the vehicle gradually along the bumpy streambed. Snow flurries began to blow around them. For nearly twenty minutes Waddell drove in silence, cautiously inching the vehicle along. Finally he couldn't contain himself. "With respect, sir. I don't think we're going to make it."

"We've got to make it," shouted Coarde. His usual veneer of calm had thoroughly cracked. "Keep moving."

The truck bounced violently. Waddell expected to hear an axle snap. With a sharp jolt the front bumper smashed against a large rock in their path. There was no way over or around it. The truck stalled.

"Jesus," said Coarde softly. He sighed deeply. "Okay, Waddell. Turn it off. Looks as though we've had it."

Breckley, who had said nothing for the past hour, began to laugh uncontrollably, his face dotted with beads of sweat.

"Shut up," Coarde shouted. "Get a hold of yourself, damn you." Breckley looked at him blankly, then quieted.

Coarde sat silently, his mind in a whirl. What to do? What in goddamned hell to do? The truck was inoperable, Breckley too sick to be of any use, Waddell terrified to move. They couldn't just stay where they were. Not with that cargo. Coarde turned to Waddell.

"Corporal, I want you to listen to me carefully. Those boxes we're carrying …" Coarde stopped, braced himself, and went on. "They're filled with gold. The two smaller boxes contain bullion from banks in Thessalonica. It was turned over to the unit about a week ago for safekeeping. The other three boxes are filled with money and gold sovereigns to pay the Greeks, part of a special fund for the Greek underground. We can't let the Jerries get their hands on it. We'll have to hide it, bury it."

Coarde climbed out of the cab and looked around. Snow interspersed with sleet was falling steadily. On the hillside above were several caves that looked like rock sandwiches with some fillings missing. He turned to Waddell. "Come on, we're going to put them up there."

For the next hour Coarde and Waddell, their uniforms drenched, struggled to lug the five boxes up the hill, where they stashed them in a cave about twenty feet deep. Using two hand grenades, Coarde blew shut the entrance. Then the two men piled small stones in front of the opening until it was totally hidden.

Pulling a pad of paper from his jacket pocket, Coarde made a rough sketch of the cave entrance and the caves around it. On another sheet he drew a map, taking a bearing on Mount Siniatsikon, which could barely be seen in the distance through the blowing snow.

"We'll back down the streambed to the road and push the truck over the side," he said. "From there we can make it on foot to the main road and cadge a ride south to get help for Breckley."

He stopped suddenly and looked firmly at Waddell. "Needless to say, Corporal, what you've just learned and taken part in is top secret, and covered by the Official Secrets Act. Any word of this to anybody could net you a long prison stretch. Understand?"

"Yes, sir," Waddell, said. He shivered as he glanced up at the cave again. It looked innocent enough now. Just an ordinary hillside that would never attract the attention of the Germans. Yet there was enough gold there to make a man and his family rich for generations. Undoubtedly, when they finally pushed the Jerries back, the army would come back and get it.

All the way down the hill, and for many years afterward, he wondered how long that would take.

PART II

SEPTEMBER 1943

War among men defiles this world.
—T. S. Eliot

1

The pilot jammed the throttle forward, careening the flimsy Blenheim down the moonlit runway. Swaying clumsily from side to side, the heavily fueled craft hurtled nearly to the end of the concrete strip before the nose lifted hesitantly upward into the warm desert night. The city was soon twinkling below as the plane circled while steadily gaining altitude. Sharply illuminated by the moonlight as the plane passed overhead, the pyramids would be the last familiar landmark before the aircraft returned from the Mediterranean and beyond.

Handed the sealed flight plan only an hour earlier, the pilot still knew little about the mission. The three darkly clothed men in the rear were to be dropped over an area near Edessa in northern Greece. They carried only light weapons, some basic supplies, and of course parachutes. Undoubtedly another sabotage team belonging to Whitehall's hush-hush Special Operations Executive. He'd spoken only briefly with the three when they boarded the craft. Two of them were Yanks. The English lieutenant, however, appeared to be in charge.

The last-minute weather report indicated rough flying over the northern coast of the Mediterranean and all the way over Greece to the target zone. A mixed blessing. Bad weather, particularly at night, was always dangerous. But it greatly reduced the chances of being caught and blasted down by fast-moving German night fighter patrols.

The pilot ambled back into the dark cargo section to check on his three passengers, still trying to make themselves comfortable in the narrow canvas bucket seats. The volatile smell of aviation fuel had nearly evaporated.

"You chaps can smoke now if you wish," he said.

"Thanks," said the English lieutenant, who immediately fished a packet of cigarettes from beneath his dark blue wool sweater. American Lucky Strikes. The pilot hadn't seen one of those in weeks. Must have gotten them from the two Americans.

"Once we get over the water," said the pilot, "it's going to get a bit bumpy. Far as we can tell, there's turbulence over most of Greece tonight. It'll get worse over the mountains, but with luck we'll find a clear spot near the drop zone so you can get down safely."

"Always wanted to leap out at fifteen thousand feet into a raging storm at night," said the younger American. "One of the things I haven't done yet."

"There's a lot of things you haven't done yet, sonny," said the other American. "This jump couldn't be half as dangerous as the one I had to make in Georgetown last year. Second-story window. Husband came home early. Barely had time to get my pants on. No parachutes either."

The pilot chuckled. Usual Yank outrage. Always amusing. "Well, have a pleasant flight, lads. Unfortunately, you'll be flying in the dark. Seems we've blown a fuse, so we have no regular lights back here. Sorry about that. We'll alert you about twenty minutes before drop time. Give you a bit to final check the gear and all that."

"Thanks, Jack," said the younger American.

The English lieutenant, about to light his cigarette, flashed a stern look in the direction of the American but caught himself before speaking. No respect for rank. Typical. The pilot, seemingly unoffended, turned and walked back to the cockpit. He closed the door behind him, leaving the cargo section in virtual darkness.

The flare of the wooden match briefly illuminated Lieutenant Timmy Devan's face. Two small eyes shifted nervously over a bushy handlebar mustache which covered most of his mouth. He briefly saw the two cocky, clean-shaven Americans as he lit the cigarette, which glowed like an orange blip in the blackness. He hadn't been amused when they told him he'd be taking the Yanks along. This part of the world had nothing to do with them. Wasn't their patch. Greece was strictly a British concern. He hadn't lost any time letting them know how he felt. Group told him to mind his own business, reminding him the Americans were helping to finance the operation. He had no choice or say in the matter.

They were the first OSS types he'd met. Not so impressive. Grudgingly he admitted they were first-class physical specimens. But both terribly unmilitary, with a shocking lack of basic discipline. It was a wonder the Americans were able to run any sort of military operations at all.

The older man, an officer, who actually permitted the younger one, an enlisted subordinate, to call him by his nickname, was almost a *Punch* cartoon stereotype—wild, loud-talking, and overfilled with self-confidence. His broad face was as typically American as a cowboy in one of those awful Hollywood films. Women undoubtedly found him attractive.

The younger one, a Sergeant Ritter, was not quite as boisterous but every bit as cheeky. He carried an eternally lighthearted look in his bright blue eyes that said as much about him as anything. He couldn't be more than nineteen, young for a mission as tough and sensitive as this, and obviously inexperienced. God, what had they done to him, sticking him with this pair? These two would have to prove they could hold up their end of things. If they couldn't, he wouldn't be responsible.

The three men dozed uneasily in the clumsily designed bucket seats as the plane glided over the northern Egyptian coast and out over the Mediterranean. The rough vibration and noise of the prop engines competed with energy-sapping high-altitude cold to make them thoroughly uncomfortable. Increasingly, as the plane neared the Greek coast and the outer edges of the turbulence, it began to bounce around, as the pilot had warned.

"Hey, Whip, you awake?" said Ritter, the young American.

"Yeah."

"Remember that crate they brought us across the Atlantic in? At least it had real seats and warm coffee. And lights."

"We aren't flying Pan Am now, sonny. This is the best the Brits can do."

Without warning the Blenheim shook violently, lurching downward several hundred feet. An unexpected air pocket. Only the seat belts hooked around them held them in their places.

Devan, the Englishman, fumbled for another cigarette. In the darkness they couldn't see his trembling hands. His knuckles pressed white against the seat edge. He didn't attempt to speak across the cabin. Even if he had wanted to, he wouldn't have trusted his voice.

"Those weather reports are always right at the wrong time," said Ritter. It was as far as he would go in admitting his own uneasiness in front of Rogers.

"Don't worry, sonny. It means the krauts won't come up after us. We're safer in a storm like this than we would be on a nice clear night. Never hear us or find us in this soup."

Ritter stroked the cold barrel of the M3 submachine gun he clutched across his lap. It was the latest design, and he and Rogers had each been issued one just before leaving the States for Cairo. The thirty-round clip could be emptied in under five seconds giving them an enormous amount of concentrated close-range firepower. The .45-caliber delivered plenty of bite, making the weapon as deadly as any other hand-carried weapon anywhere. But in the air against the weather or planes he couldn't see, it was useless. Rubbing it somehow made him feel better. He had fired the weapon well in training and enjoyed the feeling of power it gave him. He wondered how it would feel to finally use it, to kill with it.

The plane continued to bounce wildly. Ritter's stomach flipped over as he realized the English lieutenant was vomiting onto the floor almost opposite him. He tried to ignore both the retching noise and odor by concentrating on the roar of the engines. The soul-damaging vibration. The chilling cold.

Rogers was speaking to him again over the noise. "That's the guy who's going to lead us to the gold."

"Makes me sick to think about it," said Ritter.

Rogers laughed. "I know how the poor devil feels. My kid brother used to get carsick all the time. He'd puke on the backseat or out the window as we were driving along. Used to piss my mother off.

She'd have to wipe it up. My dad always pretended he hadn't noticed it very much or had to check the engine so he didn't have to get too involved in the cleanup."

"I'm too cold to be sick," said Ritter. "I think my stomach may be frozen solid. We should have brought some of that Cairo heat with us."

"Yeah, they just have to figure out how to bottle it," said Rogers.

"Say, Whip, how do you think we got tabbed for this one?"

"Who knows, sonny? Donovan doesn't exactly confide these things in me. We're just a couple of bodies on his organizational charts, pins on a map somewhere. Donovan and the Brits made a deal to find some gold the Brits lost in Greece, and Donovan wanted to make sure he was represented when the loot was divvied up."

"That's what they said. But there's more, isn't there?"

"There always is, kid. There's always more."

"Well?"

"He wants us to see what these Brits are up to. The Greeks are already at each other's throats, and the Brits are in the middle, unable to keep them apart. Donovan thinks the Brits may be playing politics instead of fighting the Germans. Churchill wants to make sure the monarchists come out on top at the end of the war. Wouldn't be in keeping with the British plan for things if royalty became a casualty. Might give somebody else ideas elsewhere. But the leftist power is growing, and already they are an important fighting force along with the Communists. We need them to fight the krauts. Hell, that's all we care about."

Ritter, just out of high school in San Diego, knew little about politics or Greece. Weren't they all on the same side fighting the Germans? The political quarrels made no sense. He didn't want to get involved in that sort of stuff. That was for the generals and the fat-bellied politicians. The plane bucked violently again. Ritter's stomach dropped and churned uncomfortably. A sour taste invaded his mouth. He concentrated on the noise and constant vibration. The endless cold. He didn't want to puke. Not in front of Whip.

A glimmer of light came from the front. The pilot opened the cockpit door and walked back toward them. He sniffed, noting one of them had been sick. "You chaps okay?"

"Yeah, okay," said the English lieutenant. He hoped the pilot didn't think it was him.

"I wouldn't recommend you as an egg or fine-porcelain hauler," said Rogers. "This thing sounds like it's going to shake apart." Ritter couldn't agree more.

"Been a bit rough," admitted the pilot. He wasn't sure which of them had been sick. "If I'd known you chaps were so sensitive, we'd have tried harder to keep it steady." The sarcasm was thinly veiled. "We're about fifteen minutes from the drop zone. Just passed over the worst of the mountains. Weather ahead looks a bit better. When the red light comes on, you have two minutes. When the green light shows, out you go. You've got to move quickly. We're only going to make one pass over the drop zone. Otherwise the Germans will be able to pinpoint you. As it is, they'll have a pretty fair idea of what's going on. Isn't picture-taking weather, you know. Good luck."

"At least the trip down'll be smoother," said Rogers.

The pilot returned, to the cockpit as the three men began double-checking their harness straps, weapons, and other gear. It was a useful way to soak up some of the last-minute tension that built up before any jump, but particularly one as uncertain and potentially perilous as this one.

Ritter kept running his hands over the M3. It couldn't help him now, but there was nothing else to do.

Rogers untied one of his boots and relaced it. Deciding the other one needed some imaginary adjustment, he loosened it and laced it back up.

Devan discovered he had vomited onto his boots, spoiling the bright military shine he had given them before takeoff. Blasted. He hoped the two Yanks wouldn't notice. He could clean them up after getting down.

The red light flashed on. Devan caught himself as he gagged again. The tension, rough weather, and fear had affected him worse than ever. He'd done too many of these. Once below the silk, he would be all right, he kept telling himself, it was just rough going now.

Ritter and Rogers glanced at each other in the bright red light as they all stood up. Rogers winked. "Always wanted an autumn holiday in Greece, kid."

Ritter offered a small grin. Rogers was more nervous than he cared to admit. It didn't matter. Whip couldn't be more scared than Ritter himself.

The copilot walked back. "One minute," he said. "It's raining out there, but the wind is not as bad as we thought. We've dropped down below the cloud cover to just over three thousand feet. You should be able to see the ground all the way down. There's a signal fire. Good luck." He shoved out his fist, showing them his thumb.

The green light beckoned them. The three shuffled toward the side door as the copilot pushed it open. Attacking his own anxieties, Devan took the initiative, leaping first into the cold wet wind. Rogers followed him, and then Ritter. The mandatory count and then the rip cord. A heart-stopping delay, then the comforting rush of silk as the parachute puffed out and formed the lovely umbrella overhead with a reassuring jerk that grabbed deep in the groin.

It was raining harder than Ritter expected. To one side, as the co-pilot promised, he could see the marker fire as he and the two chutes below drifted toward it.

Above, the Blenheim faded into the cloudy distance, turning back toward the warm comforts and security of Cairo. Who needed it? This was it. He'd waited a long time for this awesome, lonely moment. Finally some real adventure. Some action. And then suddenly he wished it had never come. He could distinctly see flashes. Small-arms fire popped below. Perhaps aimed up at him.

The wet, stony earth rushed up and slammed into Ritter, jarring him thoroughly. Stunned, he fell roughly, bruising his leg and arm on the sharp rocks that covered the clearing. The wind gusted frantically into his still-billowing parachute, threatening to drag him across the treacherous clearing. With a determined effort he fought his way to his feet and charged at the chute, pulling the cords in and finally collapsing it. The sound of small-arms fire was now only sporadic. He rubbed his hand across his water-streaked face, trying to clear his eyes. The rain was steady. He was already drenched. And cold. He estimated he had landed about eight hundred yards from the fire, which he could just see over the edge of a small rise. No sign of Rogers or the English lieutenant.

Rifle shots about one hundred yards to one side in a clump of trees and heavy underbrush startled him. Crouching quickly, he began to untwist the M3 and its strap from around his body. A scraping sound behind him. He pivoted. Too late. A dark figure leaped at him, jamming him back onto the stony ground, knocking the wind out of him. The strap of the M3 was partially caught over his right shoulder and arm, restricting his movements. His fast-moving attacker pinned his left arm, shoving a forearm against his throat. Struggling to get at least one arm free, Ritter managed to wiggle his right hand down to the broad-bladed knife strapped to his boot. The pressure on his throat persisted, but finally he reached the knife, yanking it free with a single fluid motion. He made a desperate move to bring it around into the back of his attacker. Without warning a sharp painful rap against his hand and wrist broke his grip on the knife, which clattered onto a stone. There was another harsh blow, then blackness.

No sound except the wind. The cold rain. An awful ache in the back of his head and eyes. Sharp searing sensations in his hand. Pain. He was alive. He slowly opened his eyes, rubbing the throbbing knot on his head. No blood. Skin not broken. Two dark figures loomed over him. He was shaking badly. It wasn't just the wet cold. The large, stockier one was pointing a rifle at him. Ritter carefully edged his hand down to his boot to confirm what he knew. The knife was gone. So was the M3. No sign of Rogers or Devan. The sound of gunfire had stopped. Fantastic. Two seconds on the ground and he was already a prisoner. Some commando. What would Rogers say?

The man with the rifle spoke, a strange guttural sound.

"I only speak English," said Ritter.

"English?" said the other. The voice stunned him. Wildly out of place. It was the voice of a girl. "You are English?" she said.

"Californian."

"America?"

"As apple pie," he said wearily.

The girl spoke to the man in Greek and turned to Ritter. "I am sorry," she said. It almost sounded as if she meant it. Her accent was strong but not unpleasant. "We did not know you were Americans. The Germans have been dropping agents into the hills around here."

"Who was doing the shooting?" Ritter rubbed his temples, trying to neutralize the distracting ache.

"We were."

"At us?"

"Bandits."

"Bandits?"

"Reactionaries. EDES. We followed them out here tonight and watched them light the fire. We heard the plane. Then the shooting started. We saw you coming down. We assumed you were Germans."

"Christ, Alice."

"Alice?"

"A friend of mine with a pet white rabbit and lots of interesting friends."

"I don't understand."

"Doesn't matter. Mind if I get up?"

"Oh, I am so sorry. Please let me help."

"Don't bother." Ritter climbed slowly to his feet. The chill of the wet predawn cold was soaking into his bones. His head ached badly. His arms and legs were sore from the landing and subsequent fall. His right hand also hurt—two fingers were badly bruised. He thought briefly of the warm rolling surf in San Diego. The girls. The bronzing sun. This was madness.

They walked about a half-mile before he saw the dying fire, sizzling in the steady drizzle. A group of about ten figures clustered around, absorbing as much of the diminishing warmth as they could collect. Shadows danced wildly across them as they held out their palms toward the flickering embers. He could now make out Rogers and Devan among the craggy-faced Greek mountain men. The two appeared to be unharmed, enjoying the fire with the others. Even from a distance the Greeks looked tough. In other times they were peaceful farmers and shepherds, hardworking men who spent their entire lives quietly in the outdoors with their crops and sheep. Now they were partisans, guerrillas banded together in the fight against a common enemy. The girl shouted at the group in Greek. He understood her to make some reference to Americans.

Rogers and Devan, he suddenly realized, were arguing. "You Brits are great organizers, Devan."

"Don't be stupid, Rogers. These are Communists. They obviously chased off the people we were supposed to meet."

"What the hell difference does it make? They're Greeks, aren't they? They're fighting the krauts, aren't they?"

"God, you Yanks are naive," Devan shouted. His mustache quivered with indignation. Why in God's name had they stuck him with these clumsy clods?

With a mixture of amusement and bewilderment, the large Greek in baggy black trousers who appeared to be in charge watched Rogers and Devan argue. He also was eyeing Rogers' M3 and Devan's Sten. Ritter noticed the Greeks carried bolt-action rifles that were out-of-date at least one war ago. The man nodded at the girl.

"We cannot stay here any longer," she said. She was apparently the only one among the Greeks who spoke English. "It is not safe. We must go now. It will be dawn soon."

"You don't have much choice, Devan," said Rogers. "Unless of course you're going to hang around out here in the rain and wait for your unseen friends to come back, or maybe win the war all by yourself."

Devan glowered at him. "Just remember who's in charge here, Rogers. This is a British show."

They moved out, with the big Greek leading the group.

"Welcome to Greece, sonny," said Rogers. "What happened to you? You look awful."

Ritter told him, then asked, "What are you guys arguing about anyway?"

"Politics, kid. The Greeks are badly split between those who support the return of the king and those who want to set up a socialist democracy at the end of the war. There have been shooting incidents and killings between the two sides. Some people think there could be a civil war when this is all over. Devan and the Brits thought they had arranged for us to be met by EDES, the pro-monarchy group. But apparently this bunch turned up and chased them off. So we are now with leftist partisans instead of the royalists. Devan's upset because he's supposed to be liaisoning with and helping the monarchists. The gold is supposed to go to them. He doesn't want anything to do with these people."

"But what about the Germans?"

"Both groups are supposedly fighting the krauts in a common effort. But between you and me, kid, they are much more worried about each other. They figure either the Brits or the Americans will eventually run the krauts out for them. Then the real fighting can begin."

They walked for more than an hour along a series of ridges through pine forests and around small sleeping villages. As the rain stopped, the black sky gradually turned gray and then split wide open with a magnificent burst of orange fire.

"You like our Greek sunrise?"

The girl had stepped up beside him. In the warm morning light, he could see her face for the first time. Her dark eyes were round and surprisingly soft, even compelling. Her muddy, loose-fitting dark trousers and jacket could not hide her youthful figure. She walked with the kind of athletic grace that cannot be learned. He felt himself softening toward her. He nodded.

"You are not mad at me?"

"Mad?"

"For knocking you down."

"You came damned close to adding a steel rib."

She laughed, the warmest sound he had heard all morning. "You mean the knife?"

"I don't think you would have found it so funny."

"How is it you Americans say? All is well that stops well."

"Yeah, I guess. No blood. No tears."

The girl looked at him again. She liked what she saw. Ritter was fair-haired, with the beautiful tanned skin Europeans acquire in the summer. His blue eyes sparkled despite his obvious weariness and discomfort, a great contrast with the dull dark-eyed men in her village. Ritter had a casual, dashing air about him. He was obviously his own man. She liked Americans. She certainly liked this one.

"What is your name?" she said.

"Brian, Brian Ritter…. And who are you?"

"Melanie Thouriakis."

"What are you doing out here?"

She seemed annoyed by the question. "Fighting the Germans. And the EDES."

"You should be in school, learning to cook or something."

"I am eighteen," she replied indignantly. "My country needs me."

"It's the fashion these days."

"The fashion?"

"Never mind. Where are we going?"

"Sssssssst." A sharp warning sound sliced through the morning freshness. They hurled themselves onto the ground. A motorized patrol cruised deliberately along the dirt road about 150 yards below them. A Wehrmacht officer with binoculars was scanning the hillside, obviously searching for something. The officer swept the glasses in their direction. At first he appeared to pass the glasses over their position but suddenly he swing back. The patrol stopped.

The big Greek stood up and walked down the hillside toward the Germans. He had decided to brave it out, convince the Germans he was a lone shepherd in the hills. The officer dropped the binoculars to watch the man make his way down through the scrub to the scout car. There were three cars, each filled with about five gray-uniformed men, all pointing their weapons at the Greek.

Ritter had no idea who started the shooting, but it could only be defined as murder. The old Greek caught between the two sides never had a chance. The Germans, although armed with automatic Schmeissers, had little cover and quickly collapsed under the sudden unexpected assault of concentrated fire from the group on the hill. Ritter hesitated slightly before starting to shoot. He finally opened fire, with the sound of Rogers' M3 chattering in his ear. The confused Germans tried to jump to safety behind their vehicles, but the volume of firepower was too much for them. One of the vehicles exploded and started to burn. The fight ended quickly.

Cautiously, they made their way down the hillside to the decimated patrol. The girl was beside Ritter, carrying the Enfield she had been firing.

He had never seen a German before. He stared with fascination at the lifeless, bloodied bodies at his feet, mostly fresh-faced young men who would not have been out of place on the San Diego beaches. He had never seen anyone die before. It was an odd, disquieting feeling, not particularly pleasant. As he watched the Greeks loot the German bodies, one of them stirred, raising a pistol toward the girl. "Melanie," Ritter shouted. He swung his M3 and fired. Click. Empty. Without thinking he lunged at the German. The movement distracted the man, who swung his Luger toward Ritter and fired just as Ritter slammed into him. A loud blast. A searing sensation burned through him. For the second time that morning, Ritter was plunged into painful darkness.

2

He was conscious of something vaguely familiar. Something comforting. An odor. The same hospitable smell he had known years ago in the warm security of his grandfather's north Arizona cabin. Woodsmoke. But somehow different. The accompanying smell of tobacco was more aromatic, slightly sweeter than the stuff his grandfather smoked in his oddly shaped briar pipe. There were other smells, essences he couldn't identify, more pungent but curiously agreeable. Goats' hair, milk, garlic, curds, unwashed wool clothing, aged damp wood, and least definable of all, centuries of Greek history soaked into the walls and timbered floor.

The pain returned with his awareness. From the base of his skull it gnawed all the way over to the back of his eyeballs, a cruel monster trying to destroy the inside walls of his head. He partially remembered now. He'd taken a bad bump when he was attacked after landing. But there was something later. The recollections were surfacing slowly, dredged up from some remote uncontrollable area. Something during the attack on the Germans. An explosion in his ear. His hand moved awkwardly to his head. A bandage. He squeezed open his eyes. Dark. No, not entirely. Light to one side, flickering in a fireplace. He tried to focus on the scene. Too much. He closed his eyes again.

"You almost bought the farm, kid." He knew the voice. Only one person could make such a wonderfully dumb comment.

Ritter forced opened his eyes again. It was Rogers, hovering over him, grinning like he had lost his mind or recovered a friend.

"Couldn't have been much closer," Rogers was saying. "Looks like you're going to make it. It's the advantage of having concrete instead of brains."

Ritter groaned and closed his eyes. Maybe Rogers would take the hint.

"Hey, Melody," he could hear Rogers saying, strangely detached and distant, almost unrelated. "Looks like lover boy here is coming around."

Ritter opened his eyes again as the girl bent over him, wiping his face carefully with a warm moist cloth. "Something to drink?" she was asking.

Ritter wanted to nod. The effort was too painful. "Water," he whispered.

She got up and quickly brought back a crudely made tin cup of cold spring water. Placing a soft hand gently behind his head, she raised him slightly and put the cup to his lips. It had a curious metallic taste. The cool, clean sensation in his mouth followed through to his parched throat. He hadn't realized how thirsty he was.

"Not too much," she said. "Not yet."

What did she know? She wasn't the one who was thirsty. But he was too weary to argue. She moved him slowly back to his pillow, and he fell asleep.

* * *

Two days later Ritter was able to get up for the first time and make his own way out to the smelly little house in the back. The oppressive headache that threatened to paralyze him was receding. He was able to focus his eyes without effort now.

The charred wall above the fireplace where he'd lain testified to the age of the farmhouse. It had been at least several years since the walls had been whitewashed. A thatch roof covered the large open room that served as a combination living-dining-and-bedroom. A black curtain covered the single window near the front door. Rogers and Devan had disappeared, leaving Ritter totally in the care of the girl who had eagerly adopted him. She had been sleeping on a mat on the floor near his bed, a fact that flattered as well as aroused him.

"Where are they?" he asked.

She shrugged. She didn't miss them.

He fingered the bandage, a surprisingly professional dressing. "How did I get here?"

"We carried you. At first we thought the Germans had killed you. Your head was bleeding and you did not move. But the Englishman shot the German before he could shoot you again."

"Devan saved me, huh?"

"You don't like this Englishman, do you? I don't think your loud friend does either."

"Ah, he's okay, I guess. Just don't know him very well. I don't think he really wanted us to come along."

"He does not like us. I don't think he trusts Andropolous. Andropolous will not trust him."

"Who's Andropolous?"

"The leader in this area. He is very important. He is fighting not only the Germans but also for Greek democracy." She was obviously making references to the leftists Rogers talked about.

For the rest of the day Ritter rested in the large main room of the farmhouse. The girl was never very far from him, responding to every movement or need.

"Someday I want to go," she said. "To California. What is it like?"

He wasn't sure what to tell her. Finally he spoke of the beaches, the deserts, the majestic mountains, and the fertile green valleys. The coastal highway to Monterey and Big Sur. San Diego, San Francisco, and L.A. Hollywood. She hung on every word. He enjoyed his own stories. They produced nostalgia, but curiously no homesickness.

During the day a number of people wandered in. They would glance at him, sometimes smiling or making a polite bow in his direction. An old woman dressed from head to foot in black worked endlessly in the kitchen, just off the main room. The old crone smiled toothlessly when she brought him food but did not speak beyond an unintelligible grunt in reply to his thanks.

Ritter kept worrying about Devan and Rogers. They obviously couldn't hang around, waiting for him while the war went on.

A distant out-of-place rumble interrupted the stillness. Cars. The girl was instantly on her feet. She scurried to the window, drawing the curtain back slightly. "Germans," she whispered.

Ritter reached for his M3. He was in no condition to run. "House-to-house search," she hissed. She grabbed Ritter's hand and pulled him toward the fireplace. "Here," she pointed, indicating he should lie down. She quickly covered him with a blanket, then something heavier. He realized she was stacking wood over him.

A loud rap at the door. The muffled sounds reaching him indicated two or three men in hobnail boots. They crashed around for a few minutes, coming near him several times. Tension exploded in his throat. A sneeze was building. He tried to stop breathing. Then silence. His instincts told him not to move. A distant sound of engines cranking up. He could sense the wood being removed. He sneezed violently. The dust was too much. She laughed in relief at his timing.

After an evening meal of lamb cooked over a spit in the large open fireplace, he fell asleep thinking about the Germans, the San Diego beaches, and the willing, eager eyes of the girl. She was obviously interested.

"How do you do it, kid?" he heard Rogers saying. Ritter opened his eyes to find Rogers standing beside the bed. He sat up.

"You're looking better than I expected. How you feeling?"

"Okay, Whip."

"These people think you're a hero. They know you saved Melody's life by risking your own. She is the daughter of a well-to-do Edessa merchant who has been backing the leftists. This is apparently their farm. But be careful, sonny. You don't want to get involved."

"Anything you say, preacher." Ritter smiled. "Where've you been? Where's Devan? What's going on?"

"Easy, easy. One at a time. Devan has made contact with the monarchists at Kilkis, trying to arrange some sort of reconciliation between the two factions in this area. He talked to Cairo on the radio and they've given additional orders. He's set up a meeting for sometime next week. In the meantime, he wants to go out and look for the gold shipment the Brits lost. Think you can make it?"

"Yeah, Whip. No sweat."

"You're lying kid. But I can't leave you here any longer. The krauts have come through once, they'll come through again. They have patrols out everywhere trying to find us. They were pretty upset about us knocking off their bunch. They burned the village where it happened and shot a couple of local shepherds in reprisal. If you can walk, we're taking you out. I've convinced Devan to wait until tomorrow morning. Give you another night's sleep."

Rogers curled up in a blanket near the fireplace. A fat log thrown on the fire just before they turned in burned all night. At dawn the ashes still glowed as Rogers woke Ritter. "Okay, sunshine. Your holiday is over."

Melanie also was up. "You're going?" It was not really a question.

"My general commands." Ritter smiled.

"I will go with you."

"Sorry," said Rogers. "Not this time."

Ritter glanced at Rogers in brief appeal. "Devan says no," said Rogers firmly.

She wanted to argue but knew it was useless. Her lower lip signaled her open disappointment. As they gathered their gear, she gave Ritter an old wool cap to pull over his head to conceal the bandage. Impulsively she grabbed Ritter's hand, leaned forward, and kissed him on the side of the face. He wanted to grab her and kiss her properly, but the time wasn't right. He settled for an encouraging wink—a signal they shared some marvelous secret. Her responding glance released a wave of expectation through him. A definite promise.

She was still standing in the doorway when they reached the ridge top and descended into the neighboring valley. As they crossed the ridge, a German patrol drove into the village below.

"We could have taken her, Whip," said Ritter.

"Devan wouldn't tolerate it. She's with the Communists. He's afraid if we locate the gold, she'd tell the leftists where it is. The Brits want it all to go to the monarchists."

"If we find it."

"If we find it," echoed Rogers.

* * *

They found Devan waiting in a small village farmhouse with a chubby middle-aged Greek, apparently a guide assigned by EDES.

Devan greeted them stiffly. "Hello, Rogers. Sergeant Ritter. Glad to see you on your feet again."

"Thanks to you, I gather."

"Not at all, Sergeant." Turning to the Greek, he introduced the man. "This is Milo."

"Hiya, chief," said Milo brightly. Devan grimaced at the Greek's obvious American accent. "Where you boys from? I lived twenty years in Brooklyn. Finally deported when they decided I was an illegal immigrant."

Rogers laughed, the kind of laugh that usually swept others along with it. "All this way out to East Jesus to find a Fulton Fish Market exile."

Milo didn't understand. "Vegetables, chief. My uncle owns a vegetable store near the fish market." Rogers was still laughing. The thought of Devan stuck with a Brooklyn Greek was too good to be real.

The Greek was the proud owner of an ancient Dodge pickup he used to haul farm products to Athens and other points in the south.

"Despite the petrol rationing," said Devan, trying to return a note of seriousness to the conversation, "Milo has ways of getting fuel. Also, as part of the food-delivery system to the German high command, he has a pass that will take the pickup through German checkpoints."

"What about us?" said Rogers.

"Milo knows the system well, and the Germans know him. If we move at certain periods over certain routes, there is a good chance of avoiding the known checks. There are not enough Germans in this part of the mountains to control anything but the larger towns."

"If we're stopped, we can always hide under the turnips," said Ritter.

"Where are we going?" Rogers asked.

"Ptolemais," Devan said. "The truck carrying the gold shipment was last seen there by a New Zealand unit. It never reached the checkpoint at Kozani, so we must assume it disappeared between those two places."

"What about those in charge of the shipment? The driver? Guards?"

"The records are incomplete," said Devan. "In the haste of the general retreat, brigade records were either partially lost or improperly handled. We know there were two officers and an NCO. Unfortunately, both officers are now dead. They were killed before a proper search could be established. The enlisted man has disappeared. The records don't even show who he was. One of the officers signed for the shipment. The name of the enlisted man was never entered in any of the surviving records. It's a blank."

"What do they think happened to the gold?"

"Best guess is the three men got stuck in refugee traffic and were burned out by German planes, or maybe they had an accident and had to abandon the truck."

"You really don't know what happened to this stuff, do you?" said Rogers. "How are you going to look for it? This war won't last long enough for you to search under every bush and rock in northern Greece."

"We'll survey the basic route and see what we can find. Look for abandoned or wrecked army vehicles. We can ask around and see if any of the locals have information that would help."

"The odds of finding this gold are roughly the same as finding the good fairy," said Rogers.

"That's not your concern, Lieutenant," grumbled Devan, unhappy with the implied criticism.

"Another Brit in search of never-never land," Rogers said softly to Ritter. "Rampant Peter Panism."

Devan pretended he didn't hear. He had his orders. It didn't matter what the insolent Yank thought. They badly needed the gold to finance EDES operations and to give the rightists a financial boost over the Communists.

Milo pulled up in his shabby orange pickup. "Okay, you guys, let's haul ass," he said. The vehicle looked like it was already ten thousand miles beyond its limit, but in a war, one couldn't be too choosy.

"My uncle drives a Caddy," said Milo. "Little snazzier than this heap. But I manage to keep it glued together. Never let me down yet. Hop in, you guys."

Devan winced visibly and crawled into the front cab with Milo. He was obviously not excited by the prospect of spending several hours talking nonstop with the irrepressible Greek.

Rogers and Ritter settled into the back. It was half-filled with lettuce heads. "Guess this is what will be known as my salad days," said Ritter.

"You're obviously feeling better, kid. Hope you can stand all this. The lettuce head in the front is leading us off into a real weed patch. But what the hell. We got nothing else better to do."

"Except stay alive."

"Look who's talking. You don't seem to be trying overly hard, kid. By the way, I think that girl Melody's sweet on you."

"Her name is Melanie," said Ritter slightly defensively.

"She's definitely got her eye on you," said Rogers, ignoring the correction. "Don't see why she should find a kid like you any more … ah, interesting than a seasoned stud like myself."

"Musta heard you're married, Whip."

"Yeah, that must be it. You didn't tell her, did you, kid?"

The pickup jolted along the dirt roads for several hours, hitting every possible pothole and crater. They passed through a number of villages without encountering any Germans, and Ritter wondered how the Wehrmacht could control the area, being so conspicuously absent.

The rough movement and constant bouncing were exhausting. Ritter could feel his headache crawling back behind his eyes. Rogers leaned against the lettuce heads and dozed.

At dusk they pulled into a village where Milo appeared to know everyone. After a brief discussion with a sharp-eyed local elder, they were taken into one of the farmhouses, fed, and given places near the fire for the night.

"It ain't the Waldorf, boys," said Milo. "But ya can't beat the price."

At dawn they were awakened by the lean-faced old man, and after a cold-water shave and a breakfast of warm mountain bread, drove out to the two-lane road running between Ptolemais and Kozani. Ritter was feeling better after another night's sleep. He could feel his strength and confidence gradually returning.

They drove along the road for less than ten minutes before finding the first truck skeleton. The vehicle had obviously been damaged in an explosion and burned. But the significance of the find was quickly dissipated by a close inspection. The wreckage had been given a thorough going-over by scavengers. Everything that could be pulled away from the frame—including wiring, the engine block, and the axles—had been.

"Picked clean," said Rogers. "I have a funny feeling about your shipment, Devan. If it was left behind on something like this, we aren't going to find it."

Devan said nothing. They continued along the highway, stopping at more than twenty rusting, burned-out wrecks. In each case, the story was the same. At the end of the day they were back at the old man's farmhouse.

"Impossible," muttered Devan.

"That gold was absorbed into the local economy well over a year ago," said Rogers. "I doubt if you'll get any Greeks to step forward to offer it to the monarchist war effort."

* * *

Four days and several dozen burned-out vehicles later, Devan gave up.

They returned to the small village of Kali shortly after dark.

Melanie came to the door. "Brian," she shouted, more exuberantly than she perhaps intended. She greeted Rogers and Devan, who had left Milo in a neighboring village. Milo hadn't wanted to venture into such a leftist stronghold.

"Andropolous is here," she said. "He has been waiting for you."

Andropolous was an enormously sturdy man, just over six feet, tall for a Greek, commanding attention with a powerful, confident voice and an overwhelming sense of presence. He was the kind of man who inevitably dominated any situation.

He was the first Greek Ritter had met who didn't look silly in the baggy peasant trousers the mountain men wore. Andropolous wouldn't look silly wearing anything. Beautiful white teeth flashed under a bushy black mustache and against his swarthy complexion, evidence of the years he had spent in the mountains.

"I am sorry I was not here to receive you earlier," he said, extending his strong right hand. "I gather you had a rather dramatic arrival. We are very pleased to welcome representatives of our great allies."

He motioned them to join him around the fire, which blazed cheerily. Melanie produced glasses of bitter-tasting retsina wine and took a spot beside Ritter. The old crone in the kitchen brought lamb for them to eat. Delicious. Ritter had not enjoyed a meal so much since leaving Cairo.

"I must apologize again for the circumstances surrounding your arrival," said Andropolous. "Unfortunately, EDES refuses to share or cooperate with us. They did not tell us you were coming. In the past few months German agents have dropped into the hills here to spy on our groups and damage our operations. If they had only told us it was you, the reception would have been much different. Much trouble would have been spared."

"We are frankly not pleased by this," said Devan. "His Majesty's government supports a united Greece that will fight the Germans. This is no time for civil strife. The job is to throw the Hun out. If you remain divided, it can't be accomplished."

"I fully agree. But we must also protect ourselves. It is a basic matter of survival, for Greece and for our movement. The EDES refuses us funds or weapons. Last month they murdered one of our men during a mission to Athens. There was no need to kill this man. This is an act that must be answered for. We must have revenge."

"I heard about that," said Devan, aggravated that he was being drawn into a pointless discussion he didn't want and couldn't control. "EDES said the killing was a personal act, not a political one. They claim the man had been involved in the shooting of one of their own a week or so earlier."

"A lie. Typical of the way EDES distorts the truth to suit their own selfish needs."

"We can't solve this tonight," said Devan. "But I urge you to put this behind you. If you let these incidents grow, there will be more killing. Who will benefit? You? EDES? The Allies? No. Only the Germans. Is that what you want? Do you want the Germans on Greek soil forever?"

Andropolous breathed in deeply. "We are in a position not unlike you Americans before your revolution," he said, turning his appeal momentarily to Rogers and Ritter. "But we are not only under the yoke of a foreign power, but also of a monarchy we do not want. Tyranny is corrupting our land, the very land where democracy first flourished. The time has come for the Greek people to rise up and restore the democratic system to our homeland. The monarchists are interested only in holding on to their own narrow power. The king means favors and riches for a privileged few. We want to open the society as you Americans have done to all classes."

Rogers and Ritter were openly intrigued. If they were meant to be impressed, swayed to Andropolous' side, they were.

Devan was not just unimpressed, he was disgusted. For him, it was empty talk. He made little attempt to disguise his feelings. He could see the Greek was getting through to the Americans and that irritated him further. Communists never hesitated to use fancy words when it suited their aims. In the end it always came back to the same thing—dictatorship run by a party elite where individual workers had far fewer rights than in any European kingdom. These Americans were too naive to understand.

The argument between Andropolous and Devan continued for more than an hour. Ritter's attention wandered dramatically when he realized the warm feeling on his leg was Melanie's hand. He stole a glance at her. She was looking down toward the floor as though she was deep in thought following the debate, but the trace of a shy smile on her lips confirmed that talk was the furthest thing from her mind. He slipped his own hand over hers. She wiggled her fingers in response.

"All right," Andropolous was saying. "I will attend the meeting. We will cooperate in the attack on the train. We will show you we are not opposed to doing our part. We favor cooperation. But we demand to be treated equally, and the next drop of weapons and munitions and money must be divided fairly with us."

"That depends on how much you are willing to cooperate," said Devan. "It's late. I have much to do tomorrow. I'm turning in."

Ritter felt Melaine squeeze his hand again. He knew he wouldn't get any sleep.

As soon as the sound of snoring drifted over from Andropolous, she was beside him. She placed her index finger on her lips and motioned him to follow her. They made their way quietly through the kitchen area out a rear door into the crisp cool night.

They silently walked to the barn less than fifty yards behind the house. It was filled with freshly cut hay stocked for the coming winter.

Melanie was wearing a rough brown dress that hung loosely over her body. As they entered the barn, Ritter drew her close and pulled her face to his. Kissing her, he moved his hand onto the upper part of her dress. Fumbling with the buttons, he opened them and slipped his hand over her bare breasts. They were firm with youth and excitement. She awkwardly pushed herself against him, frantically biting his lips and tongue. They sank into the warm, soft hay together.

She writhed and twisted beneath him, yielding to his every move. Ritter had scored many times with the beach girls in San Diego, but never with a girl so ferociously passionate as this one.

Afterward, she nestled against him as he played with the delicate cross around her neck. It was a beautiful artifact, exquisitely crafted with the highest-quality silver.

"Brian?"

"Hmmm?"

"Did you like it?" she asked anxiously.

"Very much."

"You are not angry?"

"Angry?"

"It was the first time for me."

"I know."

She blushed. "I love you," she said.

Ritter was not prepared for this. "I love you too," he said. It seemed like the right thing to say.

3

After his long talk with Andropolous, Devan left Edessa with Rogers to meet with the monarchists at their stronghold in Kilkis. Ritter, still recuperating from his head wound, was left behind in Melanie's care. Andropolous watched the young couple with tolerant amusement.

He liked Americans. They were open and forthright. Their humor was rough and earthy. Of course, they were a little naïve. They understood nothing about Greece or Greek politics. But eventually they could be useful, not just with the British, but also in Washington. One of these days he would need contacts. It was good to begin cultivating them now.

Planning for the raid had gone well. Those selected were alerted and prepared. Two days before the raid, Andropolous had sent Donas, the second son of a shepherd in his village, to Thessalonica. Late in the afternoon, when the youth did not reappear, he began to feel uneasy. Donas had been due back in the middle of the afternoon. By nightfall, he still wasn't back.

Melanie thought the boy had probably been delayed by a German patrol. It was possible, Andropolous said, but he didn't feel right about it. He was suspicious because he knew that by now the monarchists had probably learned from Lieutenant Devan where he would be operating while readying the attack.

After a meal of bread and hummus, they sprawled out before a comforting wood fire. Andropolous told stories about his days in the mountains, his adventures against the Germans, and about his wife and children in Thessalonica. Ritter told them of Cairo and about the new fad of riding the ocean waves on a board in San Diego. Andropolous listened politely, laughing at the right moments. But he was having trouble concentrating on the conversation. He grew distracted, and they mutually agreed to turn in early.

They all heard the noise around midnight. A single vehicle, probably a car, drove into the village, turned around, and drove out the way it came, from the east. These days one never heard vehicles drive into the village at night, particularly never heard them reverse direction in the street. Perhaps someone was lost, or maybe a late-night German patrol was turning around at a preassigned place. When there was no other noise, people went back to sleep.

Except Andropolous. When he awoke, the glow from the fireplace revealed the girl and the young American were missing. He laughed to himself. They were young, in love, enjoying each other. He had known such times himself not so long ago. He wouldn't spoil theirs. He also wouldn't do anything to embarrass the daughter of a key supporter of the movement. She was old enough to know her own heart on these things.

Ritter and Melanie also heard the vehicle, but they did not let it interrupt their lovemaking. It was the fifth night they had stolen out to share their bodies, and only once did Melanie express apprehensions about Andropolous awakening and noticing their absence. "He is a good friend of my father," she said, "but I don't think he would say anything." Ritter never worried about it at all.

Just before dawn, having slept briefly in each other's arms, they moved quietly back into the house. Andropolous was snoring peacefully.

An agonizing scream shattered the stillness just as they returned to their separate beds in the main room. A hideous chilling shriek that sliced its way into Ritter's soul.

Andropolous was quickly on his feet pulling on his heavy leather boots. Ritter rolled onto the timber floor, grabbing for his M3. He and Andropolous both scrambled for the door.

The night was just breaking up. A chilly gray cast already was in the sky, pushing aside the predawn blackness.

Another awful scream cut the air as Andropolous and Ritter dashed into the cold. An old woman, up early to begin the day's chores, rocked back and forth over a dark form in the road three or four houses down. Ritter and Andropolous ran toward her. She was convulsed in uncontrollable sobs.

Andropolous was horrified but not surprised. Ritter was simply sickened. It was the young messenger Donas. Or what was left of him. Among other things, his tongue had been cut out of his mouth.

Quivering, swinging his arms in anger and grief, Andropolous stared at the mutilated corpse. Fighting back tears of rage, he slipped off his jacket to put it over the body. Ritter, seeing Melanie approaching, turned back to head her off. She was not to see this.

"What is it?" she said, rushing toward him.

"Get back," he barked.

"What?"

"I said get back." He ran at her, roughly intercepting her, turning her around.

"What … ?" She glanced back just as Andropolous placed the jacket over the body, but not before catching a glimpse of the corpse. She gasped in horror. "Oh, no …"

Andropolous knelt, weeping over the boy's body, muttering something that sounded to Ritter like "Voko."

* * *

The British Special Operations Executive first began dropping sabotage teams with weapons and radios into Greece in the fall of 1942. The Germans were annoyed and often inconvenienced by this behind-the-lines activity, but the threat it posed never reached much beyond harassment because of the limited amount of men and materials the British could spare for such operations.

In some ways the overall SOE activity in Greece had less to do with the war effort than the country's postwar future. Prime Minister Churchill and ranking members of the Foreign Office were determined to preserve the throne of the exiled King George, who just happened to be the grandson of British Queen Victoria. Thus, as a matter of basic policy, SOE teams were expected to favor the royalists. In some respects, this policy got off to a slow start because the original British SOE commander tried to remain neutral in the Greek political struggle, thus coming under strong attack by both sides who felt the British were not playing fair. This resulted in his eventual replacement by the son of a British baron fully in tune with Churchill's thinking—the monarchy had to be restored after the war. It was no coincidence that most of the materials and radios the

British dropped into Greece ended up in the hands of EDES and the monarchists.

The radio at Kilkis had arrived during the spring of 1943 and was used in setting up and coordinating the late-September arrival of Devan, Rogers, and Ritter. It also was subsequently used by Devan in contacting Cairo to report their failure to locate the missing gold. Cairo reacted calmly. There was obviously little hope of finding the money now. The wrecks of the British army vehicles had all been thoroughly looted and picked apart. It was impossible to imagine boxes of gold still lying around this long after their disappearance. Cairo said the matter would have to be further studied and analyzed.

Then they transmitted Ops Order G-5786, the go-ahead for the assault on the Istanbul-Berlin Express. Devan and the two Americans were dropped into Greece knowing that SOE and OSS headquarters in Cairo were contemplating such an attack. They were expecting word from agents in Istanbul on the departure for Berlin of a German courier who would be carrying intelligence reports of potentially great value to the Allied war effort.

Normally, the train followed the direct line from Istanbul north through Bulgaria along the Marcia River to Sofia, the route of the legendary Orient Express. But with the railway yard at Plodiv bombed out, the Germans were forced to reroute the twice-weekly train through northern Greece by way of Serrai in the Strimon Valley. Cairo predicted the express would pass through the attack point at about 2300 hours. Sorry, they could give no details on the identity or appearance of the courier. But it was important the papers be found and delivered to Cairo as soon as possible. A plane would be dispatched immediately to make the pickup. Good luck. The transmission ended.

Devan and Rogers glanced at each other as the stocky Greek operator slipped the earphones off his head.

"Two days," said Devan. "A bit tight." He cracked his knuckles. "I suppose we can make it." He looked over at the other Greek, an unpleasantly thin man with an artificial smile. "Hmmm?"

"It can be done," said Voko. "You can count on EDES."

"Better let Andropolous know right away," said Rogers.

A frown flashed across Voko's face, quickly consumed by a plastic grin. "As you say. But we could easily do this without the Communists."

"We have an agreement," said Devan, dismissing the suggestion. "Send the liaison man with this." He wrote out the time and assembly point for the leftists—1900 hours, Skoutari. "Don't think you chaps would want Andropolous and his men coming here to Kilkis."

Voko said nothing, but his steel-cold eyes only thinly hid his contempt for the Englishman. He took the paper and left the room to pass it to a messenger.

"I wouldn't trust him with my garbage," said Rogers.

"Easy, old boy," said Devan. "He's a bit pushy perhaps, but basically well-meaning. And he's on our side."

"He's on his side," said Rogers. Voko, an off-duty policeman, gave him the creeps. Of all the Greeks he had met so far, this was the slimiest. He was the kind of guy who would smile broadly and let you have it as soon as you turned your back. A real greaser. Someone had said Voko was a killer. He didn't doubt it. Rogers made no secret of his feelings. Voko wouldn't hesitate to double-cross Devan or anyone else if it served his needs. But at the moment he needed British and American money and supplies. So he was superficially, at least, cooperating with Devan and the leftists. Rogers didn't want to be around when that ended.

* * *

They could hear it laboring up the valley nearly ten minutes away. The aging Austrian-built steam engine wheezed and puffed as it struggled up the grade toward the gorge where they waited.

Ritter, his face blacked with burned cork, looked at his watch. Even the Germans couldn't run their trains on time these days. The express was nearly twenty-five minutes late. He checked his M3 again and glanced over at Melanie, giving her a wink and a sample of the Ritter grin. Smiling back at him through the burned cork, her eyes sparkled with excitement and affection.

In the brilliant moonlight he also could see Rogers, Devan, and one of the Greeks making last-minute checks of the explosives on the tracks. Nodding their heads at each other in agreement, they scrambled up the embankment above the single-track line. It was a simple plan of attack. The dynamite was to be detonated directly under the engine. The force of the blast would derail the rest of the train. From the safety of the darkness above, they would have free fields of fire directly into the wreckage. A classic massacre.

Ritter and Melanie had arrived with Andropolous and the other members of the leftist team at the little village of Skoutari. The Greeks tensed noticeably when the rightists appeared with Rogers and Devan. Ritter had the feeling that if the foreigners hadn't been around, shooting between the two factions might have broken out. Andropolous looked at each member of the monarchist group obviously searching for someone. He gave no indication he found who or what he was looking for.

Ritter told Rogers about the killing of the boy. Devan broke in. "Germans, obviously."

"Andropolous doesn't think so. Not their style. Thinks it was one of your chums, Devan. Somebody named Voko."

"Yeah, Devan," said Rogers. "One of your buddies. But he's on our side, isn't he?"

Devan turned without replying and walked away.

"Who's Voko?" asked Ritter.

"Some asshole Greek with EDES," said Rogers.

"Which one is he?"

"Didn't come along. He's organizing the alert and backup teams."

"Probably a good thing," said Ritter. "Andropolous thinks he had a hand in killing the boy. If he had turned up, I doubt he would survive the attack."

The sound of the train was growing louder. The powerful pulsating hiss was pushing closer and closer as the massive drive wheels drove their way up the grading. Belching sparks and steam like an enormous iron monster, the locomotive appeared at the end of the entrance to the gorge. The single front headlamp flashed bravely down the track, revealing nothing out of the ordinary. The four passenger cars behind the massive coal-gray engine were dimly lit, carrying diplomats, off-duty military personnel, and their families to Berlin. Six other sealed freight cars brought up the rear. Although this was the most dangerous part of the journey, the Germans surprisingly had taken few if any safety precautions. There were no signs of outriders or special security crews. The Greeks had never attacked one of their trains. Perhaps it had not occurred to them that this was a possibility.

A brilliant flash and an enormous series of explosions shook the earth. The engine halted, rose up, tilted with an awkward slow motion, and then, still grinding forward, pitched wildly onto its side with a mighty wheeze and a roar. With a squeal of twisting iron and metal, the cars behind pitched and buckled, the forward ones slamming into the engine and tender, splintering and crumbling like miniatures and settling back in broken agony. A momentary silence was swiftly interrupted by escaping steam and cries of the wounded. Without warning the Greeks began shooting from above into the cars, raking the wreckage with hundreds of rounds of small-arms fire, followed by the small concentrated explosions of hand grenades. Ritter held his fire. He couldn't make out any specific targets and he didn't want to waste the M3 ammunition until he was sure what he was shooting at. He watched in fascination as the Greeks poured hundreds of rounds into the smoking wreckage. One of the overturned cars caught fire and began to burn, illuminating the overall scene.

As the firing gradually died down, Ritter could see the Greeks cautiously beginning to make their way down the hillside to the wreckage. Across the gorge he spotted Rogers and Devan watching, deciding whether to move down themselves. Off to the left, Andropolous was almost all the way down when another enormous explosion erupted from one of the rear cars, jolting the entire gorge. Two twisted forms were thrown into the air and plunged with a sickening thud back into the wreckage. Ritter knew the ugly repulsive odor was burning human flesh. It was mixed with the strong odor of burning oil, wood, and foodstuffs.

Melanie trembled silently beside him. The killing seemed to excite her in a strange way. She was holding his left arm tightly, her eyes bright and wide. Something told him he could have taken her right there at that moment.

Rogers and Devan were now making their way down the hillside. Ritter stood up, and followed by Melanie, scrambled down the rocky embankment toward them. An occasional stray shot still rang out. The flaming car illuminating the scene would burn for at least two more hours.

Andropolous joined them. "Very professional," said Rogers admiringly. "Your explosives man knows his stuff."

Andropolous smiled in acknowledgment of the compliment. "Not much time," he said. "The Germans will come quickly. You have about twenty minutes to find what you are looking for."

Carrying large hand lights which the Greeks had brought along, they began combing through the remains of the four passenger coaches. "Collect any papers you see," said Devan. "Documents, identification papers, briefcases, anything that looks official or even unofficial. We'll sort it out later."

Broken bodies, most of them men, littered the wrecked coaches. There seemed to be an equal mixture of those dressed in German army and air-force uniforms and civilian clothes.

Ritter felt uncomfortably ghoulish picking over the still-warm bodies. A briefcase had broken open, its contents scattered all over the coach. It would take at least twenty minutes to reassemble just that batch. He gathered what he could hastily and decided to leave the rest. Reaching into the pocket of the man's suit jacket, he pulled out a large leather wallet and proceeded to the next body. Moving through the first coach, Ritter found three army officers and a civilian. The body of a woman in an elegant pink wool suit was half-covered by a seat. No time to try to reach her. Nearing the rear of the car, he could hear sobbing. It was a boy, blond, probably not more than eight, probably German. Behind him, Andropolous apparently had read his thoughts. "We'll see he gets back safely," he said, picking up the frightened child in his large arms.

At the end of the coach Ritter flashed the light onto the bloody corpse of a man dressed in a well-tailored wool suit. He knew right away he had found what they were looking for. An expensive-looking leather briefcase was chained to the man's wrist. Ritter swung the M3 around and with a brief burst of fire severed the chain.

There was a sudden flash of light outside the car. He looked up. A green signal flare. Germans on the way. Scrambling out with the briefcase and other papers he had collected, Ritter saw Rogers emerging with Melanie from the next coach.

"Hey, Whip," he shouted. "Anything?"

"Just a lot of papers. Hard to say. What'd you get, kid?"

"Jackpot, I think."

Devan came running up. He also had a clutch of papers under his arm. "No time to examine it all now, chaps. Let's move on smartly."

The four of them scrambled up the embankment. Ritter looked back. Beneath them lay a remarkable and sobering sight, one he would never forget. The broken train, twisted and smashed, lay in the glow of the burning car and brilliant moonlight, smoldering and inert, like a giant chopped-up metal serpent. The Greeks had broken into the rear cars and were carrying away boxes of supplies. The flare warning of the German approach still hadn't scared them off. Clambering over the wreckage, they looked like large ants feeding on a fresh corpse.

The crack of a rifle shot echoed through the gorge, followed by several answering bursts.

"Germans," said Melanie.

Devan sighed, exasperation and panic rising in his voice. "No, not yet."

Gradually the rate of fire escalated to the level of a serious small-arms battle.

"Bloody Greeks," Devan groused, "squabbling over the spoils. That double-crossing Voko. He fired the flare to get us and the leftists out so they could carry away most of the stuff for themselves. Andropolous must have figured it out." He turned to Rogers. "Here, take these," he said, pushing the sheaf of papers he was carrying at the American. Devan turned and began trotting back toward the gorge.

"Devan," shouted Rogers, "it's not your battle. Stay the hell out of it. You'll get your imperial ass shot off down there." He moved quickly, grabbing Devan by the arm, pulling him back. "You can't do any good now. Neither side wants to hear anything you can say at this point."

Devan, restrained by the grip on his arm, hesitated and looked back at Rogers. He had actually begun to like the noisy American. "Got to break it up, Rogers. They'll muck up everything. If I can just reach the rightists, they'll listen...."

Rogers looked sternly at Devan. A bit pompous, but he was a brave man with a strong sense of duty. "Listen, Devan, you've been right all along, that's why you can't go down there. You've got to choose one side or the other. Playing the middle is obviously impossible. I just don't agree with the side you've picked."

"Thanks, Rogers," said Devan. "It was picked for me. I've got to stop this nonsense. If we don't settle it now, it'll become a blood feud. It'll ruin any hope of a combined effort against the Jerries." He was breathing heavily. With a sudden effort he wrenched his arm away from Rogers' grasp and headed toward the gorge.

"Devan, you stubborn idiot. Don't go down there. Those bastards are crazy. We've got what we came for."

Devan ran to the edge of the gorge, looked around briefly, and started sliding down. Rogers and Ritter, trailed by Melanie, followed him to the edge and silently watched him make his way down. Suddenly he appeared to slip and fall. He tumbled head first down the steep slope.

"Shit, I knew it," yelled Rogers. He handed the papers he was holding to Melanie. "Wait here, kid. Be right back."

"You crazy, Whip? You'll get it just like he did. Those fuckers are shooting at anything moving."

"No guts, no glory, kid." Rogers headed down the hillside.

"Goddammit, Whip. You can't drag him up out of there by yourself." Ritter handed the leather attaché case to Melanie. "Now you've got it all. Just wait here with it." Melanie, bewildered and somewhat frightened by the bizarre behavior of the Americans and the Englishman, nodded anxiously.

Ritter scrambled down the hillside behind Rogers. Several shots popped into the stony ground around them.

"Some asshole's shooting at us," shouted Rogers.

"Over there," said Ritter. He leveled his M3 and fired a short burst in the direction of the flashes he had seen. The sniper fired at them again. Ritter let go of another, longer burst. The sniping stopped.

They reached Devan at the bottom of the slope, sheltered from the shooting by the wreckage of the locomotive. He was breathing irregularly, blood oozing from his mouth. Rogers propped him up. The wound in Devan's chest was messy, ugly, obviously one lung punctured, probably both.

"Papers to Cairo," said Devan, forcing the words out. He coughed harshly, spitting up more blood.

"Come on, you limey bastard. Don't quit on me now. I'm carrying your ass right out of here." Rogers handed his M3 to Ritter and picked Devan up, throwing him over his shoulder.

Ritter led the way up the slope, followed by the heavily perspiring Rogers, who clutched Ritter's M3 strap with his free hand. As they neared the top of the slope, the firing beneath began to die out. New sounds in the background. Truck engines. Motorcycles. A flare burst brilliantly over them just as they reached the crest of the slope.

Melanie was standing silhouetted against the bright green flare, still holding the papers and the attaché case. "Germans," she said. This time she was right.

They laid Devan gently on the ground. He was having visible difficulty breathing. Blood foamed from his mouth in large amounts. "Sorry, Yanks. Should have listened," he gasped.

"It's okay, Devan," said Rogers. "Just take it easy."

It was too late. He was gone.

4

"Easy, Whip. She's having trouble keeping up."

"Come on, kid, move her along. You don't want to spend the rest of your life in these mountains."

Ritter glanced back at the girl, struggling for breath, straining to keep pace with two superbly conditioned athletes, even though Ritter was carrying her weapon as well as his own, plus the briefcase. The run had been grueling. On the go since the Germans poured into the gorge, forcing them to abandon Devan's body, they jogged steadily over the rocky hills and through the rich valleys, putting as much distance between themselves and the Germans as they could. It was already dawn. Just another two miles or so to Kilkis and the radio. They had to make contact with Cairo and order the pickup.

Melanie hadn't heard them. She was too exhausted to pay attention to anything except staying on her feet, keeping up. The pain in her side was nearly paralyzing. She concentrated on just putting one sore foot in front of the other.

The run had been tough even for Ritter. A star quartermiler at San Diego, he had always been in top shape. But nothing could have prepared him for this sort of cross-country jaunt over rocky hills in heavy boots. The remarkable thing was Rogers, in unbelievably good shape for such an old fart. He was at least thirty-five.

They jogged on in the moist morning, with Rogers continuing to force the pace, Ritter holding back as much as possible so they didn't lose Melanie. An autumn ground fog had wrapped itself like a soft gray cloak around them, shielding them from the eyes of searching Germans or anyone else. It was unlikely that the Germans were still behind them or even looking for them. They presumably had their hands full trying to salvage what they could from the wreck and rounding up the Greeks who had scattered when they arrived.

Rogers had another important reason for hurrying. He wanted to reach Kilkis and the radio well ahead of Voko or the other EDES partisans. After what happened, he wouldn't trust Voko with a K.P. detail. The last, thing he wanted was for Voko to know anything about the pickup point. Rogers couldn't wait to get away from Greece and the Greeks as fast as possible. As soon as the pickup was set, he and Ritter and the girl would disappear. Hide out until the plane arrived. The girl, who had fallen hard for the kid, was sticking with them. That was okay. They needed someone they could trust as a translator and guide.

As the mist burned off the hills in midmorning, the three of them staggered exhausted into Kilkis. They walked directly to the rundown farmhouse where the radio was hidden, pushed open the door, and collapsed onto the timbered floor like small beached whales, gasping for breath, fighting for relief. A middle-aged woman with rough skin and dull eyes working over the fire in the hearth was startled by the intrusion, but not particularly alarmed. Since they had hidden the radio in her house, she had become used to the unexpected. She also recognized Rogers and quickly brought them water—their first drink in nearly twelve hours.

They sipped gratefully, slowly regaining their strength and their relationship to a stationary world beneath their feet. The woman brought goat cheese and warm bread, which they greedily and quickly consumed. They looked at each other, pleased with themselves and their returning vigor. There was a lot to do, but they had already accomplished a great deal.

Rogers did not permit the pause to be extended into a real rest. As they ate, he began sifting through the mass of papers and documents they had carried from the train. The loose material was a collection of travel orders, passports, family letters, business papers, administrative reports, and other miscellaneous documents.

"Don't see how you can read that stuff, Whip. It's Greek to me." Ritter laughed.

"It's actually easier to read than it looks. My mother's a kraut, you know. Also I minored in German lit back before it was frowned on."

Rogers chuckled as he continued to sift through the documents. Many were interesting and would be useful to Cairo. But he hadn't yet found what they had come for. "Well, it's got to be this," he said, pulling the still-unopened attaché case to him. He slid his commando knife out of the boot sheath and slashed the rich brown leather case open. It was crammed with papers, most of them marked "VERTRAULICH" or "STRENG GEHEIM."

Rogers sucked air through his lips as he excitedly leafed through the files.

"That it, Whip?"

"Diarrhea special, kid."

"What the hell does that mean?"

Rogers continued with great intensity to leaf through the pages, fascinated by their revelations. "Krauts have doubled some agents working for us and the Brits in Istanbul. Cairo is going to shit when they see this stuff."

"Too bad we didn't find the gold too, huh?"

"Ahh, that was impossible," said Rogers. "Devan was a pretty good guy, I suppose, but he didn't really have a clue to where that stuff had gone. Some Greek's probably got it buried in his backyard, waiting patiently for the war to end so he can buy up a fleet of ships or something. That gold can be forgotten about. It's gone."

The radio operator and owner of the house appeared breathless in the room. He had heard of the Americans' arrival and had returned hastily from his olive grove. A short man with thick arms and a neck the shape of a beer barrel, he stared at the papers strewn around. If the Germans were to find any of these in the village, it would be the end for all of them.

"Call Cairo," said Rogers, looking up. Melanie repeated the order in Greek, just in case the man hadn't understood.

"Net doesn't open for another eight hours," said the Greek in heavily accented English.

"Use emergency procedures," snapped Rogers.

"Wouldn't work," said the man, shaking his head.

"Try it," insisted Rogers.

"Such an extended call will alert the Germans. It will give them time to pinpoint the transmitter, this house. It is safer to wait until Cairo calls. The outgoing transmissions will be much shorter."

"You'll have to risk it this time," said Rogers.

"Voko forbids it."

Rogers moved his hand over to his M3. He laid it across his lap, clicked the bolt into firing position while scowling directly at the Greek. "I just authorized it. Do it now."

The Greek frowned. With a shrug of resignation he shuffled to a corner of the room, and pulling up the floorboards, brought out the battery-powered transmitter.

After three or four minutes to warm the tubes, the ancient set began to crackle and hiss. Tuning the receive channel across the band, the Greek passed through a noisy selection of pulsing radioteletype signals, high-pitched whines and screeches of jamming transmitters and sunspot interference, general Morse traffic, and finally someone singing "Lilli Marlene" in German. Rogers shifted the M3 in his lap. The Greek began the emergency-procedure call.

"Calling White Owl. Calling White Owl. This is Blue Jay. Over." The Greek repeated the call several times, trying to catch the attention of the full-time radio room in Cairo, hoping the operators would quickly hear the emergency call words and respond.

Minutes slipped by. Long, agonizing minutes that also gave German counterintelligence radio teams valuable moments to spot the call and make a fix on it.

Finally the crackle of a faint reply. "White Owl. Come in, Blue Jay."

Rogers grabbed the microphone. "White Owl. This is Barrister," he said, giving Devan's private call sign. "Request soonest prosperous flamingo for hotcake number. Advise. Over."

"Wait, Barrister. Over."

More tense long minutes ticked by. Cairo transmitted a pulsating beep to verify its continuing presence on the frequency. The Germans knew this transmission was coming from Cairo and thus the fix meant nothing. But it also alerted them for a local return call.

The faint but distinct beep emphasized the long wait. Ritter could feel a warm moist sensation spreading under his arms.

"How long do they need to find us?" Melanie asked.

"Hard to say," Rogers said. "Sometimes only minutes. Depends on how busy they are, what general interference problems they have, the German response time, luck, lots of things." Ritter, still watching silently, realized he was chewing on his nails. One finger was bleeding slightly. He sucked it clean.

The beeps continued. More static. Then a faint voice. "Hello, Barrister. This is White Owl. Confirming flamingo at …" The signal faded.

"Ahh, fuck," shouted Rogers.

The radio crackled. The Cairo carrier signal drifted back, but the message was over.

"Hello, White Owl. Say again, please. Say again. Over."

More static on the carrying signal. And then faintly: "Flamingo at pumpkin echo. Designation Prosperous. Confirm. Over."

"Roger, White Owl," said Rogers with obvious relief in his voice. "Love to Cinderella. Out."

Rogers glanced down at his watch. Just after 1045 hours. "Let me see the map," he said.

The barrel-necked Greek left the room and returned with an area map. Prosperous was one of two emergency pickup points they had memorized before leaving Cairo. It was in a valley sheltered by a small stand of mountains south of Anxioupolis, about twenty miles from Kilkis.

"Better get moving," said Rogers. "We've got almost nineteen hours, but it's a pretty good walk."

Ritter looked at Melanie. Dark semicircles had formed under her eyes. She looked like she hadn't slept in weeks, but she registered no reaction to Rogers' comment. She wouldn't complain.

Rogers saw the exchange of looks between Ritter and Melanie. "You can get your beauty sleep once we get to the site. With a bit of luck, there'll be time to rest before pickup."

"With a bit of luck," said Ritter.

A small explosion not more than two hundred yards from the house blasted the late-morning stillness of the village.

"Germans," whispered Melanie.

Rogers moved like a cat to the window, peering cautiously out. "Wrong again, Melody. Your countrymen are up to their usual tricks. The leftists must have already gotten word about the double cross at the train and decided on a little catch-up ball."

Melanie swore in Greek. "Fools," she shouted. "They're like children. It's always shoot first, think last." She was shaking with anger.

"Hold the speeches," said Rogers. "We'll have to leave your countrymen to settle this one on their own." He spotted a shepherd's knapsack in the corner. "Put all the stuff in here."

They quickly assembled the papers and crammed them into the sack. Without a word, Ritter grabbed it and slipped it over his arms onto his back. Melanie looked at Rogers. He winked at her and smiled. He understood her anger. He liked her, and approved of her and Ritter. She hadn't been sure.

The barrel-necked Greek picked up a bolt-action M1903 and charged out the front door, looking for the intruders.

"No time for formal good-byes," said Rogers. "Have to send thank-you notes from Cairo. Now, Melody, if your boys will just concentrate on their fellow Greeks, we'll get out of here."

"This way," the girl whispered. She peered out the back door. The shooting seemed to be concentrated on the other side of the village. They made their way out cautiously, dashing for the base of the hillside behind the house. Once over the crest, they would be safely away.

They scrambled upward, leaving the sounds of battle in the village below. Less than fifty yards from the top, shots popped around them. Ritter looked up. Two or three men were firing at them from a concentration of rocks about one hundred yards along the ridge top slightly above.

Rogers pulled a white handkerchief from his pocket and waved it "Let 'em know we're neutrals in this one," he said. "America—" he started to shout. He never finished the word. A single shot crashed into his forehead just above the right eye, blasting directly through his skull. He twisted and fell back, his mouth open, without making a sound. Melanie screamed.

"Whip!" Ritter shouted. Crouching, he lowered his M3, aimed it at the ridge, and fired the entire thirty-round clip in a single blast. No answering shots. He reached over, grabbed Rogers' M3, and dashed up the hill where the shots had come from. Whoever had fired them was already gone. He had a brief glimpse of two men dashing down the other side of the ridge between the rocks, already well out of effective range. He fired the thirty-round clip in frustration and anger.

Ritter turned and scrambled to Melanie, who was stooped over Rogers. Tears were streaming down her drawn face. Ritter couldn't speak. He didn't dare. Biting the insides of his cheeks, he knelt and shoved his fingers under Rogers' jaw below the ear. Nothing. Rogers was not going back to Cairo. Ritter leaned back, barely able to hold himself together. A taste of blood in his mouth. He wouldn't cry. Whip wouldn't approve.

Reaching into Rogers' shirt, he found the dog tags around his neck. He yanked them off, stuffing them into his pants pocket. Methodically he went through the rest of Rogers' pockets, finally locating a small leather wallet. It contained a U.S. Army identification card and a badly creased picture of an attractive young woman sitting on a chair in a garden. There also were three letters written in faded blue ink in an elegant female hand that looked as if they had been read at least one hundred times. He shoved them into his pocket with the leather billfold. Drawing the eyes closed, he stripped off Rogers' jacket and laid it gently over his friend. No time for a proper burial.

Ritter slipped his hand under Melanie's arm and pulled her to her feet. She clutched at him, and shuddered as she choked back a sob. It could have been any of them.

* * *

They arrived at Site Prosperous sometime after dark. Hungry and exhausted, still shocked by the death of Rogers, they were both badly chilled. It would be a long, uncomfortable night.

Prosperous was an 800-yard-long meadow cleared by EDES partisans for quick landings by SOE resupply and pickup flights. Twice a week a local shepherd brought his sheep onto the meadow to keep the landing-strip grass the right length. He also used the time to pick up any rocks or other debris that had surfaced or otherwise made their way onto the crude strip, keeping it clear for aircraft. Both from the air and on the ground it looked like just another clear meadow area, a bit flatter and less rocky than most, but generally there was nothing about it to give the ordinary observer any suspicions about its use.

Ritter and Melanie lay down under some gnarled olive trees at the edge of the meadow, using the paper-stuffed knapsack as a common pillow.

"What time will they come?" she asked.

"Just after dawn. About five o'clock," he said. "Pumpkin is midnight. Echo is the fifth letter of the alphabet. Childishly simple, but easy to remember. Hopefully no one listening was clever enough to figure it out." She nodded her head. She was not really listening.

"I liked Rogers," she said. "I'm sorry he's dead."

"Me too," said Ritter. There was a lot he didn't say. It was hard to accept that the loud, hearty voice was gone forever. Rogers had meant more to him than just about any other person he'd ever known. And now with a simple and irretrievable act, he was gone. It would be a dark void in his life for a long time to come. He heard Melanie say something.

"Uh?"

"I said, why did he always call me Melody?"

"Cause he liked you."

She didn't understand. It didn't matter. They moved closer together, too exhausted to make love, but more loving than they'd ever been. The crisp autumn cold chilled them both, but it was too dangerous to light a fire at this time. Uncomfortable, unhappy, exhausted, they finally slept.

Ritter suddenly opened his eyes around 0330. Still dark. But he knew it wouldn't be much longer. The motion of looking at his watch woke Melanie.

"Must have dozed off," she said, rubbing her eyes. "What time?"

He told her.

"Quickly," she said. "We must get the fire going. Without it, they will not land."

As they stood, fighting the stiffness that had attacked their bodies, a trace of gray cracked the sky. They began collecting scraps of wood and brush that would easily ignite. They worked steadily for over an hour, gathering and stacking into a large heap anything they could find. Because they didn't have any fuel, the dew-moistened wood would be hard to light. Hopefully some of the drier loose material would be enough. They didn't dare start the fire until they heard the engines. Two passes were all the pilots ever made. If they were not satisfied with what they saw from the cockpit, they went home.

Large streaks of blue began to crowd out the morning oranges and reds. It was going to be a brilliantly clear day.

Ritter thought he heard the faint drone of motors. He fished around in his pockets for matches. Suddenly it was over them. A Blenheim, just like the one that had brought him and Rogers in.

"Quickly now," she said. "The fire." He needed no prompting. He struck a match and lit the loose dry material. Blowing on it, he coaxed it along. The brush caught quickly, starting to smoke. It was a good signal. The Blenheim passed over, wiggled its wings, and turned back. The pilot could tell from the smoke which way the wind was blowing.

"Got us," said Ritter. "Here he comes."

"Brian… I love you," she said. "When will you come back?"

"As soon as I can," he said.

She pushed hard against him and kissed him with desperation. She wanted to believe what he said.

The Blenheim was turning into the approach. The wheels were extended. Slowly it drifted down, bouncing onto the grassy strip.

She undid the top button of her blouse and pulled at the silver cross she wore around her neck, sliding it off and slipping it over Ritter's head.

"It belonged to my grandfather. We believe it will bring good luck to whoever has it. Wear it until you come back."

He smiled. "Stay away from Voko and his boys, Melanie. I'll be back as soon as I can."

The Blenheim taxied up, the wash of the propellers blowing hard against them. The rear fuselage door swung open. It was the same pilot who had ferried Ritter in. "All right, old boy, let's go. Haven't got all day, you know."

Ritter turned back to Melanie, kissed her again, and ran for the plane. Grabbing his outstretched arm, the pilot pulled him up. Suddenly bullets smacked into the side of the fuselage. The pilot slammed the door. No time for even a last wave.

"Roll it, Max," the pilot shouted over the roar of the engines to the copilot.

Several more bullets hit the plane as it hastily taxied down the strip and roared off. Ritter walked forward to the flight deck behind the pilot, who had returned to his seat.

"Close," said Ritter.

"Fairly routine, I'm afraid, old chap. Where are your pals?"

"Couldn't make it," said Ritter.

They gradually gained altitude and then circled over the strip, heading south. Ritter looked down. A line of German trucks and open cars had pulled up just beyond the olive trees. Some gray-uniformed men were firing upward at the Blenheim. Others were running after Melanie. He fingered the cross around his neck as the plane banked around and she was lost from sight.

PART III

EARLY 1975

Weaving a fiction which unravels as you weave,
pacing forever in the hell of make-believe.
—T. S. Eliot

5

"Martha, I don't see why this is so bloody important. You, know Chelsea's playing West Ham tonight."

"Don't speak to me in that tone of voice," snapped the woman. "We've already settled it. I know very well it's your telly night. But the doctor says he doesn't have much longer. And he specially asked you to come over tonight. God knows why, you've been rude enough to him over the years. I shouldn't think he'd want to see you under any circumstances. But you ought to at least show him some respect now."

"For God's sake, don't go on about it. I said I would go, didn't I? Even if he is dying, what could be so important? We all gotta go sometime, don't we?" His voice cracked into a noticeable cockney accent when he became irritated, revealing a trace of the past he had worked hard to overcome. The argument with his wife about missing a televised football match to visit his drunken brother-in-law aggravated him. He was irritated partially because he would miss the match, but even more so because he knew she was right. He had been rude to Jimmy frequently over the years. In fact, there were a few times when the rudeness had bordered on outright cruelty. But he couldn't help it. The man was a no-good drunk. He couldn't even hold the most simple job. How many times had Jimmy touched him for a fiver with the promise he would pay it back? The story was always the same. He needed the money to help land a job. The cheatin' old sot. He just needed more funds to pay his pub bills.

"Well, come on, Alfred. We ain't got all night. They'll be waitin'."

Yes, Jimmy would be waiting with his long-suffering wife, Maggie. She was the only decent one of the lot. Having put up with Jimmy all these years practically qualified her for martyrdom. She had worked bleeding hard, scrubbing floors for some lord or other and later working as a sales clerk at Marks and Spencer to hold the family together. To send their son to school. To pay Jimmy's bills. What had she got out of it? More complaining, more drinking, and more trouble. She'd be better off when Jimmy croaked. "Hold your knickers on," he said. "I'm coming."

The new year was only a week old, and Martha packed a Christmas pudding to take along as a present. They had visited the Waddells only once over the holidays, a disastrous encounter on Christmas Day that broke up early when Jimmy fell into a coughing fit and began shouting about the Japanese. When he was drunk, he often ranted about the nips. Maggie began crying, and in disgust Alfred insisted they leave. As he had done so many times before, he vowed it was his last visit.

The January night was sharply cold. Alfred pulled his coat and scarf tightly around him, trying to hold in as much warmth as possible. He wasn't as young as he used to be. Unfriendly winds cut through him much easier these days. In addition, arthritis was creeping steadily through his legs and back, making it harder for him to get around. He was most uncomfortable. He and Martha waited disagreeably in the biting night air nearly fifteen minutes for a 97 bus to pick them up for the four-and-a-half-mile journey to the depressing row of Victorian cottages, the government-subsidized council housing where Jimmy Waddell had lived since returning from the war. Neither Alfred nor Martha said much. In fact, neither of them really looked forward to the evening. Although Jimmy was the only living relative on her side of the family, his drunkenness had always made things difficult. Alfred, who by hard work had moved them beyond their simple beginnings, had never been sympathetic. He regarded Jimmy as a layabout, and it had been increasingly awkward to integrate Jimmy and his family into their lives. Visits over the years became less and less frequent.

Alfred, his eyes glued on the corner, waiting for the bus to finally appear, tried not to think much about it. Admittedly, Jimmy had had a hard time of it. Nearly four years in a Japanese prisoner-of-war camp would be enough to unnerve any man. But lots of people suffered in the war and somehow muddled through. Jim Waddell never did. He drifted from one job to another, first as a railway guard, then as a dustman. In between, there were visits to the soldiers' hospital, where they tried to dry him out and straighten him up. But the drink always got to him and yanked him back down. The jobs vanished, his health and general appearance deteriorated.

Alfred felt he had survived a modern ice age when the red double-decker finally slid around the corner. They rode in silence all the way to Bowers Lane and walked the final five hundred freezing yards to the Waddell house. Like most of the cottages on the block, it was in shabby condition. It looked like years since the trim on the windows and doors had been painted.

Maggie opened the door. "Hullo, Martha," she said with a woeful smile. The two women embraced. "Hullo, Alfred," she added, her face straightening. Alfred knew the woman didn't like him. He couldn't blame her, really. And strangely, he admired her for it. Years ago, his feelings for her had been a good deal warmer, but the atmosphere around Jimmy had poisoned their relationship. She had not accepted Alfred's rough treatment of Jimmy. He tried to tell himself it didn't matter that she didn't like him. In any case, there was nothing he could do now to change it.

"Hello Maggie," he answered. She offered a cool cheek for him to peck. They entered the tattered drawing room. Jimmy was seated at one corner in the big worn easy chair wrapped in a blanket. An electric heater glowed nearby.

"Hullo, Martha, Alfred. Come in." His voice was weaker than usual, and somehow, it seemed to Alfred, more subdued.

"The doc says I ain't got much time left," Jimmy said in a surprisingly cheerful way. Maybe he's looking forward to it, Alfred thought. Everybody'll be better off, that's for sure. "Glad you could come. Sorry about the other night. Guess the booze got the best of me again."

"Ah, forget it," said Alfred as unconvincingly as he could. He ambled across the room in the direction of Jimmy. His wire-rim glasses had fogged up and he had them off rubbing them back into use with a handkerchief that once had been white.

"Sit down, Alfred. Warm yourself up. Looks really cold out there. Reminds me of that last winter in Japan. It wasn't really as cold as it is tonight. But we didn't have much to wear in the camp. There wasn't much food or anything else to keep us warm. We froze. A lotta the chaps died...." Jimmy's voice trailed off. "Can I pour you a pint?" he said after a brief pause. "Got nothing else in the place. Maggie had to have a new coat. It's left us a bit hard up this month."

"Well, just a pint," Alfred said, putting his glasses back on. He had promised Martha he would be polite. Besides, every one he put away would be one less for Jimmy to down. He hoped he wouldn't have to listen to the Japanese bit again tonight, but it looked as if he was in for it.

Across the room, Maggie watched apprehensively as Jimmy emerged weakly from his cocoon to go to the kitchen. Alfred saw how haggard she looked. She had aged remarkably in the past few years. At one time she had been a lovely young woman. On her wedding day to Jimmy he had secretly envied his brother-in-law. But for Maggie the excitement of marrying a young man who went off to war quickly diminished and then disappeared entirely as the dreadful reality of Jimmy's life engulfed them. During the four long years he was away, she remained loyal, only to find when he returned that she had been waiting for someone else, not the broken man who came back to claim her. At first, she dared to hope it was a temporary disaster that could be overcome. But this time love was not enough. As her hopes gradually dried out, so did her youth and freshness.

Jimmy brought in two large glasses of English bitter, and handing one to Alfred, sank back into his blanket.

"Damn, this house is cold," he grumbled. "I keep telling Maggie we ought to get one of them gas heaters, but she never gets around to it."

Alfred, anticipating the ill-heated house would be drafty and cold, had purposely worn a heavy woolen sweater under his jacket, and with the electric heater close to one side, managed to remain fairly comfortable. Only his feet were cool.

"Well, it won't be much longer anyway," said Jimmy. He coughed hard. A deep rattle in his chest shook him. The violent cough emphasized his point. "It's the lungs, they say. The fags done it. But a man's gotta have some pleasure in life, ay? Without the booze and the fags, it wouldn't be worth it anyhow."

Alfred said nothing. The man disgusted him. His teeth were badly decayed. Several were gone entirely. The others hung darkly in his mouth, adding an obnoxious odor to his already foul breath. His skin was blotchy and his eyes dull. They had died long ago. Alfred sipped his bitter and reminded himself for the tenth time he had promised not to be disagreeable.

"Alfred, you and me ain't been all that close over the years," said Jimmy suddenly. "I know you been busy with yer shop and yer trips to Spain and all that. And I been ill a lot. I've had me ups and downs with the sauce. It ain't been easy. But there's something I been meaning to tell you for some time. I just never got around to it before."

Oh, Christ, thought Alfred. Here comes another bit of nonsense from this bore.

"I've told you before about my time in Jap prisons."

Maybe a hundred times, thought Alfred. Maybe a thousand times. If I have to hear that claptrap again, I may vomit. He took a sip of bitter, not interrupting.

"There's something that happened before I got to Burma. I been thinking about it for a long time. I always wanted to tell somebody, but it was an official secret. It doesn't matter now, I don't think. It was a long time ago, thirty-four years, and besides, there's not much they could do to me now. They wouldn't put a dying man in prison, would they?"

Alfred pulled a pouch of tobacco from his jacket pocket along with a package of thin white papers. With experienced moves of the fingers, he skillfully slid one of the papers from the packet, curled it with one finger, and carefully tapped in a small portion of tobacco. With a quick lick of his tongue he created a saliva seal to finish the cigarette. He lit it with a wooden match and listened with increasing interest to the story.

"It was the spring of '41, right after we left. You remember, we went first to Cairo and then up to Greece. There were several cooks in the brigade, so they made me a lorry driver. It wasn't bad duty. It was better than being on the front lines, anyway.

"When the Jerries finally attacked, I was driving a lorry with a secret cargo and a coupla officers. They was intelligence types, on some kind of classified mission. Very 'ush-'ush and all that. I was allowed to talk to nobody about it.

"Maggie, a couple more jars of bitter."

"Jimmy," she said pleadingly. "You promised the doctor not to overdo it." Her face was weary. Alfred looked at her again, searching her eyes for traces of the beauty he had once yearned for. It was long gone, drained away by unspeakable burdens.

"Aww, come on, Maggie. We're only goin' to have a couple. Not a big piss-up. I promised ya, didn't I?"

She had caved in so many times before, another time really didn't matter. Wearily she rose and returned with opened bottles of bitter for the two men, then went back to her conversation with Martha across the room.

"Ahh, that's it," said Jimmy, taking a long gulp. "Nectar of the gods, ay?"

Alfred raised his glass in a neutral fashion. "Cheers."

"So where was I? Oh, yes. We was really suffering from the wet and cold. Anyhow, the major decides we should take this back road. Wasn't much of a road really, just a dirt track. I knew we couldn't make it, I kept tellin' the major, but he wouldn't listen. He was a bit hardheaded, I remember. We finally got stuck. I knew we would. But sometimes you can't tell them officers nothing.

"The major was scared stiff. Thought them Jerries was going to get ahold of his secret boxes. You know what?" Jimmy lowered his voice to a stage whisper. "Turns out there was gold in 'em. Lots of it. Belonged to some Greek banks or somethin'. Some of the gold was ours to pay the Greeks, the major said. There was five heavy boxes. Must be worth at least a million pounds at today's prices."

Alfred said nothing. It was the first time in years Jimmy had something to say he wanted to listen to.

"Anybody who could get ahold of them boxes today would be rich. I think they're still there where we left 'em."

"Why do you say that?"

"We was the only ones who knew where they were."

"But after the war, certainly the army sent a party back to retrieve them. Anything that valuable wouldn't be left lying around."

"That's just it. I don't think the army knew where to look for 'em. If somebody didn't know exactly where to look, they'd never find 'em."

"What do you mean?"

"Don't you see? They was killed in the war. I heard the major—Coarde was his name—he went on to Libya and got it in the desert against Rommel. The lieutenant, Breckley, was on the same ship as me from Greece. And in the same unit that went to Burma. When the Japs attacked us that night, he was killed. Saw his body just before the Japs got us, had a nasty head wound. Almost didn't recognize him. Anyhow, with them two officers dead, that gold must still be there. 'Cause I ain't told nobody about it before tonight. The army never asked me. I guess they forgot about it. There was no way anybody could ever find that gold. Me and the major hid it too well."

"Do you remember where it was?" Alfred asked cautiously, struggling to conceal his interest.

"Flamin' right I do. The major drew a map. I watched him do it. Never forgot it. Drew it a hundred times in that blasted prison camp. Kept me sane, it did, gave me something to think on besides those bloody Japs."

"Do you think you could redraw it now?"

"Already have."

"What?"

"I got it hidden in my upstairs chest of drawers. Like to see it?"

"Yes, it might be interesting." Might be interesting, indeed. Alfred could feel his heart beating in his throat.

Waddell got up from the chair and slowly plodded up the stairs. In a few minutes he returned with a brown envelope. He pulled out a large white piece of paper and carefully unfolded it, revealing for the first time to anyone the big secret of his life. Waddell had thought of the treasure many, many times. He had dreamed of going back and digging it up and becoming rich. Buying a nice house for Margaret, maybe buying a pub somewhere in Sussex. Living in the country in style like good folks. But he had been too sick. Too tired. And the major had warned him. Telling anyone would mean jail. He hadn't wanted any conflict with the law.

There were two rough sketches, both done with pencil. The first showed something that looked like a layer cake.

"That's what the hill looked like. One level on top of another. Counting down from the top, we put the boxes in the fifth layer down. It was a small cave. Then the major blasted it shut with his grenades. We piled stones on the outside to make it look natural and all. When we was finished, it was like nobody had ever been there."

"This other map is the location of the hillside?"

"That's it. This road ran from the main highway between Ptolemais and Kozani."

Alfred looked at the maps closely. It was hardly a believable story. A million pounds' worth of gold stashed away in a hillside in northern Greece. Still, there was no reason for Jimmy to make it up, particularly now. Not only that, he wasn't smart enough to invent a story like this. It had to be true. Vaguely, Alfred remembered hearing a similar tale, but he couldn't quite place it.

"What are you going to do with the maps, Jimmy?"

"I ain't got much longer, you can have 'em. I know you got friends who go in for that sort of thing. Maybe they could get it, or maybe you can. I only ask one thing. Share it with Margaret. I ain't been able to give her much in life, except trouble. I owe her somethin'. If you can find that gold, just make sure she gets a fair share."

* * *

The coal fires of the Dicken's era were long cold. But the musty atmosphere, the ambience of old England, was very much alive in the shop, now one of the more established antique and map shops in Mayfair. The sign on the outside said simply "Antiques, prop. J. Alfred Thompson." A bell jangled each time the door opened, introducing a visitor to a cluttered room filled with valuables and junk of the distant and recent past. On a wooden table by the entrance was a painted wood carving of Saint George slaying the dragon. Around it were wood chests with elaborate brass fittings, brass pots, elegant eighteenth-century rural French andirons, and a number of

Ming-dynasty plates. One corner of the room was devoted to sundials, in brass, wood, and even ceramic, all of them well over a hundred years old. At least a half-dozen globes were scattered around the shop, displaying maps made by cartographers of the seventeenth and eighteenth centuries.

Shuffling around in the shop was a fleshy, spectacled figure with the melancholy of a basset hound, J. Alfred Thompson, dealer in antiques, curios, and old maps in Mayfair for nearly thirty-five years. The lifeless graying hair which once graced the top of his head had shifted with age to the back of his skull, straying carelessly over his collar. He looked so much a part of his coffee tweed suit it would have been difficult to imagine him wearing anything else. He was, after all, himself a fixture, a curio, as much a part of the shop display as anything else in it.

Dealing in antiques, both real and fake, provided Thompson a comfortable living. But his real interest was maps, particularly treasure maps. As a young man he had learned to read and speak Spanish with a workable degree of fluency. This later led to his particular interest in old treasure maps of the pirates and Spanish adventurers. A number of times he had closed shop and gone to Seville on commission from professional hunters in the Caribbean to research documents in the Spanish national maritime archives for traces of long-forgotten galleons that carried treasure and booty.

Thompson was good at this. And reliable. He had a reputation as a meticulous researcher, honest in his dealings with hunters who commissioned him to search Spanish and occasionally English records.

For the past several weeks the map given him by his brother-in-law had been locked in his safe while he tried to decide what to do with it.

Waddell had died only a week after giving Thompson the map. As a result, Thompson never had a chance to talk to him again, to ask the many questions that had formed in his mind since that January night. Was there any chance Coarde made an official report to someone about the gold before he was killed? How much had the boxes weighed? Was he sure no one else knew about the treasure? But above all, if he was sure the gold was there, why hadn't he gone after it? Was it just that he was afraid?

At the funeral, Maggie said nothing about the maps. She apparently regarded the whole affair as another of Jimmy's drunken fantasies. Without saying so, she gave the impression she thought the whole business was rubbish. A few tears slid down her face as Jimmy's casket was lowered into the ground. But Thompson knew she didn't weep for Jimmy. She wept for herself, for the life that might have been, for a young love that turned stale and then as rotten as Jimmy's teeth because of the cruel restrictions life imposed on her. Thompson wanted to say something, to comfort her. No, she wouldn't understand. There was nothing more he could say. It was done.

All that was left of Jimmy was the map. It was hard to decide what to do. Alfred himself was far too old. The arthritis made it impossible for him to go off into the Greek mountains to look for something that might not be there. If someone was to go, it would have to be someone else, someone younger. But that was the problem. Who should go? One evening, sorting through some Caribbean maps, it came to him. He finally recalled the story he had heard several years before, and he suddenly knew who should go to Greece.

6

It was, Brian Ritter realized, an absurd moment to be pondering the words of a dead German. A toss-off phrase from long ago, a notion that had lingered, was now, in the most deadly crisis of his life, adding to his torment.

He struggled frantically with the line, trying to free his foot. As pressure built steadily, uncomfortably in his lungs, the implications of it all panicked him.

They would slouch around on the dock staring at his gray flesh, asking how it happened. Police would arrive. A doctor would certify what they all could see. The ambulance attendants would make quips about another hunk of meat, while the boys from the boat grimly shook their heads trying to explain.

How had Thomas Mann put it? "A man's dying is more the survivors' affair than his own." An offensive thought. He was not ready for it. He couldn't accept it.

Ritter tugged furiously on the line again. His breath was nearly exhausted. He instinctively raised his arm and realized for the first time there was air in the darkness just above him. Air. If he could only get his foot free. With a final desperate effort he doubled up pulled on the line with both straining hands, and yanked his foot loose. He rose immediately to the small air pocket, a few inches of life-supporting oxygen between the briny water line and an unknown surface. The cool air rushed into his gasping, grateful lungs.

When the boat capsized, Ritter had lost his bearing and sense of direction. Now it was totally dark. It was obvious which way was up, but he had no idea which way was out. He rubbed his hands along the surface just above his nose as he continued to tread water. A wall? The ceiling? He had been in the cabin when they hit the rocks. Which way out now? The air was beginning to sour. The limited oxygen already was running out.

Deep shit, he thought. Got to get out. Find one of the doors. Escape. The boat couldn't be too far down. The sea was no more than twenty to thirty feet deep where they hit the rocks. With luck he could reach the door, open it, and swim safely to the surface with a single effort.

Ritter groped along the pocket, searching for a clue to his position. How well he thought he had known the cabin. Now everything was strange. The table, upside down. Bolted to the floor. So it was the deck above him. The damned boat had somehow turned completely over.

The air was getting worse. Not much time left. He had to use precious reserves to find an exit from this soggy would-be coffin. He might have only one chance, at best two, to make it. He tried to concentrate, to remember where the cabin door was in relation to the table. Keep calm. No panic now. Remember how the cabin was laid out. He realized there was no way to know which side was which. The table was in the middle of the cabin. Any direction was a crapshoot. He tried to relax for a moment, sucked in another breath, and slipped down in the uncertain darkness, heading for a side that hopefully would have a door. He groped his way along. A bench and a shelf. Damn. Wrong way. He pulled along the wall, across the corner. His lungs were straining again. He reached the doorway. Light suddenly began streaming through a nearby porthole. The wreckage was shifting. For the first time he could partially see. Movement of the wreck meant the storm was still roaring or the wreck was caught in a current. Pain seared his lungs. Tough to concentrate. He had to return for more air. But now he at least knew where the door was. He could return directly to it and open it. Safety. He rose back up to the air pocket. Originally fresh and cool, the air was now warm and stuffy. Unsatisfying. Not much oxygen left. He fought to catch his breath, sucking, gasping. Get ready for the last dive. One way or the other.

Ritter took one final breath, gulping all the oxygen left in the air pocket, then pushed off from the deck above him and slipped back under the water. As he did, the boat shuddered and lurched, a loud disturbing noise, distorted in the water. The light began to fade. He swam frantically for where he thought he had left the doorway. He touched the side. The door had shifted. Which way? Damn. Lost the bearing again. Tortured lungs bursting. Darkness tightening in on him. Another loud noise. Thoughts of his body on the dock.

* * *

The rain had stopped. Half a dozen persons who saw the boat capsize on the reef at the height of the squall hovered around him, looking down. His normally bronzed skin had a deathly gray tone to it.

"He's coming around," said the man kneading the muscular back with strong, experienced hands. He'd been breathing his own breath into the lifeless form. "Come on. Move back," the man shouted. "Let him get some air."

Ritter coughed, regurgitating salty, slimy liquid. His lungs were gradually clearing.

"Close call," said someone in the crowd. "If we hadn't reached the cabin when we did, he'd been a goner."

"Godawful lucky," said the man with the strong hands, continuing to press down on Ritter's bruised back. "He was down there a long time. Didn't think we could get him." He shook his head. "He's either got the greatest set of lungs in the business or he's the most resourceful man alive. Must have taken us at least fifteen minutes to find him."

Ritter was making a low moaning sound. He was going to make it. The man rolled him over. Ritter coughed up more fluid from deep inside. His breathing was becoming more regular.

"Let's get something over him, keep him warm. He's suffering from shock."

"Yeah," said the man, dropping an offered jacket over Ritter's trembling body.

"Cool, this guy, you know. A survival artist. None of the rest of us woulda made it. No way."

No one contradicted him.

*　*　*

The hotel's glass-bottomed boat sputtered into silence and glided through the rolling surf toward the beach. Guests who had spent the morning spearfishing and skin diving off a coral reef two miles east of the bay expectantly gathered together their belongings. Two ebony men leaped over the side of the craft to pull it to the beach, their muscular bodies glistening with dripping sea water and sweat as they struggled to tug the boat to the edge of the sand.

The newly tanned guests, some loaded with scuba-diving gear and others holding aloft strings of fish for those on the beach to admire, climbed over the side of the boat. A well-shaped young woman barely covered by a black string bikini and a diving mask pulled back onto her head brought a noticeable scowl or two from pudgy sunburned wives whose overweight husbands eagerly jumped up to inspect the catch.

"Now there's a great looking honey," Ritter clicked his tongue in an approving way. "We should have gone diving this morning, after all." A lazy smile eased over his face. It was a face not handsome by Madison Avenue standards; one could never imagine Ritter modeling shirts in *The New York Times Magazine*. His ears were slightly too big and his infectious grin was sometimes almost too broad. He was only of average height and his nose was slightly crooked, the result of a war injury. Yet Ritter's almost casual, relaxed approach to life proved irresistible to women. His muscular body, strong arms and legs, his tight belly, added to the appeal. His sandy hair had begun to thin out, but he still carried the eternal-beachboy look. A bright silver cross hung around his neck over the blond hair on his chest.

Ritter and Nelson, a lean wiry man who, like Ritter, looked as if he had spent his entire life somewhere on a beach, gazed out over the sunny scene from the cool comfort of the hotel's bar. The circular room was walled with large green-tinted glass panels extending from the floor to the ceiling, through which the pair could see the girl. Leafy green plants and strategically placed palm trees along with an artificial waterfall produced the effect of a cool indoor jungle.

Ritter ran a large, weathered hand over his hair and glanced down at his glass. His ears framed a face that only hinted at his nearly fifty years. His blue eyes were filled with bright enthusiasm, but if one looked carefully, the furrows around them and on his forehead, baked into place by years of hot tropical sun, revealed he was not as young as his well-proportioned body suggested. Constant work as a diver had kept him in the excellent shape that much younger men envied.

Ritter and Nelson had arrived at the hotel the previous afternoon for a few days' relaxation in one of the luxury spots of the Caribbean. For the past seventeen months they had labored recovering treasure from the wreckage of three sixteenth-century Spanish galleons off the coast of Barbados. The dive nearly ended in disaster when a sudden storm capsized one of their boats, trapping Ritter underneath. After settling their expenses, the partners had flown to Jamaica to unwind, enjoy their joint profits and contemplate their next move.

The Barbados dive had brought Ritter more money than he had ever known at one time in his life. As he sat sipping his drink and looking at the bikinied girl, he felt very glad to be alive.

"Come with me to Greece," he said to Nelson. "Thompson wouldn't have written unless he thought he was onto something good. Years ago, during the war, I looked for some gold in Greece, but never found it. Always wanted to go back."

Nelson shook his head. Since he and Ritter had gotten together nearly five years before, things had gone well. They had brought up a number of treasures, and now Nelson was pressing for another big hunt right where they'd just come from, Barbados. He couldn't understand Ritter's interest in some fantasy gold at the other side of the world. They'd talked about it many times, but Nelson remained adamant. No Greece. This time, Ritter would go it alone. Although he knew he'd miss Nelson, Ritter felt an odd surge of excitement at the thought of pushing back the clock nearly thirty years.

* * *

For most of the morning, Thompson thought of little else but Ritter's arrival. This was definitely the answer to his problem. Too old and arthritic to go himself, Thompson needed someone trustworthy. Assuming the gold was really there, a split would not be a bad deal. After all, the gold would be deposited in a Swiss bank, sold off on the Zurich market, and the money put into secret numbered accounts. The tax people would never have to know about it. Half a million sterling tax-free was more than most people ever saw in their entire lives.

Thompson had known Ritter for more than a decade. Although they had met only twice before, when Ritter came to London looking for a Spanish researcher, and later during Thompson's only trip to the Caribbean, their relationship had always been warm. Ritter was meticulously honest in their dealings, paying on time and twice even paying more than they had agreed on as a result of successful dives. In fact, of all the treasure hunters Thompson knew, Ritter was the best. He liked none better. But above all, Ritter had once told him about a missing British gold shipment in northern Greece. Maybe this was the same gold. Maybe not. But Ritter at least had some experience in the Macedonian mountains, he was smart, and he had always been trustworthy.

Ritter showed up amid Alfred Thompson's curios at noon. The two men repaired to the pub around the corner almost immediately, Thompson hanging a neatly lettered sign on the door that announced "Out to Lunch."

"You appear to have survived in excellent shape," Thompson said, running his eyes up and down Ritter. "But I see you still have that scar on your temple."

"Compliments of the Wehrmacht," Ritter said, settling down in the Pig and Grouse, known to local residents for its old London atmosphere and tasty bar snacks, the British equivalent of haute cuisine. "So, what about this big find in Greece?"

Thompson told him about Jimmy Waddell and his maps.

Ritter's eyes went wide with surprise. "That sounds familiar," he said, launching once more into his own unsuccessful treasure hunt during the war.

"I'd like to try again," Ritter said, "but I don't speak the language. A hunt through those mountains will require a guide, someone fluent in Greek."

"I know someone who might be persuaded to go with you."

"Is he Greek?"

"Half and half. The other half is Lebanese. He's a smooth operator. Just might be interested in this."

7

The hush of big, serious money filled the room. Whether crowded around the roulette tables, perched on stools playing blackjack, watching or being watched, no one spoke much above a whisper.

It was the nearly religious reverence for the arrogant and ostentatious wealth that made the scene possible. The holy devotion to smart looks, large diamonds, expensive clothes, and the exhilaration of winning or being able to afford to lose. The self-fascination of the beautiful people at play. The smoky, alcoholic atmosphere was further stimulated by the distinct presence of fear. Or, perhaps more accurately, the electric tension generated by the imminent loss or possible gain of thousands of dollars on a single turn of a wheel or a card over which only fate had control. At best there could be misplaced and often desperate hope, or in some cases, foolish but nearly mystical faith.

Above the general murmur, plastic chips clicked gently on the padded green tables. Mechanical voices of the stonefaced croupiers could be heard sorting out winnings and losings, preparing for the next suspenseful journey of the little metal ball around the edges of the large red-and-black wheel.

Men in billiard-green jackets scurried about emptying ashtrays, dusting away imaginary flecks of dust, occasionally picking up fallen chips from the plush red carpet and handing out scoring cards for those who took an orderly or pseudo-scientific approach to the mysteries of roulette-table numbers.

Gambling has been widely regarded as a form of pleasure, a game of chance in the name of sport, relaxation, or good fun. Few here showed it. Most of the casino guests affected grave expressions, particularly those with money at stake.

Drifting through the crowd of Pierre Cardin-suited men and Dior-dressed women was the evening's prize show-off. Her hair was dyed nearly white to match her floor-length gown, which was molded over her breasts and slit down the front as far as her navel. Obviously conscious of the attention she attracted even among such a sophisticated gathering, she wore an artificially bored expression and puffed continuously on thin plastic-tipped cigars.

As usual on Friday nights, one end of the elegant casino hall was roped off for a backgammon tournament. The players, mostly men, huddled over expensive leather boards, tossing dice onto them to provide firepower for opposing small armies of polished marble stones.

Elias Khoury swore, first in Arabic, then in Greek. The dark-eyed man opposite him pretended not to notice. He had just rolled a double four, permitting him not only to knock a key Khoury stone off the board but to block the return of the stone to the board. The game was the tie-breaker in their match, and Khoury, muttering quietly to himself about evil luck and certain parts of the anatomy of the man's sister, had almost certainly lost. Like many men of the Middle East,

Khoury considered himself one of the best backgammon players in the world. That self-centered belief reflected as much about the game of backgammon as about the mentality of Khoury's joint Greek and Lebanese heritage.

Backgammon, often known as "the cruellest game," is largely a matter of chance. Rolls of the dice primarily determine the outcome. But it also is a game of odds, and an experienced player with an intimate knowledge of those odds has a strong edge over a lesser player. The cruel hazard for any experienced player is that a novice, with the help of cooperative dice, can in a given situation overcome even the best player. Intellectually, all good players understand this. Emotionally, it is impossible to accept.

The dark-eyed man, an Egyptian reputed to once have been a high-class procurer for King Farouk, was in a winning position and obviously enjoying it. He said nothing, but with every roll of the dice he puffed triumphantly on a Cuban cigar. The match between him and Khoury had been close, as is common between evenly matched players. But a series of good rolls in the last and deciding game had put the Egyptian in an unbeatable position.

Khoury glanced across at the woman sitting behind the Egyptian. She wore a black brassiere under a sheer yellow see-through blouse. The brassiere was tightly wrapped around a fleshy, overweight frame that might have once been regarded as attractive, but now too many nights of overeating, overdrinking, and general indulgence had taken their toll. Khoury wondered whether years ago she might have been one of Farouk's favorites and a big earner for the Egyptian across from him. The Egyptian rolled the dice again, spilling them out of a heavy leather playing cup onto the board. A four-six. Khoury had lost for certain. The roll permitted the Egyptian to begin lifting his stones off the board while still blocking Khoury from playing.

Typical of my luck these days, Khoury thought. In the past year or so things had certainly not gone well. In the Turkish invasion of Cyprus, Turkish bombs hit a dry-goods store he owned in downtown Nicosia, wiping it out. The insurance company refused to honor the policy, saying it did not cover war damage and thus the stock as well as the business was a total loss. Just over a year later at the height of the Lebanese civil war, a group of Palestinians looted a jewelry store he owned with his brother George. Losses again were heavy. On top of these two setbacks came yet another, the most expensive and unexpected of the three.

During a lull in the fighting in the banking district of Beirut, members of the Syrian-controlled Palestinian Saiqa group broke into the burning branch of the British Bank of the Middle East and looted it. Among the millions of dollars in cash and valuables scooped out of the vault and safe-deposit boxes was $650,000 worth of cut diamonds Khoury had stored to cool off. The diamonds were the haul from the robbery of a Belgian diamond merchant the year before. As an investment, Khoury bought the stones through a French intermediary at a cost far below their market value. Because the stones were cut and thus possible to trace, they were purchased with the knowledge that they'd have to be stored for at least five years before they could be gradually released back into the market through Khoury's own jewelry store.

The combined setbacks cost Khoury well over a million dollars in little more than a year.

The imminent hundred-dollar loss to the Egyptian, of course, was relatively minor. For Khoury was not exactly broke. But his current fortune was not endless, and the series of reverses had shaken him.

Over the past decade his fortunes had ebbed and peaked like the tides. A nightclub he bought attracted the beautiful people for a season, then fell out of vogue and folded.

An investment in a publishing house seemed promising until a couple of nonsellers reversed his fortune, putting the company in the red. After a few years Khoury had sold out.

At one point he backed a treasure hunt for a cousin who brought up a modest fortune from the wreckage of a Spanish merchantman off the coast of Bermuda. His cousin cheated him out of what he was due, he was sure, but did repay the original loan plus ten percent. So Elias Khoury was not able to complain loudly.

Khoury's fortunes had taken another of their turns in Paris when he met Dr. Hermann Straussmann, who had achieved an unwelcome degree of notoriety in World War II as a top official of the Nazi Sicherheitsdienst, or SD, in Yugoslavia. The SD was the sadistic security arm of the dreaded Gestapo, the front-line unit in Hitler's campaign to eliminate the Jews. At the end of the war Straussmann escaped to Italy and with the help of friends in the Vatican made his way to the safety of Egypt, where he became a friend of Prince Abbas Halim, King Farouk's pro-Nazi cousin. In the years that followed, he became one of Europe's most notorious gun-runners, selling to anyone who could pay, cash up front. Among his customers were the Muslim Brotherhood of North Africa; a number of black African underground groups, including the Mau Mau in Kenya and the Biafran rebels in the Nigerian civil war; Kurdish nationals in Iraq; the IRA; various Palestinian groups; and both Christian and Muslim private armies in Lebanon. On a more limited basis, Straussmann also sold small arms to the EOKA Greek Cypriot terrorist organization. The link between Straussmann and EOKA was Elias Khoury.

Working through contacts of his mother's family in Greece, Elias Khoury arranged over the years a number of small shipments purchased through Straussmann. A typical shipment included submachine guns and hand grenades shipped to the Greek-controlled port of Famagusta in crates labeled "engine parts."

EOKA sympathizers in the customs service assured the shipments reached their destination unmolested.

Initially, of course, EOKA activity was directed against the British colonial government. When the Union Jack was hauled down and Cyprus became independent, the new EOKA-B group led by Colonel George Grivas targeted itself against the regime of Greek Cypriot President Archbishop Makarios. The churchman was accused of being too soft on the volatile Turkish issue and dragging his feet on joining Cyprus politically to the Greek mainland.

In the wake of the 1974 overthrow of Makarios and the resulting Turkish invasion, the EOKA-B organization was badly damaged. Many were killed battling first Makarios supporters and only a few days later the Turkish Army. The EOKA-B groups also used up large amounts of their military supplies, and with the Turks having captured Famagusta and effectively closing Nicosia airport, normal resupply channels were badly disrupted.

When Makarios finally returned triumphant to the badly bruised island, the remaining EOKA-B elements were forced further underground. Shortly after, one of the leading EOKA-B cells regrouped, and with financing from a well-to-do Greek businessman, decided to institute a cross-the-border guerrilla operations against Turkish occupation forces firmly entrenched on the northern half of the island.

A mainland Greek, Dimitri Metaxas, whose cousin was a key leader in the cell, was asked to make contact with Khoury to acquire automatic weapons and explosives.

At the moment, Metaxas was playing backgammon at the table next to Khoury. Earlier, he had given the agreed recognition signal by pulling a red silk handkerchief from the breast pocket of his gray suit jacket at an appointed time. Khoury caught the move and answered by coughing loudly across the room and then pulling out his own handkerchief to wipe his mouth.

The Egyptian, oblivious of any of this, in fact oblivious of anything except the board and the dice, grunted with satisfaction as he rolled a final double six. With his pudgy hand he reached down and picked his last four stones off the board.

On the previous roll Khoury had managed to get one stone off the board, thus preventing a humiliating loss of a double game. The Egyptian forced a smile, his yellowed teeth showing through his liquid lips.

Khoury extended his hand across the board. "Congratulations," he said in Arabic. "You played well." He really meant the Egyptian had been damned lucky.

"Thank you, my friend," responded the Egyptian. "I was fortunate." He meant, of course, there was no question his superior skill had showed itself.

Khoury excused himself politely, and still muttering to himself about the Egyptian's luck and sexual deviations of the man's sister, drifted downstairs to the bar.

He waited only about half a scotch and water before Metaxas entered, nodded in recognition, walked to his table, and sat down. "The gods were unkind to me tonight," Metaxas said in Greek. Khoury answered, also in Greek, with the expected reply to the verbal identification signal. "That is sad, brother, but one cannot expect to win all the time."

They quietly introduced themselves, and Khoury signaled for a waiter. "What will it be?" he asked as the man approached. "Double scotch," Metaxas said, looking up as the waiter reached them. The order was acknowledged and the man quietly disappeared.

"How was your luck tonight?" asked Metaxas politely. "I gather the Egyptian had the dice with him."

"Acch," muttered Khoury.

The younger Greek, sensing he had touched a tender nerve, quickly tried to change the conversation. "Well, win some, lose some," he said with a casual wave of his right hand. "Who was the woman with him?"

"One of the whores he used to provide for Farouk," said Khoury unpleasantly. His anger over losing was subsiding slowly. The waiter arrived with the drink for Metaxas. Khoury ordered another for himself. He looked again at Metaxas. He saw a rugged man, probably in his mid-thirties. Perhaps he was a sportsman or managed to spend a lot of time outdoors. There was healthy color in his face, and his eyes were attentive. They were the eyes of a man in the prime of life, filled with confidence in himself. Khoury was not unimpressed.

There was a moment of silence as each man sipped his drink, carefully, like two wrestlers sizing each other up.

Metaxas looked closely at Khoury. Khoury's premature double chin indicated he was not in top physical shape. Probably does little exercise, thought Metaxas, and doesn't push himself away from the dinner table quickly enough. On the other hand, Khoury was very much at home in the elegance of the casino. He wore the surroundings as easily as his expensive white suit. Despite Khoury's temperamental outburst about the backgammon game, there was an obvious sophistication to him that could not be lightly dismissed.

Khoury, sensing he had gone far enough, broke the silence. "Well,"—he laughed artificially—"it was not a major loss. I'll have another crack at him. And then we shall play for real money and I shall show him how the game is played. But enough of that. Tell me, what brings you to the Riviera?"

Metaxas relaxed slightly, although his instincts cautioned him against letting his guard down too far. There were times even a jackal might seem harmless. "I assume our mutual friend told you something about the purpose of my trip?"

Khoury nodded. Metaxas' cousin, with whom Khoury had dealt years ago, had written saying friends were interested in buying some land. A further exchange of letters had established the meeting arrangements.

"I understand you are interested in real estate."

Metaxas laughed. "Yes, if you are talking about plots," he quipped. "We have need of some items I think you could provide."

"It is possible," countered Khoury, still fencing with Metaxas, cautiously feeling him out, avoiding the first move.

"Can you provide Sterlings?" Metaxas referred to the British-made 9-mm submachine guns introduced in the mid-1950's to replace the Sten gun in the British armed forces.

"Depends. What model?"

"We need the kind with built-in silencers. Folding stocks. Thirty-four-round magazines. The usual."

"What quantity did you have in mind?"

"At least fifty. We would take delivery of sixty, with ammunition of course. Fifty magazines with each item. We also need one hundred hand grenades. U.S. military specs."

"Hmmm. Could be expensive. What's the delivery point?" Khoury was now doing what he loved most, dealing. The words slipped out of his mouth as smoothly as the patter of a Persian-rug salesman.

"Larnaca."

Khoury thought quickly. It was a small order, but a potentially profitable one. He tried to calculate his profits against the cost of each item and the cost of getting them safely to Cyprus. He scratched his chin, trying not to show he was already adding up the money involved. "How soon would the order be needed?"

"How soon could you deliver?"

Khoury did not want to lose the initiative. He parried the question with yet another. "Would forty-five days be suitable?"

Metaxas nodded.

Sensing the right moment, Khoury made his move on the key point. "Each Sterling will cost three hundred U.S. dollars paid in advance. In addition, it will cost you thirty dollars for each magazine and fifty for each hand grenade. Delivery in Larnaca port guaranteed."

Metaxas grunted. The order was going to cost even more than they had allowed for. "Your price is high," he said softly, a slight tone of accusation in his voice. He looked straight at Khoury.

The older man had expected a strong response and was ready for it. "This equipment is not cheap. It is also the best available. There are many expenses involved in addition to the purchase price of the weapons. Customs officials must be looked after. Documents must be purchased. They also are not cheap." There was another factor he did not have to mention. It was virtually impossible for EOKA-B to obtain weapons in the quantity they needed in any other fashion. Since the collapse of the junta in Athens, supplies from mainland Greece had dried up.

Metaxas picked up his drink and sipped again. He did not speak for a few minutes. He needed time to consider his next words. Khoury was in no hurry. He knew there would be no serious argument.

Looking for a way to avoid showing the obvious, Metaxas decided a further stall was necessary. "I shall have to consult my friends of course on a matter involving so much money and so far over our budget. You are asking perhaps more than we can afford. We have had many troubles. Our funds are limited."

Khoury smiled in a condescending manner. "I understand," he said. "But I hope you also will appreciate my problems. Things are not as simple as they used to be. Palestinian terrorist operations have made it more difficult than ever for us. Authorities have tightened up everywhere. Checks that once were routine are no longer so. In trying to cut off the Palestinians, the German Baader-Meinhof gang, and others like the bandit Carlos, many have been hurt. Expenses have gone up all around."

There was another strained pause.

"Inflation also has taken its toll," said Khoury, speaking sooner than he wanted to. He caught himself. "Let's have another drink." He didn't want to seem anxious, to spoil the deal. It was nearly $100,000 and his profit would be over $50,000. It was not a large amount of money, but it would not take a great deal of work, and he could well use a new injection of capital, even such a small amount.

8

Elias Khoury didn't actually dislike Hermann Straussmann. They had done business successfully together too often for that. And Straussmann's jovial exterior was not altogether unpleasant. But lurking below the surface was something sinister, cobralike, that aroused in Khoury a sense of extreme caution. With a cobra, the snake charmer weaves and bobs to hypnotize the snake, to lull the dangerous serpent into a mood of placid serenity. The danger is that the mood can be easily broken if the movement of the charmer is interrupted, and the snake can suddenly strike.

With Straussmann, Khoury always felt it necessary to remain fluid, to keep his back to the wall, to conduct their meetings in public places. On one level Khoury didn't really think Straussmann would ever cross him or do him harm. It would be bad business. Yet, instinctively, he knew Straussmann would remorselessly snuff him out if there ever was any advantage in it. True, Straussmann was not as young as he once had been, but there are certain poisons that become more lethal with age.

As was customary, Khoury had written to Straussman in care of a post-office box in Zurich. Five days later the reply, stamped in Luxembourg and enclosed in an envelope with no return address, had come back advising Khoury of the meeting arrangements. By mutual consent, the meeting was always in one of the large classical European cafés such as the Kempinski in Berlin, the Sacher in Vienna, or Fouquet's in Paris. This time the note said, "1330 Thursday. The Ritz."

London. And by previous understanding, two days and one hour earlier than stated. Tuesday at 1230.

Khoury had not seen Straussmann's passport, but he assumed the German never traveled under his real name. Although the statute of limitations had expired for crimes committed during World War II, a man like Straussmann undoubtedly had many enemies, people who would pay well for a tip-off to his whereabouts. Straussmann's caution was understandable.

The Ritz was one of the few major hotels in the world that did not have a large sign outside advertising its name and being. Its imposing stone exterior gave the impression of a private club or perhaps some special unmarked government office. It was assumed that those who count knew where and what the Ritz was and to whom it catered. Over the decades its guests had included European royalty, international movie stars, American millionaires, and Arab oil sheikhs. Recent years, however, had not been kind. More modem and flashier hotels had been built. The elegant large rooms with polished brass beds and pool-size bathtubs in spacious bathrooms were no longer profitable in the modern hotel market. The imposing old building had become increasingly expensive to maintain and heat. Tastes changed and so had loyalties. Old money had been overtaken by the nouveau riche, with emphasis on the newest and most modern. Yet, like dethroned royalty, the Ritz lingered on in regal dignity, a relic of past glories.

The one link between its flourishing past and the present was its dining room. The Restaurant Louis XIV still boasted one of the city's most qualified chefs, a Frenchman, of course. The wine list was widely regarded as one of the most sophisticated in Great Britain, with a selection ranging from Château Guraud-Larose '62 to Richebourg '64. The service remained definitely old-world.

It was immediately obvious to Khoury that Straussmann's care and feeding of his stomach had not been neglected. He had not seen Straussmann in nearly twenty-eight months, but in that time the German had added ten to fifteen pounds, mostly, it seemed, around the waist.

"Elias, how are you?" boomed the big German as he strode across the once luxurious lobby. He was immaculately dressed in a heavy British pin-striped wool suit, double-breasted, and carefully tailored. Business must be good.

"*Ca va,* Hermann? How have you been keeping?" Khoury patted his stomach. "Not too badly, I see."

"Ha, Elias, the food is always, how do you say, too good to refuse." Straussmann laughed heartily. His English was basically fluent, but he had never lost the heavy accent so distinctive of many Germans.

They walked into the mirrored gold-leaf dining room, where the formally clad maître d' smartly escorted them to a table overlooking Green Park. An attentive junior waiter immediately poured water into crystal goblets as the headwaiter handed them expensive printed menus.

Straussmann ordered for both of them. As they began working through a consommé madrilène, Straussmann dropped the small talk. "So, Elias, what shall it be this time? A few helicopters? A small howitzer or two perhaps? Or even a used U-boat?" He laughed again at his joke.

"Unfortunately, Hermann, nothing so spectacular. Just 9-mm Sterlings, L34Als. We need sixty, with fifty magazines for each weapon. We also need one hundred hand grenades. American-made, if you have them."

"Sounds like a big hit somewhere, eh, Elias?"

Khoury did not answer. He had no intention of giving Straussmann even the slightest hint as to the weapons' ultimate destination. It was possible Straussmann could figure out or find out for himself, but Khoury wasn't going to help. The grilled sole arrived. Khoury lifted a bite-sized sample to his mouth. It was delicious. He could not resist a satisfied "Hmmmm."

"You like this fish, eh, Elias? I tell you. The fish we used to catch in Yugoslavia. Wunderbar. We had no butter in those days, but fresh out of the stream, cooked in a flat pan, Elias, that was eating. How do you say in English, that was the good old days."

Khoury, chewing on a bite, nodded. The good old days. Playing God. Slaughtering Yugoslav civilians and Jews. Must have been a thousand laughs.

"Yes, Elias, I can get your Sterlings for you. As always. The current price for reconditioned Sterlings is one hundred and twenty dollars each."

"Reconditioned" was a polite trade phrase for "used." At least they were cheap enough.

"The magazines will be fifteen dollars each. And at a discount price for an old customer, thirty-five dollars each for the hand grenades. American-made, of course."

"The magazine price is too high, Hermann."

"Achh. Come on, Elias. It is only money."

"The last time I bought, they were only ten dollars each. And we had several bad ones."

"You never complained about that before."

"It was too late. What were we to do? Stop the action and demand our money back?"

"Okay, for you, a special discount, fourteen dollars each for such a large order." Straussmann's eyes hardened. He didn't like being bargained down, particularly on such a small deal. "Cash in advance, Elias."

It was time for a soothing movement. "As always. Hermann. Forty-eight hours before delivery."

"And the delivery place?"

"Antwerp. The crates should be labeled 'machine parts.'"

"That vill be no problem. Delivery in ten days."

"Agreed. Payment in the usual manner, I assume?" Deposited into a numbered Swiss bank account.

"Natürlich."

A waiter brought them strawberry tarts and poured one of the house specialties, a Chateau Coutet '66.

"So, Elias, I drink to your health. And your good business sense. It is always a pleasure."

"Here's to you, Hermann."

Khoury sipped the light wine and glanced across the table at Straussmann, who winked cheerily at him and drank deeply. His alcoholic flush was becoming more pronounced. Damn, thought Khoury. I should have driven him down on the price of the Sterlings. At least he's paying for lunch.

Khoury watched the German disappear in the backseat of a black Austin Taxi that wove its way steadily through the traffic down Piccadilly toward Hyde Park Corner. The deal was sewn up. He had the rest of the afternoon before catching the evening flight back to Nice. Time for perhaps a bit more business.

He strolled through Mayfair past the fashionable shops, seeking one he had previously visited some years before. It belonged to a map dealer he had hired to handle research for his cousin's treasure dive in the Caribbean. A pleasant old man with a sharp eye for a profit. The brief note had asked Khoury to come around when convenient to discuss a potentially interesting situation. It was not the kind of note Khoury was in a position to ignore. He finally found the street and immediately recognized the distinctive Tudor-style storefront, although he had not seen it in years. It appeared to be virtually the same. The same white paint and black beams and Old English script lettering on the sign. Same old junk in the windows. Who in the world bought such stuff?

A bell jangled as he walked through the door. In the back of the shop he saw J. Alfred Thompson look up at him, peering quizzically through the wire-rim frames. Although it had been several years. Thompson recognized his visitor immediately. Khoury had come just about when he thought he would. He was a bit plumper, a double chin was spreading out under his already round face, but he had not changed that much.

"Elias, come in."

"Hello, Alfred. You have a good memory."

Thompson remembered Khoury well. He had paid generously for the research in Seville. That in itself was enough. But there was also something else. He had not forgotten that Khoury spoke English, French, Arabic, some obscure African dialect, and, of course, Greek. It was unusual to find someone fluent in so many languages.

"Have a cup of tea, my friend," Thompson said. "It's been a quiet afternoon. This isn't the antique season. People are still licking their Christmas wounds, and the tourists aren't here yet."

Khoury regarded the English as almost Oriental in their affinity for tea. While not as ritualistic as the Japanese, they were nevertheless every bit as serious about a cuppa.

"Thank you, Alfred," said Khoury, accepting a steaming cup and a biscuit.

"Elias," said Thompson, draining his own tea, "you are probably wondering why I asked you to come by. Would you be interested in a new and potentially very profitable business venture?" He pulled out his tobacco pouch and papers and began rolling a cigarette.

Khoury hesitated. He did not wish to appear too eager. It was never wise. "I am always ready to consider a good venture, Alfred. What do you have in mind?" He spoke as if he were merely trying to be polite.

"A treasure hunt."

"Another Caribbean dive?"

"Not exactly. I am talking about a hunt for buried treasure."

"Pirate stuff?"

"More modern."

Khoury stared at a blue-and-white Ming vase. "Why me?" he said, scratching his inky sideburns. He hoped he looked distracted.

"Several reasons." Thompson was not fooled. He sensed he had piqued Khoury's interest. He pulled out a small box of wooden matches and lit his newly rolled cigarette. "I should go myself. But I'm too old. My legs are ailing with arthritis, among other things. Someone's got to go for me. I also need a bit of capital to put into the hunt. As you know, the Inland Revenue chaps take a punitive bite out of what we British earn. As a result it's tough to keep this place open, much less accumulate any capital. There is another important reason. You speak Greek. Another cuppa tea?"

Khoury stirred in his chair and handed over the bone china for a refill. "What kind of treasure is this, Alfred?"

"Gold. Bullion and coins. From what I can tell at this point, about a million pounds' worth. Maybe more, maybe just a fraction less. But certainly well worth going after. If you're interested."

"That much money is always of interest," Khoury said, struggling to keep his voice at flat as possible. "Just where is the gold?"

"In northern Greece. Left behind by the British Army in World War II."

"How do you know where it is and what it is?"

"I'll explain later. But first, I need to know if you'll accept my terms. I will need a cash investment and at least a month of your life. You will not have to go to Greece alone. An old friend of mine will be with you. He can provide the muscle. He is an American, seasoned, reliable, and nobody's fool. The project is too complicated to be handled by one man. Getting the gold out of the ground and out of Greece will he difficult. I am thinking in terms of a three-way split."

"How much investment?"

"I should think five thousand pounds sterling would be more than enough. That would cover basic travel costs, the purchase of tools and a vehicle, and miscellaneous expenses we can't foresee at this point."

It was not Elias Khoury's kind of project. Normally, he expected others to do the heavy, dirty work for him. But this was obviously different. A million pounds cut three ways, even in these inflationary times, was still a lot of money. Khoury leaned back in his chair and looked at Thompson. He saw a much older man, probably in his middle sixties. What was left of his hair was gray, but his permanently sad eyes, framed by the wire-rim spectacles, sparkled when he was excited, as he was now. It was basically a crafty face, but also the face of a pragmatic man.

"I'm in the middle of a deal that will take ten days to two weeks to clear up," Khoury said. "Once it is settled, I might be able to give you a month. The investment money is no problem. But there is one obvious condition. I must be convinced the deal is worth the risk, that it's on the level, before I consider it. I don't have time or money for a flutter."

"That is understandable. I have no doubt you will be convinced and enthusiastic once you have been briefed."

Thompson didn't say so, but there was another reason for having both Ritter and Khoury on the hunt. Not only would the two men complement each other and make a good team, but it was plainly in Thompson's interest that the two keep an eye on each other.

9

The water-blurred sign on the inside of the door said "Closed." Ritter tapped on the wet glass. The early-spring rain was gushing down London-style, bathing the city and assaulting endless black umbrellas whose stoic owners wistfully dreamed of holidays in the sun. Cold drops crept into the collar of his tightly zipped jacket. A figure in the back stirred. It was Thompson shuffling forward to open up for him. Thompson, an odd old duck. How ironic for him. All these years studying maps and researching treasure hunts for others while unknowingly only a drunken heartbeat away from his own. How ironic also that it was apparently the same treasure he and Rogers and Devan had looked for in 1943. Ritter couldn't get over it. After all these years.

A muffled voice said, "Brian, come in, my boy." Thompson pushed open the door with a loud click. Ritter stepped quickly inside and peeled off his jacket, shaking away some of the water.

"You should get yourself a brolly."

"You should get yourself some sunshine."

Thompson chuckled and motioned Ritter in. Mopping his head with an already damp handkerchief, Ritter moved past the old man and made his way to the back of the shop.

A swarthy man of about forty was seated next to the desk. At first glance he struck Ritter as a Mediterranean antique dealer who had come in to sell Thompson expensive used furniture. He had the smooth look of a commercial man, the polished well-groomed appearance that often grows on those who spend their lives in expensive clothes, good restaurants, and the company of chic women. The man stared intently at Ritter as he moved toward him.

Khoury, who had not known exactly what to expect, was impressed by the American. His athletic bearing encouraged confidence. He was a man who had taken good care of himself, and although obviously well into middle age, still had a lot of life left. He was a man of the outdoors, a man who could handle himself. Yet there was a deceptively leisurely manner about him, the air of a man seldom rushed, seldom in a hurry.

Thompson squirmed between them to make the introduction. He had brooded nervously about the moment all afternoon. The more he thought about it, the more his stomach hurt. What if they didn't hit it off? What if their personalities clashed so badly they couldn't work together? Khoury was intense and secretive. He was a man of the drawing room, a negotiator, an expert in deals and bargaining. There was something shrewd, perhaps even cunning about him. Thompson admired and in fact envied Khoury's smooth command of so many languages. This was the mark of a sophisticate, a man of the world. An inside man with all the accompanying skills. On the other hand, Ritter, easygoing and basically an open person, spoke only English and a smattering of Spanish. He had spent most of his adult life in the outdoors, diving in the West Indies, a more physically oriented but decidedly more provincial existence. Ritter's treasure-hunting experience had taught him patience, diligence in seeking the hard-to-find. Thompson was certain Ritter was the type who would remain cool in a tight and dangerous situation. A man who had spent as much time underwater as Ritter was not one to panic or scare easily. The two had little in common. A dot and a dash. Salt and pepper. But they would need all their combined skills and talents to find the gold and get it out of Greece. If they didn't take to one another, the entire project could be endangered.

Khoury rose slowly and extended his hand. Ritter grasped firmly, making Khoury even more aware of his excellent physical condition. Khoury defensively squeezed hard. Ritter noticed the hand was smooth, not overly muscular.

"How do you do," said Khoury cautiously.

"Greetings," replied Ritter in his languid manner. The visual sizing-up process was only momentary. To Thompson, as the two men briefly examined each other, the moment seemed to last much of the evening. The chairs scraped loudly on the stone floor as they sat down. Thompson busied himself making the expected tea, letting the chemical laws of nature take their course. One of the men cleared his throat.

"Bit wet out there." Khoury broke the stiff silence.

"Yeah," said Ritter. "Like rain in the Amazon. Falls in sheets. Then suddenly, like a spigot, turns off."

"In Africa the rainy season was the same way. Used to drench everything. Often caused flash floods in Conakry. Left mold everywhere, in shoes, clothes, everything."

Thompson let them talk. The casual conversation burned the tension out of the air.

"Gentlemen, a cup of Darjeeling's best." The two accepted the tea from Thompson and he sat down to join them.

"I've been figuring," Thompson said, "that if each of the three strongboxes my brother-in-law Jimmy talked about took three men to lift, they could weigh as much as one hundred and seventy pounds. Assuming the basic weight of each box was already twenty pounds, we are talking about four hundred and fifty pounds of gold. The other two boxes contained perhaps another two hundred pounds. That's a total of six hundred and fifty. At today's prices, I conservatively make it at least a million and a half dollars, maybe almost two million. Shared three ways, it would be about half a million each."

He paused. The only noise was the pelting of the rain and the loud breathing of Ritter and Khoury. Thompson was having no trouble holding their attention.

"Alfred, I'm convinced this is the same gold we were looking for in 1943," Ritter said. "Too many basic points overlap for it to be anything else. But I don't think it is a good idea for us to run into the mountains unless we can find some corroborating evidence. There must be records that can confirm the basic facts."

"I agree," said Khoury. "If we can confirm the two officers were definitely killed, then I am prepared to fully accept the story. We must be sure one of the two didn't somehow survive and hasn't already returned and dug up the gold."

"I'm most concerned about the maps," said Ritter. "It's a basic rule of any kind of hunt, whether it's a dive or a search for buried loot. We must check the sketches against some real maps. Are the roads where Jimmy claimed? Does it seem feasible the burial site could be where he claimed it was? I don't want to go up there unless his sketches correspond to some good maps. If the sketches and maps don't match up, it could be pocket pool whether the gold is there or not."

"The Imperial War Museum can be a starting point for research," Thompson said. "We should be able to verify many of the basics there. The Public Records Office also should be helpful. The official war diaries are there. The maps can be checked at the Royal Geographical Society, and further research can be made through the Ministry of Defense."

A flash of blinding light and a sudden clap of thunder shook the shop. Khoury ducked down, and then, sheepishly, gradually pulled himself up. His face was as white as a lily at a funeral. The noise had startled Ritter too, but Khoury was really shaken.

"Thought they'd gotten me," said Khoury with a weak laugh.

"Let's go out and get a drink," said Ritter.

Khoury had pulled out a handkerchief and was wiping his face. His color was coming back. "A good idea. Let's go, gentlemen. I'll buy."

All three men began putting on their coats. Ritter looked again at Khoury. An interesting man. Obviously intelligent, shrewd. But there was something about him. The idea of depending on him in the treacherous mountains of northern Greece gave Ritter a slightly queasy feeling.

10

After the successes and relatively easy profits of the 1960's and early '70's, Elias Khoury never imagined he would ever again have to hustle like a beginner for a relatively small deal. But the setbacks of the past twenty-four months had stung more than he cared to admit. As a result, the moderate profit he stood to make on the EOKA-B deal was most welcome.

An unexpected setback, however, suddenly made the money more than just welcome; it was urgently needed. Khoury flew from London to Nice to collect three months' rent from an investment company which leased two floors of a small office building he was still paying for. Troubled when he found their offices closed, he was horrified to learn they were bankrupt. All they could offer toward a settlement was the office furniture and appointments. But there were other creditors, lawyers, and it would take months or even years to straighten it all out. Finding a new tenant could take months. In the meantime, Khoury was faced with a hefty mortgage payment on the building. To default would mean the building would become the property of the bank and he would lose his already considerable investment. As a last resort, of course, he could sell the building. But in a city like Nice, word of misfortune spreads fast, like loose dollars in a hurricane. He would never get a price near what it was worth.

Despite the growing pressure, Khoury was calm. The EOKA-B deal, after all, was set. After his meeting with Straussmann, there was little to worry about. For all his idiosyncrasies, Straussman was a proven performer. Khoury had never known or heard of him defaulting on a deal. An agreement with Straussmann was probably not as secure as an investment with AT&T, but profits in percentage terms were always far higher.

A week after their meeting, just as Khoury reached Nice, Straussmann cabled that arrangements were set. As always the cable was brief. "Eloise says all is well. Will arrive as planned on the fourteenth. Asks her ticket reach her no later than the twelfth. Regards. Rachad."

Trust Straussmann to come up with an Arabic signature. The crates would arrive in Antwerp on the fourteenth. Payment of $52,700 would have to be deposited in Straussman's account not later than the twelfth. Khoury was ready now to collect the 50-percent down payment from EOKA-B.

If all went well, that money would be received in plenty of time to make a payment to the bank and give him breathing room to find a new tenant for the building. In addition, he would have the capital to finance the Macedonian gold hunt. It was curious, the gold thing. It had come at just the right moment. A half-million dollars would be more than enough to get his business dealings back on a solid footing. Most of his current loans and debts could be paid off, and there would be enough left over to even finance a new venture or two. He would once again be well-fixed.

The idea of the hunt itself excited him. It wasn't his line, really, lurching off into unknown mountains to look for something they might never find. Roughing it in the mountain villages of northern Greece also had no appeal. It would mean separation from some of the luxuries of modern life he no longer regarded as luxuries, and it would mean temporary separation from Brigit, the secretary who had lived with him for the past year and a half. But the inconvenience would be worth it, if the hoped-for profits were there.

Besides, Ritter amused him. He was open and uncomplicated. A man who never worked too seriously, a man who had devoted his life to the hedonistic pleasures it could provide, a man who, in fact, detested work as most people in the world know it, but a man who could appreciate a chance to make a quick easy hit. Ritter was smart, but not particularly cunning. That would place him at a disadvantage in some situations. But Khoury felt he had enough brains for both of them. Still, Ritter was a hunter by profession. He was making a living at it, and the implications of that could never be underestimated.

Khoury rolled over and looked at the clock. Nearly eight a.m. Brigit was sleeping peacefully beside him. Something last night had really turned her on, and that had turned him on. She was exciting when she got wild like that. He looked at the clock again. He still had more than three hours to get dressed and get to the airport. By early afternoon he would be in Paris. A few hours later he would have the EOKA-B money for the Straussmann payment. There was still plenty of time. He slid his hand under the pale blue sheet onto Brigit's wonderfully smooth bottom. It was time she woke up anyhow.

* * *

Had it not been for Hermann Straussmann, Emil Berbir probably never would have become an agent for Milli Istihbarat Teskilati (MIT), the Turkish CIA.

He probably would have ended up a moderately successful Middle East correspondent for a number of French and German newspapers, providing them with a steady flow of inflated expense accounts and marked-up telex charges as well as colorful copy chronicling the region's bloody revolutions and evolutions.

Emil Berbir was an ambitious and aggressive journalist. He was also one of the early members of the Phalangist party of Lebanon, a move prompted by his basic fascist leanings. In 1935 he was approached by a first secretary at the German embassy. Would he be interested in a position with the German Nachrichtendienst? The German term "Nachrichtendienst" is intriguingly ambiguous. In a strictly civilian sense it means and is used for press agency. In military terms it means intelligence service. In the minds of many, the two are often confused.

Without asking which the German meant, Berbir said yes. Thus it neither shocked nor surprised him when he was asked to report privately on certain matters, particularly those regarding French military affairs in Lebanon and Syria.

When war broke out, Berbir was sent to Turkey, where he spent a year learning Turkish as well as filing news stories and intelligence reports. Using his newsman cover, he operated successfully for a number of months before being transferred to the German-occupied Balkans. It was in Yugoslavia he first met the dashing young captain Hermann Straussman. A series of articles about the heroic exploits of Straussmann's unit was deeply appreciated by Straussmann, who was as vain as he was ambitious.

As the war turned against the Germans in 1943, Berbir was ordered back to Berlin. In 1945, because he was not German and spoke English, he was hired by the American occupiers as a translator. Under the circumstances it was a good thing, until he decided to make it even better and was consequently arrested and jailed for black-market dealings. Berbir was released from detention in 1949 by the new West German government, and he returned to Lebanon to resume his journalistic career.

In August 1952, a few weeks after the overthrow of King Farouk, Berbir was in Damascus on the trail of a story for a Paris paper. In the souk he recognized a familiar face. It was Straussmann, freshly arrived from Egypt. He was accompanied by two swarthy men who were not Arabs. Berbir was certain of this because he knew one of them. They were Turks.

Straussmann was at first startled, then suspicious when Berbir called him by name. After a tense moment, Straussmann recognized the young journalist who had interviewed him years earlier in Yugoslavia. They sat down together for coffee. The Turks, who Straussmann had met while working for Egyptian intelligence under Farouk, were with MIT. Berbir remembered meeting one of the two men casually during his Turkish days. Within a month, Berbir was working for them and on his way to Paris.

For over twenty years Berbir had operated out of Paris, keeping his eye on pro-Communist Turkish students and politicians and Greek intelligence operatives of interest to Ankara. It was not an unpleasant existence. Berbir lived comfortably in the Sixteenth Arrondissement in a five-room apartment with his French wife, Marcelle. The work was not overly demanding and only occasionally even remotely dangerous. Twice, he was asked to eliminate persons the Turks considered threatening. One had been a Turkish Communist who was in a position to blackmail the then newly appointed defense minister. The other was a Greek agent highly regarded by Ankara. In both cases, Berbir dispatched them with relative ease, using a 9-mm Italian-made Beretta automatic pistol. Berbir regarded these acts as potentially hazardous but also as a more or less expected part of his duties and he carried them out with cool efficiency.

Now Berbir, who had managed to put away some money, was thinking of calling an end to it. During two decades in Paris, he had managed to accumulate a modest apartment in Monte Carlo and a bank account in Geneva that would permit him and Marcelle to spend the rest of their years in relative security. Part of this had been made possible by the discovery of some $150,000 in cash in the apartment of the Greek agent he had shot. Berbir never saw any reason to mention the money to Ankara.

"Marcelle," he said looking out of the kitchen window over the park as they shared morning coffee. "Maybe you are right. Perhaps we should go to Monte Carlo this summer."

The woman looked at him. Although she had nagged for the past three years about leaving Paris and retiring to the Riviera, she didn't understand at first. "We are going, dear. What do you mean?"

"I mean it's time to stay. I'm getting too old for this."

Berbir was agonizing over his latest assignment, the elimination of a Greek EOKA-B agent, a mam named Dimitri Metaxas. The invasion of Cyprus and Turkish occupation of the northern half of the island had brought a great deal of international criticism of Turkey and the authorities in Ankara wanted to keep things as peaceful as possible. Any kind of incident could bring Cyprus back into international controversy. Berbir's superior made it clear. The EOKA-B agent was up to no good. Stop him!

Berbir didn't like it. He hadn't been given an assignment of this nature for nine years. He was too near retirement to get mixed up in these things. Why didn't they find a younger man for the job?

* * *

Something was not right. No one except Khoury and Nicosia were supposed to know he was in Paris. And yet, Dimitri Metaxas' intuition told him he was being stalked. Or was it just a case of nerves?

Metaxas arrived in Paris on the early Swissair flight from Zurich, as scheduled. He carried $56,500 in cash in a brown leather attaché case, half the total payment due Khoury. A security man at Zurich airport gave Metaxas a funny look when he spotted the fat stack of thousand-dollar bills during the routine check. Metaxas smiled at him. There was no law against carrying money on a plane, no matter how much it was. The man shrugged and closed the case. The flight proceeded without incident. There was no customs check at the Paris arrival. Metaxas took a taxi to the hotel with the feeling all was well.

As planned, he checked in at the Hotel Pavilion on the Rue St. Dominique around the corner from the Invalides. The hotel was chosen because it was small and inconspicuous, only twenty rooms in a modest brick building some fifty yards quietly off the street. The hotel was patronized mainly by low-budget travelers in need of something clean and respectable. From the busy street a narrow passageway under a sign that said simply "Hotel" led back to a pleasant brick courtyard. It held a white garden table and four matching white chairs with blue cushions. The hotel had a lazy L-shape formed around the courtyard. The rooms in the front overlooked the yard. Those in the back faced onto an apartment building.

Because the courtyard provided the only entrance to the hotel, anyone with a front room could carefully monitor all comings and goings, thus providing a very basic security arrangement. That is, if one knew whom one was on the lookout for.

Metaxas was scheduled to meet Khoury at six o'clock at the hotel. The room would provide proper security for counting and exchanging the money. After his arrival, Metaxas, on his first trip to Paris, decided that with five hours to spare he would treat himself to a bit of sightseeing. It was an easy stroll, the girl at the desk explained, to the Alexandre III bridge and across onto the Champs Elysées. It was during this excursion that Metaxas first began to get the feeling someone was interested in him. He looked around several times, trying to pin down his suspicions. The streets were filled with jostling pedestrians and traffic. It was virtually impossible to pick out anyone showing him unusual attention. Maybe it was just nerves. Carrying around this much money would make anyone nervous, he reassured himself.

Metaxas cut short the walk and returned to the hotel room. He told the girl at the desk he was expecting a visitor around six o'clock. At first glance everything seemed to be as he had left it. But the pillow on the bed looked as if it had been smoothed out. And the closet door was closed. He was sure he had left it partially open. Ah, of course, he told himself. One of the maids had been in the room to tidy up. He was behaving like a child. He locked the door from the inside, deciding to take a nap and wait for Khoury to arrive.

Metaxas stretched out on top of the bed and dozed off. He was awakened by the sound of someone tapping lightly on the door. He looked at his watch. It was almost six. He had slept longer than he intended. Khoury was a bit early.

"Khoury?" Metaxas called out.

"Oui," came the reply.

Metaxas unbolted the door and opened it. In the dark, narrow corridor stood a man he had never seen before. He estimated the man to be about fifty or fifty-five years old. It was hard to say what nationality he was. Perhaps northern Italian or French. His tanned face was covered by liver spots from long years in the sun. His suave gray hair was carefully combed and he was conservatively dressed in an unobtrusive brown suit. Only the man's teeth, yellowed with age and ill care, spoiled the picture of a well-to-do businessman. Oh, yes, there was one other small thing. The man was holding a lethal-looking pistol pointed directly at Metaxas' stomach.

"May I come in?" Emil Berbir asked gently.

It was not the kind of rhetorical question Mataxas felt he was in a position to argue with. Instinctively he stepped back. With a sad smile, Berbir followed him into the room.

Elias Khoury arrived in Paris on schedule, still thinking of Brigit. As he often did, he took a taxi to the George V Hotel. He couldn't afford to stay there these days, but it pleased him to at least afford the pleasure of a late lunch, weather permitting, in the garden. The weather was unseasonably warm, in fact springlike, and Khoury was soon lunching in the fashion to which he once had been accustomed and to which he shortly hoped to become accustomed again.

Shortly after four p.m. he finished coffee and decided to take a long walk before meeting Metaxas at the hotel. He was in a relaxed mood as he wandered along the Seine, thinking of last night with Brigit and the gold in Greece. He stopped at a sidewalk café for another coffee, letting the mild afternoon carry him along. Somehow the girls always looked better in spring, fresher and more appealing as they emerged from their heavy winter wraps. He looked at his watch. Almost time to meet the Greek. There was time enough to walk from the café to arrive right on schedule.

He strolled through the hotel courtyard and up the stairs to the reception desk. A young French girl with rich black hair, a light olive complexion, and a quiet voice was at the desk.

"Which room is Mr. Metaxas in?"

The girl did not have to consult her list. "Room seven, monsieur. Up the stairs and second door to the right. The other gentleman just arrived."

"Thank you," he said impassively, hiding the minor explosion in his chest. The other gentleman? There was not supposed to be anyone else. Khoury's heart pounded as he hurried up the stairs. Reaching the top of the landing, he looked down the narrow hall just in time to see a man with what looked like a pistol in his hand step into Metaxas' room.

Unarmed, Khoury groped frantically through his suit searching for something, anything, that might be useful.

Like a savage cat, he moved swiftly and silently down the dark carpeted hallway. The door was just closing.

Without hesitating, he slammed his shoulder against the wooden frame. There was a sickening thump as he followed the door into the room. The force of the unexpected blow caught Emil Berbir squarely in the back. His breath blew out of him, causing him to drop the automatic. His knees buckled. Metaxas looked on in fascinated terror as Khoury lunged through the door, fell onto the winded man, and drove a plastic ball-point pen into his neck. The man grasped desperately at his throat emitting a nauseated gurgling sound. The pen was protruding from a point just below his Adam's apple. With a final animallike cry, the man went still. His bloodshot eyes stared blankly, seeing nothing.

Khoury got up, rubbing his bruised shoulder. "Who's this?"

"Dunno," said Metaxas breathlessly. "He was going to kill me. Never saw him before. You saved my life." The young Greek was shaking uncontrollably. He felt he was going to vomit. He began to weep.

"Get a hold of yourself," snapped Khoury. "Where's the money?"

Metaxas pointed to the attaché case beside the bed.

Khoury stepped over, opened the case, and counted the bills. It was all there.

11

The girl seated at the sadly worn desk looked up. Her expression was as bureaucratically indifferent as the chipped finish on the piece of aging furniture. "Yes?"

"I have a ten-o'clock appointment with the reference department."

"Name?"

"Ritter."

The girl ran her fingers along a list. "Fill this out, please." Any cooler and she'd be a candidate for frostbite, Ritter thought. The official-looking slip of paper wanted his name, address, and the purpose of his visit. To answer the last point, he wrote simply "research." He handed the sheet back to the girl. Help keep a file clerk productively employed. In a frayed logbook she noted his arrival time.

"Roberts," she called. A small man in a poorly fitting blue uniform ambled over, one of several guards lounging in the lobby. "This gentleman to documents and books."

"Follow me, sir," Roberts said in a soft institutional way. He didn't look at the girl. He didn't like her either.

Ritter trailed him up a brief flight of steps out of the main entrance hall into a long corridor and turned. The left side was lined with display cases crammed with memorabilia of the Battle of Britain: uniforms, autographed pictures of boyish daredevils who had saved the nation, and pictures of their flimsy aircraft.

They turned again and entered an antique elevator, its insides freshly painted blue. It creaked upward to the second floor, where Ritter followed the guard up two more flights of stairs.

A whispery library atmosphere covered the circular room of the documents reference section, with its pastel green walls and dark green carpet accented by fresh gold-and-white trim. Ritter gazed up at the nineteenth century dome overhead, an expensive crystal chandelier suspended from it, evidence of more prosperous days of the empire. Four long curved tables hugged the edge of the room, with a large round reading table in the middle. On one edge of the wall, in artistic gold letters, were inscribed the Ten Commandments, credited to the twentieth chapter of Exodus. Directly opposite, a rack of contemporary magazines offered *Military Affairs, Deutsche Waffen Journal, Aerospace Historian* and *NATO Review*. A sign over a desk to one side said, "Head of Readers' Services."

"May I help you, sir?" said a young woman with receptive brown eyes, a freckled nose, and deep dimples.

"Uhh, my name is Ritter. I called yesterday about some research regarding the 1941 campaign in northern Greece."

"Yes?"

"Well, I'm interested in the period, and, uh, I'd like to get an idea of what sort of material is available."

"Certainly, Mr. Ritter. I suggest you go through the card cataloge."

"Fine." He let her sample the Ritter grin.

She flushed slightly. "Why don't you sit down here? I'll bring out the drawer with the Greece cards. You can thumb through them and see what interests you."

He sat down obediently. The girl disappeared next door into a room with wall-to-wall drawers. In a minute, she returned.

"I'm sorry, Mr. Ritter. You'll have to wait. Someone else is going through that drawer at the moment. Is there some other subject you would be interested in checking?"

"No, I'll wait."

"It shouldn't be long." She wanted to reassure him.

He looked around. A Chinese who could have been a diplomat was deeply absorbed in a thick, tattered volume. A scholarly gentleman with a German accent was discussing Libya with a member of the library staff. Others appeared to be students or academics. Except one, a particularly good-looking young blond woman with pearl earrings. She was not beautiful in a classical sense. Her nose was not entirely straight and her face was slightly too thin. But still, she was extremely attractive and smartly dressed, in a dark blue suit and cream blouse. There was something distinctly erotic about her despite the conservative clothing. Her breasts were not large, but they couldn't be called inadequate, either. She seemed deeply absorbed as she fingered her way through a drawer of cards. Her polished manner was vaguely European, but Ritter didn't think she was British.

She raised her head and signaled one of the staff, who took a number of yellow cards and the drawer from her.

In a minute the girl who had been helping Ritter appeared with the drawer he had asked for.

"If you need any help, Mr. Ritter, I'll be in that room. These yellow cards are requisition forms. When you locate something you want to see, just fill out a card giving the name and reference number. In a few minutes one of us will bring it to you."

From the top of the drawer, the tabs ran from Gatling guns through Hanoi. In the middle was one that said "512.142 Greece WWII."

He began leafing through the material. Several cards offered promising titles, mostly articles or books about the 1941 campaign in Greece. But they were very general, not likely to have the detail he sought. Near the end of the Greece offerings, one in particular caught his eye, an article in the *Journal of the Royal Artillery*, Volume LXXII, 1945, "With the First Armoured Brigade in Greece," written by an officer who had served with the unit. Jimmy Waddell's old unit. A good starting point.

Ritter spent the rest of the morning studying the article and several others. It was quickly apparent that the basic facts of Jimmy's story were true. The First Armoured Brigade had been the main unit charged with defending northern Greece when the Germans rolled over the border from Bulgaria and Yugoslavia. Overwhelmed by German firepower and numbers, the general pullback had begun almost immediately. The unit retreated down the Ptolemais-Kozani road a few days after Jimmy claimed he and the two officers put the gold in the ground. It was hard to believe but this seemed like the same gold Ritter had searched for in '43.

Around one p.m. Ritter's stomach informed him he was hungry. He looked up. The number of persons in the room had thinned out.

The girl with the pearl earrings was still deep in concentration, writing in a red notebook. He watched her for a few moments. She obviously was engrossed in whatever she was doing. He stood up and found the librarian with the dimples who had helped him earlier.

"I want to leave my books and notes here while I get a quick bite for lunch."

"Yes, I'll take you downstairs. When you want to come back up, just check in with the reception desk and get one of the guards to bring you."

"Tight security for a museum, even a war museum."

"Bomb danger mainly," she said. "The Irish, you know. Also, we just can't have people wandering around unchecked. A lot of the documents and books are irreplaceable."

"Suppose so. Know a good place to eat around here?"

"You might try the Ole Bill Café in the basement in the public gallery."

"Who was old Bill?"

She smiled. "Lots of foreigners ask that. Ole Bill wasn't anybody. That's what they called the buses that carried the boys to the front in France in the First World War. Brought' em over from London. The buses, I mean."

"What do you tell the foreigners about the food?"

"It's convenient."

They reached the ground floor. The girl started to return upstairs. "By the way …" Ritter stopped her. "That woman with the pearl earrings and blue suit."

. "You mean the American?"

"American?"

"Yes, the woman seated next to the Head of Readers' Services desk?"

"That's the one."

"What about her?"

"Do you know what she is studying?"

"She's been in the library several times in the past week. Someone said she is doing research on Greece."

The Public Records Office in London's Chancery Lane is one of the great document repositories in the world. Its dusty shelves are laden with deaths and births, land purchases, probate records, legal decisions, ships' logs, war diaries, and other bureaucratic and historical accumulations dating back nearly a thousand years. There undoubtedly would be even more but for the great London fire of 1666 that destroyed many of the city's records.

In traditional British practice, anyone wishing access to the records must produce a letter of introduction. For any British subject, this can be from a member of Parliament, a leading personality from the academic world, a recognized member of the legal profession, or someone else well placed in the establishment. For an American citizen, such letters addressed to the Keeper of the Records are routinely issued by the American embassy in Grosvenor Square upon presentation of a passport at the Special Consular Affairs section.

In a scruffy office at the entrance to the records compound, Ritter handed over his letter to a formal man, his balding head supported by a bow tie.

"What are you interested in seeing, Mr. Ritter?" The voice was middle-class Knightsbridge.

"War diaries of the First Armoured Brigade for 1941."

"As you may know, war diaries are technically classified for one hundred years. However, if you are willing to sign this waiver pledging not to make public use of any of the names you come across, we can forgo that restriction."

Ritter signed. Within a few minutes he found himself in the aptly named Long Room facing the officer-in-charge, a grim-faced girl with dark smooth skin and a Twiggy-esque figure. In terse, businesslike fashion she explained how to fill out the requisition cards after locating in the master index the diaries he wanted. The index covered every recognizable unit in the British armed forces during the Second World War, from brigade to army-corps level. After a thirty-minute search Ritter located references for the First Armoured Brigade, filled in a requisition slip, and settled down to wait. Perhaps he would go out for a cup of coffee on Fleet Street and come back.

He gazed out over the rectangular room. There were four main reading tables, each crowded with serious-looking researchers taking notes and, on the back table, pecking away at typewriters. Shelves of books and records covered one long side and the back wall of the room, partially lit by sunlight filtering through hazy windows on the outside wall.

Most of the readers were poring over old journals and logs. They appeared to be the usual collection of students, hobbyists, historians, writers—and the blond girl with the pearl earrings. There she was, sitting at the third table back, in the corner, as he had seen her before, taking notes from some papers. A bad time for coffee. He didn't want to miss her this time. But it probably wasn't a good idea to interrupt her. He watched her for several minutes. She really was lovely. As though she sensed he had been watching her, she suddenly looked up, staring right at him. Their eyes caught. She held the gaze for a moment, then looked away, out the window, then back down at her notes. Lovely, no question about it

"Mr. Ritter?" One of the librarians calling.

He stood up and went to the desk. "Yes?"

"The war diaries you requested are out at the moment."

"Oh. Can you tell me which of the readers has them?"

"I'm afraid we couldn't do that, sir."

"No, of course not." He already knew. It was too much of a coincidence. The building held millions of documents. The odds of another person having a call on the same obscure document at the same time were about the same as finding a sunken galleon on the first dive. It just didn't happen.

He walked back to the third table until he was standing over her. "You wouldn't by any chance have the war diaries of the First Armoured Brigade, would you?"

She raised her head and her eyes to meet his. Up close she was even more appealing than at a distance. Her eyes were lit with a bright glimmer and her lips parted slightly into a cautious smile. "How would you know?"

"My fairy godmother told me."

"Well, Cinderella, aren't you the lucky one? Did she also tell you it's rude to bother a stranger in a public reading room?"

"Funny. She never mentioned that."

"I'll bet there's a lot she hasn't told you." Her smooth voice was not unfriendly. She spoke American English, as expected—with a slight trace of a French accent, which wasn't expected.

"As a matter of fact, there are one or two minor things she failed to mention, such as why it's taken me so long to meet you."

"You obviously don't frequent the right reading rooms."

"You left the last one before I had a chance."

"Ah." She sighed in recognition. "The Imperial War Museum. I thought I had seen you somewhere before."

"An unforgettable face."

She leaned back in her chair, studying him, showing no haste in breaking off the conversation. "You interested in Greece?"

He wasn't quite ready for the question, "I'm, uh, writing a book. Don't tell anybody. It's a secret. What's your excuse?"

"Working on my doctorate. It's not a secret. You can tell anyone."

"About the First Armoured Brigade?"

"About the 1941 campaign in general. That is just one small aspect."

"I like your timing."

She smiled, not replying. The smile said everything.

"You live here in London?" he asked.

"Just here for a while as part of my research."

"Seeing as we're both working on similar subjects, perhaps we should get together and compare notes. Which leads me to ask an overwhelming question. When are you going to be finished with those diaries?"

"By the end of the day. If you request them now, they'll have them ready for you first thing in the morning."

"How about dinner tonight, then? You can review for me some of the more dramatic highlights."

"Well, I… Sure, why not?"

* * *

Few women in Brian Ritter's life stirred him as thoroughly as Michelle Bennett Simonet.

On his way to the Chelsea wine bar to meet her, he found himself inexplicably skittish. Women never made him nervous. Those days were long past. But he was feeling as uncertain of himself as a kid on a first date. Strange. Strange.

She was seated at the bar, a glass of white wine in front of her.

"Muscadet or German Moselle?" he asked.

"Oh, hello. Didn't see you come in," she said, looking up. "It's a Mâcon Blanc '73. A very nice vintage. You should try it."

"Sounds like you did your master's in wine-tasting."

"Not exactly. Where I come from there are certain things as natural as you might find knowing O. J. Simpson's rushing average."

"Yes, I was wondering. You're the only American I ever met with a French accent," he said, raising a glass of wine the bartender had poured. "Cheers."

"A la votre." She raised her glass. "Actually, I'm only half American. I have both an American passport and a French one."

"How does one manage that?"

"Easy, really. Just be born in France to a French mother and an American father."

"I see. Nothing to it. All carefully arranged in advance."

"Ha." A marvelous girlish laugh gushed out of her slender throat like freshly uncorked champagne.

"Your father was an American tourist with a rich tongue and fat wallet who just swept your mother off her feet."

"My father was not exactly a tourist. I was born in Vierville sur Mer, a village you have never heard of, although it is on one of the most famous beaches in the world."

"The Riviera?"

"Vierville is one of the coastal villages of Omaha Beach. My father was an officer with the U.S. Twenty-ninth Division that stormed ashore on D Day. He was wounded during the day and spent the next three weeks recuperating in a field hospital in Vierville. During his recovery he met my mother, who was working as a volunteer nurse. He spoke very good French for an American, and within a month and a half they were married. I never saw him. He was killed a few months later in the Battle of the Bulge. I was born about six months after he died."

"So that's where the Bennett comes from."

"An old-line Philadelphia family. My American aunts and uncles have been very good to me. I was born Michelle Bennett, of course. But when my mother remarried, I was adopted by her new husband and thus acquired his family name."

"Why the interest in 1941? Seems '44 would be more likely."

"I've already done that. For my master's degree at Cornell, I spun out a long study on France in 1944, the return of De Gaulle, the shattered social and political fabric and the implications of that year on the nation's life for the next twenty years. It's what they call instant history. When I looked around for a similar idea for a doctorate, I thought 1941 would be a good idea. It was in some ways the most interesting year of the war. It was the first full year of occupation in France, and the pressure and consequences of that are still being felt."

"What's the Greek campaign got to do with that?"

"Not much, really. But the weak showing put up by the British in Greece shows that a year and a half into the war, England was in an extremely vulnerable position. Lend Lease began only in March, and that kept them afloat, but financially and in terms of morale, it still looked like the end to many Europeans. People thought the Germans couldn't be beat, that they would have to find a way to coexist with them."

"And what do you plan to do with all this history?"

She shrugged. "I don't know. Teach, probably. I might try to find a job with some unsuspecting university in the States or maybe even in France. I haven't faced up to it yet. It's one of those things one puts off as long as possible, like going to the dentist or sending out Christmas cards."

"Or deciding whether to have dinner or another glass of wine?"

She looked at her watch. *"Alors.* I have been talking too much. I haven't even had a chance to ask you about your book."

"First things first. This is good wine."

She flashed him a partners-in-crime look. "I thought you'd like it."

"Another glass, then we'll find something to eat."

She took the last sip from her glass and nodded as he signaled the bartender to pour another glass for them.

Ritter wasn't anxious to talk too much about his fictitious book. But he had to face up to it. Better now when he still hadn't had too much wine.

"It's, uh, a thriller," he said.

"Spies and all that?"

"Not exactly. It's about a treasure hunt."

"How exciting. Have you written many books?"

"Uh, this is my first one."

"What do you normally do?"

"I hunt for treasure."

"You mean gold?"

"Actually, I'm a diver. I spend most of my time in the Caribbean and West Indies salvaging Spanish galleons and two- and three-hundred-year-old merchant ships."

"What in the world brings you here?"

"I needed a change. I wanted to do something different."

"So you're going to reveal the secrets of successful treasure hunting?"

"No, the book's about a treasure left behind in World War II."

Her alert eyes burrowed into him. "Left behind by the British?"

"Yeah. I thought it might make a good story."

"Sounds fascinating. How in the world did you ever get the idea?"

"From a television show."

"British army treasure. Gold, I assume?"

"Well, I haven't gotten that far. Still doing what I guess you'd call basic research." He had the unpleasant feeling the conversation was getting out of control. It needed a definite change in direction. He looked at his watch. "You must be starved. If we're going to get something before the reputable kitchens close down, we'd better move on."

"Yes, I suppose we'd better. As a professional treasure hunter, I expect you to find something good."

"Not exactly my specialty, you understand. But there are certain basic procedures in any hunt. The first, of course, is research. What kind of food do you like?"

12

The board beside the sink was strewn with culinary promise. Ripe young tomatoes, cloves of garlic, large fresh carrots, French onions, a bright green pepper, rosemary, bay leaves, a bouquet of thyme, parsley, and the best Mediterranean black olives. Michelle was cutting pork rinds into bite-sized squares which would give the red-wine sauce body as well as rich flavor. The heart of the stew, which she called *la daube,* was a rump of beef cut into squares about the size of the palm of her hand and about a third of an inch thick. After scraping the carrots, peeling the onions, and skinning the tomatoes, she sliced them all, placing them into an earthenware oven pot with the rinds and olive oil. Carefully the meat slices were laid over the bed of vegetables before placing the open pot over a medium flame. Moving with the knowledgeable ease of someone born to haute cuisine, Michelle readied the sauce by bringing a pan of red wine to a quick boil, igniting it to burn off the alcohol, and then pouring the boiling wine over the meat. Covering the pot, she slipped it into the oven and let it begin its two-and-a-half- hour simmer to perfection.

Michelle gazed through the kitchen window. Outside, it was Hyde Park and raining.

"Hmmm, smells like what they serve when you die and get to heaven," said Ritter as the rich odor of the stew spread through the large one-room efficiency flat he had rented after deciding to stay in London to research the hunt. "I guess being French, even half French, means never having to eat badly."

"They say the way to a man's bed is through his stomach." She smiled.

"Who says that? There are more direct routes, you know."

"Really?" She placed a hand on her hip, thrusting it out suggestively.

"If you just happen to wander over this direction…"

She strolled to the couch where he had been lying. Her blouse was open and she was wearing nothing under it.

In the cozy warmth of the flat, the penetrating spring cold and rain were easily forgotten. *La daube* simmered undisturbed.

They lay on the day bed together, enjoying the sound of rain outside, their nakedness and the peaceful intimate moment together. She was toying with the finely crafted silver cross he always's wore around his neck.

"Where'd you get this? I've been meaning to ask. It's beautiful."

He stared distractedly at the window. "Gift from a friend. A long time ago."

"Nice gift." She hoped to provoke more information.

"Nice friend." Offering nothing further, he closed his eyes as she trailed her fingertips along his chest and stomach.

She accepted the hint. "Brian?"

"Hmmmm?"

"I've got a question."

"Okay."

"You won't be angry?"

"Why should I?"

"Well, if you're really writing a book, why don't you have a typewriter or any papers around?"

After nearly a week of restaurants and meals produced on a small stove at Michelle's flat, Ritter realized his efficiency had a better-equipped kitchen. There had been good reason for not inviting her in earlier. His story about writing a book would never hold up. The most academic item he had in the place was a copy of *Time* magazine, so her question was not totally unexpected. "I, uh, well, you see, they're packed away.

I took a break for a couple of days and stored all the notes so the maid wouldn't get them mixed up."

"You're the only writer I ever met who could keep a flat tidy."

"That's me. Mister Neatness."

A pause.

"Brian?"

"Hmmmm?"

"How much have you written?"

"Written?"

"Your book."

"Oh, uh, you see, I'm uh, still researching it. Haven't actually gotten around to writing anything yet."

"Do you have an outline?"

"Don't need one. Story's all in my head."

She didn't believe him. For a long time they lay together silently, stroking and nuzzling each other. Ritter had never been very good at keeping secrets from people he liked. An overwhelming urge to tell her rose in him. What difference would it make anyhow? She wouldn't hurt his chances, she was too involved in her own research to mess with his. Anyway, it wasn't his nature to keep up a lengthy masquerade.

"I'm not really writing a book," he said.

"What have you been doing in the reading room, then?"

"Checking out a real hunt."

"I didn't believe you were a writer, you know."

They both laughed.

"My dishonest face?"

"Dummy. You don't talk like an author. You never discuss your work. I've known a few writers. All they ever talk about is their books. You never mentioned the matter after the first day at the library. Also, your note-taking was not organized. And when I saw your apartment, I knew it didn't belong to a serious writer."

"Spot a phony a mile away, eh?"

She kissed him. "There are phonies and there are phonies. I try not to make value judgments. In fact, there are some phonies I rather like." She kissed him again.

"Can't stand 'em myself. But I'm glad you've got room for at least one."

"You're not a phony, Brian Ritter. Just a lousy liar. Is there really a treasure?"

He nodded.

"How do you know it's there?"

"One of the guys who put it in the ground told one of my partners."

"Partners?"

"There are three of us. An older English guy whose brother-in-law was involved and a Greek guy who's putting up some money and who's going with me to Greece." He quivered as her hand ran teasingly along him. "Hey!"

"What kind of treasure is it?" she said softly, her warm mouth beginning to move downward on his body.

"British army gold," he said. His concentration slipped away with each of her arousing moves.

"Sounds like a lot of money. Are you definitely going next week?"

"Yeah." He sighed as her tongue touched him. "Research is pretty well wrapped up."

"Could I come?" she said, raising her head for a moment.

"Hmm, sure," he said without thinking, suddenly lost in the erotic, exotic pleasure of the moment. Time stopped, the treasure vanished, as he gave himself up to her deeply satisfying attention and needs.

Much later, as she lay contentedly by his side, he tried to forget the conversation. There was no place for a woman on this trip. She'd just get in the way. On the other hand, Michelle's presence could add another dimension to the hunt: body comfort. But that was crazy thinking. Khoury would never let him do it. Still, having her along would definitely help their cover. They were going as tourists, and who could imagine the two of them taking a holiday together? With Michelle along, it would be more convincing. More dangerous perhaps, but certainly more exciting.

"Could you afford to come to Greece?" he asked.

"My father's family was in real estate and commodities. The family made, how do you say, a killing in land speculation during the American depression. Anyhow, when my father died, his brother set up the fund for my mother and me. I get a check for $1,400 every month. It's not a lot, but it's very nice. I have been able to follow my studies without worrying where the next meal would come from. It's made life much easier."

Her voice suddenly rose. "Brian," she shouted, *"la daube!'* She leaped up and ran to the oven. The cooking odor had been replaced by something slightly stronger. She pulled the pot out of the oven, removed the lid with a quickly gloved hand, jerking her head back as a cloud of steam geysered out.

"Saved it," she exclaimed triumphantly. "Just in time." Standing naked in the kitchen holding the top of the earthenware pot, she was a wonderful sight. She had lovely breasts. The legendary perfect handful. Her body was slender without being skinny. Her legs were nearly perfect. And her blondness was natural.

"Time to eat," she said.

"La daube?"

A lusty grin spread across her face. "For a change."

13

Every hunt Ritter had been on needed a certain amount of planning, or more precisely, organization. A dive sometimes involved as many as fifteen or twenty people, including boat crews, divers, support personnel, and others. These people all had to be fed, bedded, paid, given days off, and looked after in a seemingly infinite variety of ways. But basically the work to be done was routine and normally followed a predictable pattern, getting the mother ship to the site, sending the divers down, searching and combing the ocean floor with the airlift, and, when something was finally uncovered, bringing it to the surface. All pretty straightforward.

This was drastically different. There was no precedent, no pattern. Although Ritter's research had convinced all of them the treasure was still in Greece, just as Jimmy Waddell had said, nothing would be cut-and-dried about their operation. Each move would be a step into the unknown, their single largest source of anxiety and, possibly, danger. The unknown factor also severely limited how detailed any plan of action could be. This was the dilemma that faced Ritter, Khoury, and Thompson as they met again to make a number of final decisions.

"And transportation on the ground?" said Khoury.

"We'll obviously have to have a car," said Ritter. "We're going to have to be mobile and independent. That means having our own vehicle. No drivers."

"A rented car?" suggested Thompson.

"Wouldn't work. Don't think we could drive a rented car out of the country, could we, Elias?"

"Probably not," said Khoury.

"Then we'll buy one."

Thompson rose to pour them another cup of tea. "You risk drawing attention to yourselves unnecessarily. How many tourists turn up in Thessalonica and buy cars? It's usually the other way round. People come from Europe with cars to sell them. In Greece, cars are expensive by European standards."

"Maybe we should drive one in from Italy," said Khoury. "That would eliminate that problem."

"Let's backtrack a moment," said Ritter. "We ought to discuss what kind of car. The more I think about it, the more complicated this could be. If there are five heavy boxes of gold, they probably won't fit into the trunk of an ordinary car. The sag in the rear suspension would draw the attention of the authorities, they'd wonder what kind of a load a couple of tourists are carrying. It would be an invitation to an inquiry and trouble. Even worse, if the load was too heavy, it could damage the suspension or lead to a cracked axle on bad roads. We can't afford any breakdowns once we've got the gold in our possession. That's all we'd need, to be stranded in the middle of nowhere with a car full of gold."

"What you need is a lorry," said Thompson pouring the steaming water over waiting tea bags in their cups.

"What kind of tourists arrive in trucks?" asked Khoury. "If buying a car will attract attention, imagine what a truck would do."

"Not a truck," said Ritter, as though he had just seen a vision. "A camping van."

"What?"

"A Volkswagen camper. It will meet all the requirements. What could be more normal than a couple of tourists buying a camper van to tour Greece and then taking the slow way home through Europe, where the van will be resold? The camper would be more than large enough to accommodate the boxes and to conceal them from those on the outside. Also, having Greek license plates will make it less conspicuous."

Thompson pushed his glasses back up on the bridge of his nose. "Likely to be any trouble finding such a camper in Thessalonica?" He looked at Khoury.

"Hardly. It's the second-largest city in the country. Yes, I think the camper is a good solution. It can also carry digging tools. If necessary, we can sleep in it."

"Which brings us to another point—our escape route."

"Escape is a strong word. Brian."

"Come on, Alfred you don't think it will be anything less than that, do you? The Greeks aren't going to give this stuff away."

"True, but those boxes no longer belong to anyone. They've been in the ground 34 years, far beyond the statute of limitations of any kind. They belong to whoever can find them. Naturally, you don't want to attract any undue attention, but that gold is ours. No one in Greece even knows it's there. No one else has a claim to it. No one will miss it when you've dug it up."

"The government might not share your point of view on that," said Khoury. "But I don't think we want to waste time now discussing such a trivial matter. It is clear we will have to be as discreet as possible. It's not exactly the kind of operation in which press coverage will be invited."

"Back to the original point, then," said Ritter. "Fortunately, there'll be no visa problems. So when we arrive in Thessalonica, we'll spend a few days looking around. Sight-seeing like tourists. Then we'll buy the camper. We'll tell anyone who will listen we're tourists who've been successful in business together and want to take five or six weeks off to see a bit of Greece and southern Europe. We'll tell everyone we're going to tour all of Greece down to the islands. We'll make no mention of leaving the country. Once we've got the van, we'll wait a day, then buy the tools. We can explain we might need them if we get stuck in mountain roads. A couple of shovels and a pick should do it."

Ritter paused to sip his tea. "Once we've located the gold and get it successfully into the van, we'll drive straight to Igoumenitsa and take the ferry to Corfu. From there it will be a relaxing overnight ferry ride to Brindisi. The final hitch will be entering Italy. It will be necessary to declare the gold. It's not illegal to export gold from Italy as long as you declare it properly when it's brought into the country."

"And then you'll drive north as fast as you can, cross into Switzerland, and head straight for Geneva. We'll meet there, go to a bank, have the gold valued, sell it, split the proceeds, and adjourn to the nearest pub for a small drink of celebration."

"I look forward to buying that drink," said Ritter.

"It's a simple, efficient plan," Thompson said. "The best kind, actually."

"A bit too simple," said Khoury.

"What do you mean?" Ritter said.

"Nothing. Except it sounds easy as we sit here talking about it. I'm not so sure it will be so simple in fact."

"Nor am I, Elias. At this point we can't expect to have more than a general outline or plan. We'll have to improvise as we go along. That's the nature of this filthy and hopefully lucrative beast."

"I am worried about one basic thing," said Thompson.

"What's that?"

"The image of you two as tourists is a bit thin. Pardon my being so blunt. But you hardly look like two persons who would go off on a holiday together, anywhere."

"I've been thinking about the same problem," said Ritter with a measured air of casualness. "And I have a solution."

"Plastic surgery? A sex change?" Thompson chuckled at one of his own rare jokes.

"A girl."

"What girl?"

"A girl I know. We could take her along."

Khoury bellowed like a wounded bull. "Have you gone mad?"

"Brian," said Thompson, his voice rising, "let's not make jokes. There is no room for another person in this operation."

"Okay," Ritter said. "Just consider the obvious. Elias and me riding around in a van in northern Greece would look damned suspicious. But with a girl along, we could pose as some sort of academics who have combined a holiday with research. It will make a much better story than the one we have now."

"How much have you told her?" Khoury demanded, a threatening tone in his voice.

"She knows I'm going to Greece on a treasure hunt," said Ritter evasively. "Not much more. She certainly doesn't know enough to endanger anything," he added, taking the offensive slightly. "She doesn't even know she's going yet," A small white lie.

"And she's not," said Khoury again. "Of all the stupid …"

"Hold on," said Thompson. A tone of conciliation. "Who is this girl? What do we know about her?"

"She's a student. Her father was an American soldier killed before she was born. He left her and her French mother a very nice trust fund she's been living on since she was born. She has completed her master's and is now working on her Ph.D. That's how I ran into her. She was doing research on the campaign of 1941 for her doctorate."

"Sounds suspicious to me," said Khoury resentfully.

"In what way?" challenged Ritter.

"I don't know. But we're in the middle of this project, and suddenly this woman turns up. I don't like it. My instincts tell me there's something not right about it."

"With all due respect, Elias," said Thompson, "you're becoming a bit paranoid. A dangerous symptom anytime, but particularly now."

"Elias, she didn't just turn up," said Ritter. "She was already at work in the reading rooms when I arrived. You're the only two who knew why I went there. I sought her out. She didn't pick me up."

Khoury grunted, the unsatisfied sound of someone losing ground in an argument. "I still don't like it."

"It goes without saying I take full responsibility for her," Ritter said.

"What about the money?" asked Khoury sharply. "There's no question of any cut for her, certainly not out of my share."

Finally, the guts of the matter. Thompson quickly jumped in. "He's right, Brian. There can be no question of the girl sharing any of our part of the gold. What you do with your share is your business.

But it must be understood that whatever you find will be split into thirds, and Elias and I each are entitled to a full third."

Ritter sensed he had won. "I have no argument with that. She will not be entitled to any part of your shares. If she gets anything at all, it will be out of my third. That's agreed."

"All right, Brian," said Khoury, accepting what he considered to be a concession. "If you want to have a good time on the side, that's your private business. But if this woman gets in the way or makes a false move, we get rid of her. Understand?" He drew his finger across his throat. It was not a pleasant gesture.

PART IV

APRIL 1975

I have smelt them, the death-bringers.
—T. S. Eliot

14

Like an ancient Greek amphitheater, Thessalonica rose from the head of the Thermaic Gulf on the slopes of Mt. Hortiatis. Huddled hillside homes and former Byzantine walls were sets for thousands of daily dramas starring the energetic and industrious people of the city. Tragedies, comedies, morality plays—all swirled around the city's glorious Byzantine churches producing the humdrum routine that was the heart of the city's life. The most enticing seats in this giant theater were to be found in the front row along the seafront, where on a cool evening, as the light dimmed over the gulf, the devoted gathered in cafés to gaze across to Mount Olympus silhouetted against the brilliant sunset.

"I don't think he likes me," said Michelle, ignoring the heavenly spectacle. Over the legendary residence of the gods. She had an odd habit of sticking the tip of her tongue into the rich Turkish coffee before sipping it.

"I don't think he really dislikes you," said Ritter. Staring across the darkening blue water into the fading light, he rubbed a hand over his sandy hair. He was glad he had worn a sweater. "He just hasn't gotten a chance to know you. You should give each other a chance. You might find he's the nicest Greek-Lebanese you ever met."

"You don't like him either." It was neither a statement nor a question. Almost an indictment.

"He's okay," said Ritter evasively. Inwardly he still had a bad feeling about Khoury. It was the same feeling he got the first time he had met the minister in Barbados who made them pay a large private fee for expediting their diving permission. But he wasn't going to confide that to Michelle. Things were already difficult enough. "Not my type, as I've said. But we get along all right. We're going to find the gold together—possibly make each other rich. That can go a long way toward easing personality conflicts."

"I couldn't believe how cool he was toward me when we met at the airport. Then he deliberately sat away from us on the plane. I don't think he's said ten words to me in the past two days. He regards me as an intruder, probably feels a woman is out of place in a situation like this. Typical Middle Eastern reaction. Maybe I shouldn't have come along after all."

"Don't be so sensitive. He wasn't … well really expecting you. That's all. He needs to get used to you. You'll find out he's not so bad. He handled himself very well today when we bought the camper."

"I must admit, arguing about the price the way he did was very convincing. All the consulting about money. Counting the traveler's checks and looking over his checkbook. The business about being tourists on a low budget was a good touch. The dealer seemed convinced."

"It was very good. If anybody takes an interest in us, that performance certainly won't hurt our case. By the way, how was the museum?"

"Not bad, if you like museums. Not much about the war. But there's not much to tell anyway. The British skipped out as soon as they heard the shooting start. Anyway, I figured out why everything in this city is so tacky, so old-fashioned modern."

"Why?"

"Thessalonica burned in 1917 except for the walls and the heavy stone buildings like the churches. Most of what you see has been built since."

A horn beeped. They looked up to see a shiny apple-green Volkswagen camping van roll into the square.

"Here comes your friend."

"Hmmmm, lucky."

Khoury parked the van, stepped out, and strolled over to them. He wore a long sheepskin coat and a noncommittal expression. Without invitation he pulled up a chair. "All set," he said.

Ritter moved his head in acknowledgment.

"Oil changed and a full tank of gas. Tires okay. Also purchased a few digging tools. We can get moving in the morning." He waved at a waiter and in Greek ordered a coffee.

"Think I'll freshen up before dinner," said Michelle, standing up.

"See you in the room," said Ritter.

She looked at Ritter, glanced briefly at Khoury, and sauntered off toward the hotel, her flowing blond hair bouncing on the back of her head.

"Don't think she likes me," said Khoury.

"You haven't exactly given her cause."

Khoury treated the remark as if it had never been spoken. "I recommend we get moving as early as possible. Dawn would be best. No sense wasting time."

"Getting up early has never been a biggie with me, particularly on holiday," said Ritter. He stretched out his arms and legs and pulled back his shoulders as if to emphasize the point.

"We're not on holiday, my friend."

Ritter had always been uneasy with people who used the term too loosely. But he let it float past him. "We're supposed to look like we are."

"With your working student along, we've got a good reason for wanting to get a good look at the countryside."

"Then maybe we also ought to be having a good time. Hardly looks like a holiday when two members of a group are barely speaking to each other."

"Okay, Brian, you've made your point. Perhaps I have been a bit, shall we say, distant with her. I admit I didn't want her along in the first place. But she's here now. And maybe she will prove to be useful. To both of us. I agree, it will look bad if we're not all getting along. I'll change that. So you can relax."

"I want to tell you something, Elias. I've always enjoyed my work in the past. The fun was somehow just as important as the money. You may find that difficult to understand, but never mind. The point is, give the girl a chance. You might actually like her. She's really got it all together. After all, it's not her fault she's along. It's mine."

Khoury released a condescending chuckle. A bit of the old massage. "Ah, Brian. You have a wonderful way about you. Let's have a real drink. Enough of this coffee." He signaled a waiter and asked for something in Greek. "Ouzo, a Greek liquor that helps to set spirits right. In Lebanon we call it arak. We will toast the beginning of our adventure. So far everything is going well. Even the weather is behaving itself."

A waiter brought two glasses of ouzo, already milky from the ice cubes.

"To a successful hunt," said Khoury.

"Amen," said Ritter.

"Brian, I've been thinking."

"Hmmm," murmured Ritter. Don't strain yourself, he thought.

"You know we're doing all the work on this hunt. Taking all the risks. It's not just."

"Just what?"

"You know, it's not right."

"What do you mean by that?"

"When we get the treasure out of the ground, we three will be the only ones who know about it."

"Thompson will know."

"That's the point. He will know only what we choose to tell him."

"Look, Elias, I don't know exactly what you're driving at. I'm not sure I want to know. But we've got a deal with the old man. I intend to carry out my end of the bargain. I hope that's clear."

"Of course. Of course it is, Brian. It was just a joke. I didn't mean anything serious. I was just thinking what a joke we could play on Thompson. Tell him we didn't find anything, then surprise him with his share."

"We'll worry about the jokes when we find the gold."

"Naturally. It was silly of me to be thinking so far ahead."

"This stuff's not bad," said Ritter. "Tastes like licorice. The Spanish call it anís."

"Same wonderful potion. Loved all over the Mediterranean." Khoury was staring across the square. The streetlights were just coming on. The illumination was dim and uncertain, but he thought he saw a familiar face.

"Brian, excuse me. There's someone I know. I'll meet you and Michelle at dinner."

Khoury stood up and walked across the square to the opposite café. It was only by chance he had seen Dimitri Metaxas. It would be a moment fraught with major implications for all of them.

* * *

"Do you think my breasts are too small?"

"I've handled bigger."

"What does—?"

"But not nicer."

"Saved yourself."

She snuggled against him. The gentle sound of splashing waves across the street on the seafront drifted through the window with a light spring breeze. The spacious room characterized by its old-fashioned elegance wore its age with grace and dignity. As a result, the Mediterranean Palace was still the city's most comfortable and preferred hotel. The room certainly was a welcome improvement from the Spartan settings of their London efficiencies.

"Brian?"

"Hmmm?" He was drifting off to sleep.

"Why was Khoury so different tonight?"

"Different?"

"You know. He actually talked to me at dinner. If I didn't know the other side of him, I would have been tempted to find him charming."

"I told you he wasn't all that bad. He's getting to like you. I told you he would."

"There's more to it than that. What did you say to him in the café after I left?"

"Nothing. He told me he was sorry he had been ignoring you. Said it had been a mistake. I may have made some comment about cutting losses."

"I don't believe you, entirely."

Ritter shrugged. "Let the events speak for themselves."

"You must have said something to him."

"Wasn't necessary."

"It doesn't matter. I still don't like him. Or trust him. There's something greasy about him. In French we would call him *visqueux*."

"My French isn't so hot. But that doesn't sound like a very nice word coming from a lady."

"Be careful, Brian. He is not to be trusted."

"Don't worry. He's not going to do anything dumb. He wants the gold as badly as anyone. Maybe more so. Khoury is a crafty, shrewd man, above all—commercial. He won't do anything to endanger getting his share. He knows he is going to need us. And I am certain we are going to need his talents in the coming days equally as much. It's a marriage of convenience, if you like. But sometimes those are the most successful."

"Just remember what Euripides said."

"That was?"

"Put not thy faith in any Greek."

"What did he know?"

"He was Greek."

"So you're putting faith in what he said?"

"You've been warned. Be vigilant."

"Don't worry, Michelle. This will work out. Let's lean back and enjoy it. It might be years before we have a chance to dig up another treasure in Greece."

"I'll let you know in a few days whether I'm going to be good for more than one."

Ritter wrapped a muscular arm around her. It was a gesture that comforted him as much as it was meant to reassure her. "Can I ask you a personal question?" he said.

"It depends."

"How'd you get this far without, uh, getting attached?"

Silence. Ritter sensed he had bared a sensitive nerve. She countered with a question. "What about you?"

"Never got around to it, I guess," he said. "I've thought about it a few times. I'd love to have a kid, a son. But I've rarely met a woman I wanted to settle down with. It's usually fun for a while, and then I start getting claustrophobic."

"Have you ever been in love?"

"During the war I met a girl. Greek, and very young. We had a very torrid week or so together. If we'd had more time, perhaps it could have become serious. The last I saw her she was surrounded by Germans as I took off for Cairo. I've often wondered whether the Germans killed her. And now I'm going back.…"

She was silent for a long moment, nuzzling his arm. Then: "Do you ever worry what will happen when you get old?"

"Don't think about it much. I've got a brother with a real-estate agency in San Diego. I suppose at some point I'll go back there and work for him. Who knows? Maybe by then I'll have found enough money so I won't have to worry about it. With one big hit I can put away enough so I'll be set permanently. This one could be it."

"If it's not?"

He shrugged. "I'll go on to the next hunt. My partner is pressing for a big one in Barbados. You know, I had an uncle who was a fairly well-known figure in the old west. Scotty O'Shea, one of the last gunfighters. When I was still in school I went out to Arizona to visit a relative who lived near where he had lived. One day we ran into an old-timer sitting outside a general store and asked him if he had ever heard of Scotty O'Shea. Christ, it was as if someone had stuck an electric cattle prod up the old man's ass. 'That son of a bitch,' he shouted. 'Scotty O'Shea was the dirtiest fighter I ever knew. Woulda cheated his own mother playing cards and then stomped her if she said anything. Why'd ya ask?' Just wondering, I said. Old Scotty must have been a rough one. My mother has a picture of him at home in the family album. He was a mean-looking bastard. Never did settle down. Must be a bit of that in the family blood."

"I treasure my independence," she said. "Whether loneliness will get me at some point is hard to say. But right now I just want to come and go as I please."

"Being alone gets all of us from time to time. I had a married friend of mine once tell me he was the loneliest person in the world. You know something? I find I'm least lonely when I'm by myself underwater on a dive unable to communicate with anyone except the fish."

"Do you think Khoury ever gets lonely?" A light question to break the sober mood.

"Only when he's not on the trail of money."

Two rooms down the hall. Elias Khoury lay quietly staring at the dark ceiling. The acrid smoke of a Gauloise cigarette drifted up and over his upper lip, lingered outside his nostrils, and then quickly disappeared into his lungs as he inhaled. The sign on the wall next to him said "Danger. No smoking in bed."

Khoury was tired but he couldn't sleep. The excitement of the hunt had triggered his adrenaline. He was finding it difficult to clear his mind.

Metaxas had been a real coincidence. He hadn't realized Metaxas lived with his family near Thessalonica. He had given Khoury his phone number and invited him to dinner. Khoury explained he was on holiday with friends and would have to leave early in the morning. He would accept the next time he was in the area.

Ritter had remained curiously detached. He had to admit, Ritter had the coolness of a professional, a man who had done it all before. Khoury almost had the impression Ritter didn't care as much about finding the treasure as having a good time. But the suggestion of cutting Thompson out had touched a nerve. He wouldn't bring it up again.

The girl. She was charming at dinner. Her smile had warmed him considerably. He had been too harsh in his initial judgment. Ritter was not dumb. She would be enjoyable to have along. As long as she didn't interfere with his share, it wouldn't be bad. Still, there was more to her than met the eye. He couldn't place it, but she had something extra. Her tight-fitting jeans showed it. She had an exceptionally appealing derriere.

* * *

The frail old man inside couldn't recall it, but another gray-haired coffee-shop veteran rocking back and forth on the terrace, his eyes clouded over with glaucoma, had not forgotten.

"Communists," he whispered, rolling his head around as though he could still see. He knew where his ideological bread was buttered. "Waited till most of the others had gone off to attack a German train. Hit the rest of us thinking we weren't expecting it. Bombed several houses over there." He pointed the cane toward the hills behind the town. "Finally chased 'em off with their tails between their legs. Haaa. Got one of them myself. Was a pretty good shot in those days. Still would be if it weren't for my eyes."

"What about the American?" prodded Ritter gently. Khoury was translating.

"Oh, yeah. He was in the village when the Communists attacked. Think there were some others with him, but never saw 'em. He got it up near the top of that hill there. Helped bring down his body myself."

"You buried him?"

"In the church cemetery." He waved his cane. The wood was as gnarled as the figures on his hands. But he could still see the town as clearly as if he had his eyesight.

Ritter found the grave in an out-of-the-way corner of the community burial ground. A small stone marker said in Greek, "American soldier. Died September 30, 1943."

Ritter leaned down and touched the stone. He wanted to speak: Hello Whip. It's been a long time. I ... He settled for a brief touch. The only sound was the wind that had whistled over the grave marker for the past 32 years.

Ritter turned, kicked a small rock in the yard, and walked slowly back to the camper where Michelle and Khoury waited. They still had a long drive to Kozani.

15

"Christ, it's worse than I thought," Ritter said. "It could be anywhere." Through the camper's rain-splattered windows loomed the dark range of mountains hung with a ghostly early-morning mist. His breath kept fogging the glass.

An hour earlier they had left Kozani following a restless night at the Aliakmon Hotel. On the drive from Thessalonica the previous day, they decided to establish their operations base at Kozani, well known as a traditional center for Greek nationalism and pro-monarchist sentiments. It was the nearest town of any size to the search area, and the hotel was certainly more comfortable and convenient than camping in the mountains. "Besides," Khoury had said, "I'm afraid I'm too civilized for nights in a tent or a camping van without a warm bed and hot water." Neither Ritter nor Michelle needed convincing. But Michelle, feeling easier with Khoury, didn't pass the chance for a light stab. "You're getting soft in your old age," she chided.

"Just more practical, my dear," he replied. "That kind of stuff is only for boy scouts, field soldiers, or the mentally demented."

They headed in the direction of Mount Siniatsikon and began driving back and forth, combing the mountains trying to locate the exact pass marked on Waddell's rough sketch. In many ways, it all looked familiar. The villages, the landscape, the mountains. The flavor of the place was just as it had been thirty-two years ago. But at the same time, Ritter recognized nothing. Time had distorted or washed out his memories. With Devan and Rogers and the Greek kid from Brooklyn, he had driven along this same road looking at the wrecks. No sign of them now. The road was paved and widened. The sparse traffic flowed smoothly. It was the same world, but different. They were starting from scratch. With each mile, the rain fell harder.

Ritter broke the long silence. "I already see this is going to be as tough as a dive."

Khoury was amused. "Yes, habibi. If it keeps up like this, we'll have to swim to the treasure, or take an ark." He was in a surprisingly good mood. The Arabic term of endearment flowed easily through his lips.

"When the research is finished," said Ritter, "you are always sure you know to the inch where the treasure is. Each dive begins with the optimistic belief you will swim right down and scoop it all up. The reality is, it usually takes days or weeks or even longer sometimes to uncover the actual site, regardless of how good the maps or descriptions are."

Ritter edged the camper slowly up the narrow winding road. The drop off the side of the muddy unfenced track was at least three hundred feet. Heavy rain made visibility increasingly difficult. "Our sketch generally corresponds to these maps, but matching it here on the ground is not so easy. All goes back to the basic problem."

"That is?"

"That is, we don't know what kind of tricks Waddell's memory played on him during the years in that prison camp and afterward fighting the drink. I was here too, and I don't recognize a thing. This clearly is not going to be your standard cakewalk."

They stopped for forty-five minutes at midday to lunch on cold chicken sandwiches Michelle had obtained from the hotel kitchen. The dark mountains and heavy rain had steadily sobered them. There was little conversation. When the remnants were packed away, they moved on. The rest of the afternoon was spent crawling along mile after dreary mile, eliminating slowly, one by one, possible sites. As darkness began to close in on them, they had established nothing positive. A valuable day was irretrievably gone. Wearily and glumly they returned to the hotel.

"I've had more exciting days," said Michelle as they finished a quiet after dinner drink and walked up the stairs.

"Certainly more productive," added Khoury.

"All in a day's hunt," said Ritter. He slung an arm affectionately over Michelle's shoulder and they headed for their room.

None of them had taken particular notice of the heavyset man with garlic breath sitting in the lobby pretending to read a week-old copy of an Athens newspaper.

* * *

"There," blurted Khoury, his voice rising. It was shortly before noon. After nearly five hours of driving, they tentatively had identified a pass and were now looking up at caves that matched the description given by Waddell.

"Like a sandwich," said Ritter. "And the streambed fits."

Michelle rolled back the sun roof and stood up through the top of the camper to survey the exhilarating scene. The rain of the day before had moved on, leaving the air cool and clear. The mist also had slithered off. The deep green mountains rich with pines and patches of snow flecking the peaks were framed by a brilliant blue sky.

They were several hundreds yards up a streamed from the small mountain road. The mountainside looming above them was covered with a dense growth of trees and brush, except, about 150 yards above, for stratalike rock formations bare of foliage, excitingly similar to those Waddell had described.

"Let's have a closer look," said Ritter, climbing out of the camper.

Khoury followed, pulling the Waddell sketches from his pocket. The rough drawing was definitely similar to the rock formations in front of them.

"Now the map," said Ritter.

Khoury carefully unfolded the map. They didn't have to look at it long. It didn't match.

"According to the map, we should be able to see Mount Siniatsikon from here in this direction," said Ritter, pointing away from the caves. "But it's over that ridge, a difference of nearly ninety degrees."

"He couldn't have been that wrong," Khoury sighed. "We haven't found it yet."

"Elias," Ritter said, "I think we ought to lunch in Ardhassa. Get to know the natives."

"You know the risk."

"Is there a choice? There are maybe ten passes up here similar to the one Waddell was referring to. There may be hundreds of rock formations similar to this. We could spend weeks trying to find the right one."

"We don't have that kind of time."

"That's the point," said Ritter, running his fingers through his hair. "There may not be a single case on record of foreign tourists stopping more than two nights in Kozani. Imagine the questions if we have to stretch this thing over four or five days. Sooner or later someone will start asking what those strange tourists are up to. The questions will eventually draw official attention. We've got to find a shortcut. That means seeing if some of the old-timers at Ardhassa remember which passes the convoys used and which one was blocked by the bombing Waddell talked about."

* * *

Ardhassa was a classic village of rural Macedonia. The heart of the simple community was the single commercial enterprise, the *magazi*, the combination grocery, bar, café, and town hall that's as essential to life in rural northern Greece as life itself. Ardhassa's *magazi* was not particularly imposing. It was a simple one-storey dwelling coated with seasons of whitewash and character. Alongside the building was a flagstone terrace that in the height of summer was shaded by a large tree and grape vines trestled overhead.

But in early spring, shade was slightly less desirable than a late snowfall. Several village men, trying to forget the harsh mountain winter and encourage the luxurious summer, were seated around three of the rusted metal tables on the patio sipping thick coffee or white retsina wine. The still-gentle spring sun offered a warm promise of better days approaching as it climbed each day further into the sky. Talk on the terrace centered on speculation about the grape crop and the reportedly illicit activities in Athens of the daughter of an absent village elder.

The older men in the group all wore traditional baggy, pleated dark blue wool trousers, heavy black wool shirts, and black boots. Several of them were leaning on carved walking sticks or shepherd's crooks. They were lean, hawk-eyed men with proud mustaches and sharp features chiseled by generations of wind, rain, sun, snow, and ice.

Conversation stopped as the camper pulled up. The men turned to stare at the visitors. It was not often Ardhassa was honored by a delegation from the outside. This was the first time since last fall.

Ritter, Khoury, and Michelle casually climbed out of the camper like admiring tourists and walked into the *magazi*. The room, heavy with a rich and unfamiliar odor, was larger inside than they had expected. Along one side were slabs of salted cod and open tubs of salted sardines and anchovies, their levels low as the winter neared its end. Other items reflected the simple life pattern of the small community—coils of rope, tinned goods, saws, bales of cotton and wool, horse nails, and small barrels of olives. Clear ouzo in large jars filled one shelf. On another wall hung mule bridles and lengths of webbing for girths, along with two leather saddles. The dust on them indicated they hadn't been touched since they were hung up at least a winter ago. Obviously it hadn't been a big year for saddle sales.

On the floor in the center of the dimly lit room a red-and-black rug was spread out. Across it lay the pelt of a wolf which had strayed one spring too close to the village from the security of the surrounding mountains.

An old woman clad in black was seated beside the open blackened hearth. She stood up in reaction to their entry. Khoury spoke in Greek, asking her whether they could get something to eat and drink.

"She says she doesn't have much, some goat's cheese and warmed-over mutton," he translated. "But she can provide a small meza, olives, onions, and, if we like, hummus."

"Sounds fine," said Ritter. Michelle nodded in agreement. They turned and strolled out onto the terrace. The men continued staring quietly, expectantly. In the mountains it was understood strangers must always speak first. "Hello," Khoury said cautiously, bowing his head slightly to all of them.

"Welcome," said one of the men guardedly.

"You are well found," said Khoury politely, offering the traditional reply to a greeting.

"Please be seated," said another of the men. They had passed the critical first test.

The three sat down on rush-bottomed chairs around one of the chipped white tables.

The old woman appeared shortly with a bottle and three glasses. Retsina wine can only be described to the uninitiated as an acquired taste. It is particularly Greek and not usually appealing to those sampling it for the first time. "Ugh," said Michelle, taking her first sip. "I've tasted better mouthwash." Her comparisons with the light wines of the Loire were even less flattering."

"They treat the casks and barrels with tar or resin," explained Khoury. "And it seeps into the wine. It is a product of nature the Greeks have accepted. You must drink the tar or do without the wine. The latter is obviously not a serious option. When Greeks think of wine, they think of the resin taste. Because of the tourists, however, some vineyards are now producing wine in glass bottles. But no respectable man in this village would touch it. For them and many other Greeks, resin is the normal taste."

After a few sips, Ritter found he was slowly adjusting to the wine. He still didn't like the taste, but each sip seemed a bit smoother than the previous one.

The old woman appeared with the food and spread it on the table. They were all hungry, and the hot mutton was delicious, as was the warm bread, the hummus, and the freshly cut onions. For a moment, refreshed by the crisp air and warmed by the food and wine, they lost themselves. For a moment it was a real holiday, an escape from the frantic aggressive outside world and their growing concern about the hunt. The villagers looked on approvingly. Khoury caught himself, but realized the mood was not unhelpful.

"The Greek word for stranger is the same as the word for guest," said Khoury, chewing on the piece of mutton. "*Xenos*. It illustrates the strong feeling of hospitality these people feel. But it also is worth remembering the word is the root of your English word 'xenophobia,' the hate of foreigners."

"What's the point?" said Ritter, looking up from his plate.

"These men here are quick to welcome us. But they will be quick to distrust us if we make a suspicious move, do something outside the acceptable pattern they have put us in."

"Don't have much choice."

"Only in style. We'll finish our meal and have a leisurely coffee. The last thing we can afford to do is rush them. We've got to lull them into accepting us." Khoury looked over at one of the older men, raised his glass in silent toast, and smiled warmly. The men at the table smiled back approvingly. It pleased them the strangers were enjoying their meal. It was a compliment to the village.

It was not lost on Michelle that she was the only woman on the terrace. "This place doesn't exactly look like a bastion of women's lib," she said.

"Hardly," said Khoury. "These places are for men only except for tourists and special festive occasions. The men enjoy seeing a pretty girl like you here. It brings them pleasure. But they would strongly disapprove of a village girl your age walking in and joining us. She would have to stay with the old woman inside. Of course, they never think about the obvious double standard for their women and those of the outside world. It is an old system here. They don't want it changed."

As the old woman brought them coffee, Khoury turned to the man at the table nearest them.

"Looks like an early spring," he said in Greek.

The old shepherd grunted. "The signs are good. A few lambs have already been born. A good sign to see them come a bit early."

"Not bad for the grapes, either. How was the harvest last fall?"

The old man proudly explained it had been a good year. Soon he and Khoury were deep in conversation about the local wine and farming. Ritter and Michelle looked on with counterfeit interest as though they could follow the conversation in Greek, occasionally nodding and smiling when it seemed appropriate.

Khoury ordered another round of coffee before the opening came from the old man.

"You tourists? You don't sound like a Greek."

"Not entirely. My mother was Greek. I was raised in Africa. Now I'm with a university in France. The girl is also a teacher doing some special studies. The man is a friend of hers." He winked at the shepherd, chancing a bit of titillation would amuse him.

"What brings you to Ardhassa?" the old man asked equably, not revealing his reaction.

"Our studies."

"What are you studying?"

"History. The last war, in fact. In particular, the German invasion of Greece." He lowered his voice slightly. "I'm writing a book," he confided.

"A book," the old man exclaimed. "Hey, fellows, this gentleman is writing a book." It was the kind of effort that impressed the simple village men. Most of them couldn't even read. Anyone at work on a book was considered an intellectual, someone to be highly respected.

Others from nearby tables drifted over to join the conversation.

"Were you here when the Germans invaded?" asked Khoury.

"Yes, that was the spring of '41, I remember. The British left in a hurry, and the Germans rolled through. Wasn't all that much fighting. Didn't come until later, when the Americans and British came back at the end of the war."

"We were interested in tracing some of the retreat routes of the British. Everybody knows about the main routes. But some of the lesser-known routes would be of academic interest. I understand there was a pass blown up near here. Some British units were trapped."

The old man pushed his coarse black wool cap back and scratched his head. "You mean Mitata Pass?"

"What happened there?"

"The German planes bombed it until a landslide finally closed it. It took the British trapped behind it more than twenty-four hours to clear a path through. By then the Germans closed in. Some British were killed. A lot of others escaped on foot to the main road on the other side."

"Where is Mitata?"

Pointing his crook, the old man indicated the pass was about four miles south of the village. They had driven over it earlier in the morning but hadn't had a chance to look for a possible turnoff. If that was it, Waddell's map was slightly wrong. But not so wrong as to rule out the pass the old man was talking about.

Khoury struggled not to show any particular interest. "Must have been an exciting time."

"Damn Germans. Came through the village the next day. Their tanks rolled through without stopping. Three of my sheep were killed, and no one ever paid me a drachma for them. We saw a lot of Germans during the war, but they never bothered us here much. Patrols came through a couple of times looking for partisans. But they didn't find anything. The partisans were too clever for them. Later the Communists came through trying to kill those fighting for the king. They were the worst."

Khoury spent the next fifteen minutes discussing the war and civil war.

At one point one of the younger men, a sullen-faced farmer who appeared to be about forty-five, asked in an antagonistic voice, "Why are you asking these questions? What business is it of yours?"

"Told you. We are from France. Studying the history and campaigns of World War II."

"We don't like strangers nosing around."

"Now, now, Marko," said the old man. "That's not a way to treat these people."

The man suffered the rebuff from the village elder in silence and sulked off. Khoury was sure he had already heard what they wanted. It was time to break off and leave. No sense in creating unnecessary tensions.

"It has been a pleasure talking with you," he said. "We must be off." He got up and walked into the *magazi* to settle the bill with the old woman. She accepted his payment gratefully. It was not often money came into the village from the outside, particularly this time of year.

Khoury waved to the men on the terrace as the three climbed into the camper. Most of them waved back, smiling. Khoury had left a generous tip with the old woman to make a better impression on the villagers.

"Take it easy, Brian," said Khoury. "All we need now is to get a ticket for speeding." They all laughed.

They reached Mitata with about an hour of daylight left. There was no trace of the deadly landslides of thirty-four years ago. Time and the normal road rebuilding had long erased the scars of the war. It was hard to imagine that the peaceful scene had ever seen men die.

They drove along the road through the pass and the village of Mouzakion before Michelle spotted it.

"There," she said. "That might be described as a former streambed."

The way was overgrown, but years before it obviously had been a streambed until some act of nature diverted the water away. The dried-out pathway moved up the hill toward the ridge at the top of the mountain in the direction of the main road.

"Let's try it," said Ritter. "We have just enough time before it gets dark." Ritter was able to guide the camper about 150 yards before the undergrowth proved to be too thick. "We'll have to walk the rest of the way," he said.

They got out and walked for another fifteen minutes before Michelle shouted, "Look!" She was pointing to a rock formation high up on the mountainside above them. The formation was very similar to the one they previously had examined. The stratalike formations looked like a giant rock sandwich on the side of the mountain. There were obviously a number of caves up there. Khoury pulled out the Waddell map, turned, and looked at Mount Siniatsikon. "Right where it should be," he said.

Ritter could feel the excitement beginning to grow in him. "Let's get up there."

They scrambled up the mountainside to the caves. One part was blocked shut by large rocks. It looked like it had been covered years before by a rock slide—"or a hand-grenade explosion," said Michelle.

"Could be," said Khoury.

Ritter looked at the mountain again. "It fits, Elias. The mountain, the description of the caves, the streambed, the pass. I think we've found it."

"Looks like it," said Khoury, trying to keep his emotions under control. The two men shook hands. Michelle gave them both a congratulatory kiss on the cheek.

"It's beautiful," she said.

"Hardly seems like it's holding two million dollars in gold, does it?" said Ritter.

Khoury looked at his watch and then up at the fading light.

"You're right, Elias," said Ritter, noticing the gesture. "It's too late to start anything tonight. From the looks of this, it's going to take a bit of digging. We'll start early tomorrow morning."

"Another night in the luxurious Aliakmon Hotel," said Michelle.

"The last," said Khoury.

"You think we can dig this out in a single day?" said Ritter, doubt in his voice.

"Highly unlikely," said Khoury. "But we've already spent too much time in the hotel. And I don't like the way the villagers reacted today. They were polite, but clearly suspicious. We must leave here as soon as possible. Some of the hotel people may already be wondering why we've hung around the area so long. Doesn't make sense."

"We'll go back and spend a final night, telling everyone we're heading on to Servia and points farther south," Khoury said. "We'll come up here early tomorrow and stay until we get the gold out."

"We might have to do a bit of camping," said Ritter.

"I know," Khoury said. "Frankly, I'd rather be back in Conakry. But we can't very well turn up at that hotel at night dirty and sweaty from a day of digging. We might as well invite everyone in the place to join us."

"Guess that makes us all boy scouts," said Ritter.

"Or mentally demented," said Michelle.

Khoury smiled. "I'm just a good soldier doing my duty," he said. "Tomorrow is P Day."

"P Day?"

"Payoff Day."

The three arrived at the hotel well after dark. Ritter knew he was tired, but the anticipation of the hunt was more than enough to keep him going for the drive back. Michelle fell asleep in the back of the camper, managing nearly an hour's nap. Khoury sat quietly in the front beside Ritter. He was intensely quiet. Whatever his thoughts, he wasn't in a mood to share them.

They went straight to the hotel bar and ordered a round of drinks.

"How was your day?" asked the bartender.

"Saw some very interesting churches," lied Michelle. "There are a number of them with fifteenth- and sixteenth-century murals in Aiani," she said, quoting from the guidebook by memory. "I'm sure you know them."

"I have lived here all my life," said the young man. "But I have never visited that village. Only tourists go there."

"The area is beautiful," said Khoury. "But we've got to move on tomorrow. Heading on down to Servia and Larissa. There are some ruins we want to see before heading on to Athens and the islands."

"I was in Athens last year," the bartender said. "Didn't like it. Too frantic for me. Too many cars and, if you'll pardon me, too many tourists."

"I know what you mean," said Ritter. "Too many bartenders spoil the drink, eh?"

The man smiled. He liked these people. They were not like the ordinary tourists who usually stayed one night on their way from Thessalonica to Athens. Or boorish Greek businessmen. They were pleasant, and that one was a pretty good tipper for someone who spoke Greek. He had the feeling the man was not entirely Greek. He envied them traveling with such a beautiful girl. One of the maids told him the American was sleeping with the girl. Lucky fellow.

The three moved into the dining room and ate a light meal before deciding to turn in.

"How about a quick drink before going up?" said Khoury. Ritter glanced at Michelle. She smiled.

"Nope," said Ritter. "Think we'll pass it up. Got a fairly heavy day … of driving … tomorrow. I want to be fresh."

"Me too," she said.

"Roger," said Khoury, smiling at them with a knowing grin. Yes, Ritter was not such a fool after all. He strongly wished he had a girl of his own, too.

They stood up and turned to the stairway. As they did, a heavyset man with a thick droopy mustache approached them. His breath was overloaded with garlic. They had not noticed him before. His shoulders were slightly hunched and the sleeves of his jacket were at least an inch too short. He reminded Ritter of a country tobacco salesman.

"Excuse me," he said in strongly accented English. "Mr. Khoury, Mr. Ritter, and Miss Simonet?"

"Yes?"

The man pulled a wallet from his pocket, opened it, and showed his identification card.

"I am Lieutenant Doriacles of the Macedonian Gendarmerie. I'd like you to come down to the station with me for a few minutes. Don't be alarmed. It's just a routine matter."

16

With a loud and disheartening clank, the metal door slammed shut. They had been told to wait. There wasn't much choice.

Michelle rolled her eyes in a silent statement on the exasperating absurdity of it all. Khoury maintained a professional coolness. These were Greeks. He knew them. His face betrayed no emotion. No one spoke. Ritter looked around the room. He was more annoyed than apprehensive. The automatic stomach-gnawing fear that would grip perhaps more worldly persons in such a situation did not trouble him. He had had little experience with police. Or police buildings. He could only think this must be drearier than most. There was a definite odor of vomit and a nasty trace of urine. The stone floor was splotchy as though it had not been thoroughly cleaned in weeks, or perhaps months. On one of the gray stone walls was a Greek flag and a creased black-and-white photograph of a well-known Athens political figure who was now president. There was one window, high up on the outside wall, placed so one could not peer out without standing on a bench or chair. The window was barred. Technically, it seemed, the room was not a cell. But to even the most naive observer, it obviously had been used as such many times.

The rough wooden benches were anything but comfortable.

As the minutes ticked by, they became increasingly less so. The colonel would see them in a moment, the man had said. About what? The man couldn't say. Ritter mentioned something about telephoning the American embassy in Athens. It wouldn't be necessary, the man explained. They weren't under arrest. The colonel simply wanted to talk to them. About what? He was sorry, he was busy. The colonel would see them shortly.

The room was cold. The situation, however, was what really made them all shiver. Restless, Khoury leaned over and whispered to Ritter. "I think we are in the hands of Colonel Voko."

"Who?" replied Ritter also in a whisper. The name seemed strangely familiar.

"Voko, the man they call the hammer. He was a famous guerrilla leader in the war. During the civil strife that followed, he was a nearly legendary government hero in the fight against the Communists. It is said he killed many men. Just as often, he is supposed to have enjoyed it. He is now chief of the Macedonian Gendarmarie."

Voko. Yes, of course. Voko. The right-wing policeman who had betrayed them during the attack on the train. Could it be the same man? He never actually saw Voko. But Whip had, and hated him. And the others feared him. Ritter didn't want to alarm Michelle or Khoury. "I wouldn't recommend his interior decorator," he said irreverently. "What does he want with us?" If it was the same Voko, he shuddered to think.

Khoury shrugged. "I wouldn't care to speculate."

Ritter turned to Michelle and in a whisper repeated what Khoury had told him.

"Hmmm, lucky," she said softly.

Ritter chuckled. He had to hand it to her. She was cool. But he instinctively sensed this was no laughing matter. He could tell by the way Khoury glared at him.

The minutes dragged by. He looked again at Michelle, who was humming lightly to herself. Khoury stared calmly ahead, as though he was used to waiting for indifferent officials. Ritter looked at the walls, the window, his hands and fingernails, the floor, his shoes, the lone electric light bulb that glimmered dimly above them, a roach exploring one dark corner, the heavy metal door. Maybe the colonel had forgotten them. No, of course he hadn't. Not a chance. Just softening them up. An old psy-war trick. The colonel wanted to let the message soak in thoroughly before talking to them. Macedonian jails were not exactly the Greek equivalent of Disneyland. Ritter looked for the hundredth time at his watch. They already had been kept waiting over forty-five minutes.

The door squeaked open. It was the heavyset lieutenant with the droopy mustache. "The colonel will see you now." "He spoke in broken English with the same tone one might expect from the chief of protocol in hell.

They were ushered into an office as remarkable for its plainness as for its grisly power to shock. A large polished wooden desk nearly filled one end opposite the door. No papers on it, just two empty trays and a pen protruding from a black plastic holder. The walls were the same drab gray. The only decoration was an oil painting depicting a public hanging. On the opposite wall a large window looked out over a small courtyard, which seemed to have been the scene of numerous executions. Three chairs stood at attention before the desk and, off to one side, a small table. On the table a human skull bared its teeth.

The room was dominated, however, by the man behind the desk who rose as they entered the room. He was not particularly large, perhaps around five-feet-seven. But in his neatly tailored uniform he was definitely striking. His black hair was slicked back with what Ritter spotted as greasy kid stuff, the kind movie stars wore in the big musicals in the early 1950's. A black pencil mustache heightened the effect. The man's eyes glowed with activity. His smile fell heavily on them. It was the kind of smile a hungry snake often affords a trapped mouse.

"Come in," he said smoothly. "I must apologize for keeping you waiting. We've been very busy." He walked from behind the desk and shook hands with each of them, pausing extra long with Michelle. Ice-cold, she thought. Ice-cold. The colonel returned to his chair behind the desk and signaled them to sit down.

"May I offer you a cup of coffee?" His English was educated, but not polished. His accent was thick, the English of someone who studied for a number of years in school but rarely if ever got abroad.

Khoury nodded for all of them. The colonel pressed a buzzer on his desk.

"Permit me to introduce myself," he said. "I am Colonel Voko, chief of the Macedonian police. It is possible you have heard of me." In a sweeping gesture he pointed to the painting. Apparently his usual act for first-time visitors. "That painting depicts an important episode from my life and the history of Greece. That was the execution of Andropolous, the infamous Communist revolutionary who tried to destroy Greece in the years from 1945 to 1948. He killed many loyal and good Greeks in the name of Communism, including my brother. It took me three years working night and day to catch him. That was the result. And that," he said, pointing to the skull, "is all that is left of him."

Ritter shivered. So Voko had finally killed Andropolous. A Communist perhaps, but a warm and generous man. A lot more man than this slime who had survived.

The colonel paused. Avenging his brother's death had been the macabre highlight of his life, but not the end of his brutality or killing. "Now I am a simple policeman," he said unconvincingly, "serving my country and people." He sucked air in through his teeth.

"Why are we here?" asked Ritter, surprised at how firm his voice sounded.

Voko laughed, a brittle, nearly metallic sound. "Of course. It is not often we have three such interesting tourists in our area. Particularly this time of year. I wanted to meet you." A note of sarcasm coated his tone.

"We are flattered by the colonel's attention," said Khoury calmly. "But it is after midnight. An unusual time for a social call."

A uniformed young man knocked and entered with a tray of small coffeecups. He served everyone and left.

The three sipped in silence, waiting for Voko to speak again. A dropped pin would have shaken the room.

"Governing Greece these days is not an easy task," said the colonel softly. "There are many currents and pressures, threats to civil order. Our civil war is, thank God, over. The Communists have been crushed. But our society still has many enemies. These enemies are a threat to the life and progress of the Greek people. One of the difficulties of being a servant of the people is protecting the innocent without harming them. This is not as easy as it might seem. Our enemies are often difficult to detect. They come in many forms. Sometimes they come from outside the country, to spy or steal. Greece, as you know, has a long history of hospitality. Unfortunately, this hospitality has been violated many times. It has made some of us, how do you say, wary. It is not a nice trait, I fear, but I have found it a necessary one."

The colonel paused. He sipped at his coffee and stared at the three people before him. His carefully programmed smile returned. "I am sure, of course, you do not fall into this category. But frankly, we have received some reports that have raised … questions. Please tell me, what brings you to Greece?"

Khoury spoke. "Miss Simonet is a student. All her adult life has been spent in one university or another. She is currently working on a doctoral thesis about World War II. Her line of studies has touched on the campaigns in Greece, particularly the campaigns of 1941. Miss Simonet and Mr. Ritter are, shall we say, close friends. Mr. Ritter himself is collecting material that he hopes will form the base of a book. He and I have been friends for many years. When he and Michelle said they were going to take a combination study trip and holiday to Greece, they asked me to join them."

The Colonel sniffed, a blatant gesture of disbelief. He sighed deeply. "I don't think you fully understand the situation," he said. "We have been watching you since your arrival in Thessalonica nearly a week ago. It is most unusual for someone to buy a camper in Greece. That alone would not have been enough to arouse our, uh, interest, of course. Foreigners sometimes do crazy but harmless things. But sometimes, not so harmless. Tell me, Mr. Khoury, about your purchase of the shovels and digging equipment."

"I can explain that," said Khoury, perhaps a bit too hastily. He had no time to ponder how the colonel knew.

"Please," said the colonel.

Ritter twisted uneasily in his seat.

"We knew we would be driving into the mountains. It is still spring. Late snowfalls are not unknown. We figured we might need such tools in case the camper got stuck in snow or spring mud."

"I compliment you on your foresight. But surely not all of the tools you bought, Mr. Khoury. They far exceed what you might need if your camper got stuck. I think they are intended for something else. That's what we would like to know. Your long drives into the countryside were not exactly normal tourist ventures. And your conversation in Ardhassa revealed more than just an academic interest in the area. What are you after?"

Voko was disturbingly well-informed. It was as uncanny as it was unsettling.

"We've already told you, Colonel," said Ritter. "I don't see why you find so much trouble believing us. As far as I can see, we've done nothing to warrant your hospitality. We've not broken the law and we've given you no reason to believe we plan to break it. Admittedly, our trip may be a bit more unusual than most, but that is more a compliment to the beauty of your country and the interest it holds for us than anything else."

The colonel smiled. Like a large cat stalking its prey, he was patient and careful, waiting for the right moment. The verbal crossing of swords amused him to some extent. It was a game he liked and was good at.

"I am flattered by your words, Mr. Ritter. It is true, you've done nothing to break the law, yet. But frankly, I need no excuse to ask you to leave the country. Suspicion of intent is more than enough. However, I don't want to give you a bad impression of Greek hospitality. You are looking for something. Why don't you tell me what it is? Antiquities? Perhaps I can help you?"

"Colonel, with your permission, I would like to speak with Mr. Ritter privately for a few minutes," said Khoury. He ignored Ritter's sudden sharp glance.

Voko arched an eyebrow. He hesitated, a cool smile seeping back onto his face. He sensed he had won. "Of course." He pressed the buzzer. The uniformed man entered. The colonel instructed him to take Ritter and Khoury back to the waiting room until they signaled a desire to return to the office. "I will have in the meantime the pleasure of getting to know Miss Simonet."

Michelle looked nervously at Ritter as he walked out with Khoury.

"Elias, are you out of your Greek mind?" There was real anger in Ritter's voice.

"Easy, Brian," soothed Khoury. "If we cannot satisfy Voko, he can and undoubtedly will throw us out of here. Or worse. There will be no treasure. It's already very clear. We can't escape him."

"But we're not going to give it to him."

"No. We've got to make a deal."

Ritter had been through a similar situation in Barbados. "Another partner, huh?"

"Another partner or no gold for anybody."

"We need another partner like we need a case of clap. How do we know we can trust him?"

"We don't and can't. We'll have to bring him in on an official government basis. There will have to be a contract, notarized by a prefect."

"I don't like it."

"Neither do I. But do you have any better ideas?"

"We could protest our innocence and let him throw us out."

"And then?"

"Come back some other time." Ritter was fishing. He knew Khoury was right.

"He'd never let us back. He would put our faces and names on alert lists at the borders. The next time one of us appeared, he would be on us like a vulture on a rotten carcass. If you'll pardon the comparison. I'm afraid we've got to deal."

"Shit!" Ritter pounded a fist against his hand. There was no sense in discussing it any further. They returned to the colonel's office.

"Come in, gentlemen, come in. Miss Simonet and I were just discussing some of the events of the war. She is indeed very well-informed. Very bright and very beautiful. A rare and most appealing combination." He bowed his head slightly to Michelle as the two men sat back down in their chairs.

"Well, gentlemen?" It was the colonel's silkiest voice.

Ritter suddenly knew how it felt for a fly to bounce into an innocent-looking web.

"As I said before, Colonel," said Khoury, "Miss Simonet is a student. Brian is working on a book. And I am a friend. But you are right, there is more to tell. We are looking for something."

The colonel leaned forward on his desk expectantly. His hands were clasped in front of him. Michelle looked over at Khoury, obviously distressed at the turn the conversation had taken.

"In 1941, the British Army left behind five boxes filled with gold. We are looking for those boxes," said Khoury.

"Very interesting," admitted the colonel. "How do you know about this?"

"Mr. Ritter was here during the war as part of an official mission to recover the gold and turn it over to the partisans. But they didn't find it then."

Voko cast a quizzical glance at Ritter.

"You were here during the war?"

"Briefly," said Ritter, pained that Khoury had mentioned the fact.

"In this area?"

Ritter nodded.

"I don't believe we met. When were you here?"

"In the fall of 1943. I was wounded," said Ritter, touching the scar on his temple. "By the time I recovered, they took me back out again. Not a very distinguished record, I'm afraid."

Voko stared at him, uncertain of the significance of this revelation. He sensed Ritter didn't want to talk about it. There was something he didn't want to say. It was not important now. "But, Mr. Ritter, if you didn't find the gold then, what makes you think you can find it now?"

"One of the men who buried the boxes told a friend of ours, our partner in London. There are currently three partners. We would like to invite you to become the fourth. Whatever we find, we would split four equal ways."

Crimson flooded the colonel's face. He leaped up slamming his fist angrily onto the desk. "What do you take me for, a fool? Do you know the penalty for trying to bribe an officer of the Greek police? I could have you all jailed for ten years," he shouted. "Typical insulting conduct from foreign vultures. Guard!"

The uniformed young man opened the door and ran in.

"Take them out and lock them up," Voko said. The guard roughly grabbed Ritter by the shoulder and pushed him toward the door. He turned to grab Khoury.

"No, wait," said the colonel, his voice calming. "Leave them be." He waved his arm, dismissing the appropriately confused-looking young Greek. He was familiar with the colonel's tactics.

"Forgive me," Voko said, sinking into his chair. "I am tired. It is late. I have been working too hard. Sometimes I react too harshly. But this is a serious situation. Those boxes or whatever, they are in Greek soil. They belong to Greece and the Greek people."

"With all due respect, Colonel," said Ritter cautiously, "only if the Greek people can find them."

"You are not in a position to offer such insolence," said the colonel sourly. He suddenly had little time for subtlety.

"Look at it this way, sir. From your side, it is valid to feel that anything in Greek soil belongs to Greece," said Ritter. "But if you found oil, you undoubtedly would have to hire foreign oil experts to come to Greece to help you get it out of the ground. That is, in a sense, what we are. We have the expertise to recover the boxes. We know where they are. From that point of view, we deserve to be compensated adequately for our services."

The colonel looked at them intently. "Twenty-five percent is not a fair share for the people of Greece. We must receive seventy-five percent."

Ritter and Khoury looked at each other. "Colonel," said Ritter, continuing to carry the conversation, "for twenty-five percent, I can safely say we would not be interested." He was surprised at his own boldness. Although the predawn chill had reached his groin, he realized he was sweating. Slight beads of perspiration had appeared on Khoury's upper lip.

Voko's eyes narrowed. "I can have you put away in this prison forever. You would never see the sunlight again. You would rot there waiting for your own undistinguished funerals which no one would attend."

"It is obviously in your power to lock us up, Colonel," said Ritter. "Whether you could hold us forever is another question. Frankly, I really don't want to find out. But if you do lock us up, you will never see that gold. And it could well be worth millions."

The magic word, "millions." The colonel gradually permitted the smile to return to his face. His voice softened. "Gentlemen, I admire your courage. And I admire Miss Simonet. It would be a shame if you came all this way for nothing. I must agree, throwing you in jail would not solve the problem. Frankly, it would bother my conscience to take years from the life of such a beautiful and charming woman. Let us be friends. Let us agree to a compromise. For the people of Greece, fifty percent. And fifty percent to you as compensation for your efforts. That is my last offer."

Ritter and Khoury looked at each other. Finally, Ritter twitched his mouth in a signal of resignation. "You drive a very hard bargain, Colonel," he said. "I guess we have no choice. We accept."

"A very reasonable decision," said the colonel. "What do you say, Miss Simonet? We've heard nothing from you?"

"I am not a partner in the venture, Colonel. It is up to them to decide."

"Ahh, Miss Simonet. As gallant as you are beautiful."

"You realize, Colonel, we must have this in writing, officially notarized by a judge or prefect," said Khoury.

"Of course, gentlemen. It is not a matter of trust, but a matter of correct procedure. You are absolutely right." Voko suddenly remembered his watch—still on his wrist. "It is late. I fear I have kept you too long. The lieutenant will take you back to your hotel. We all need some sleep. I will contact the necessary legal experts tomorrow and we will have a document drawn up. When it is finished, I'll contact you. We can sign it and get things organized. In the meantime, I fear, you will have to remain in your hotel. You are not under arrest, but considering the circumstances, I do not think you would consider it unfair of me to make such a small request. Let me add I am honored to have a former colleague in the fight against the Germans visiting us. We must get together in the next few days and talk about it. But now is not the time. I bid you good night." He shook hands with Khoury and Ritter and made a show of amorously kissing Michelle's hand.

As they left the room, Ritter looked again at Andropolous' skull and realized how tired he was. The skull seemed to be grinning at him.

***

The first rays of sunshine began to speed through the gray skies as Michelle turned over, fitting her warm, nude bottom tightly against Ritter's side.

"Wish Khoury hadn't mentioned my wartime experience here," said Ritter.

"Thought something was bothering you."

"Oh, I don't suppose it makes all that much difference. But I took part in an attack on a train that involved Greeks from both sides. Voko was one of the leaders of the right-wing group."

"You knew him?"

"Only of him. Never actually met him. But we regarded him as poison. Anyhow, during the raid on the train, Voko betrayed the left-wing group. They were led by Andropolous, whom I did know. And liked."

"Who?"

"The guy on the coffee table."

She sucked in her breath. "How horrible."

"Yeah. Voko tried to fool the left-wing group into believing the Germans were coming, so he and his boys could collect all the booty from the train for themselves. The leftists caught on quick, and it resulted in a shoot-out that led to the death of the British guy who was with us, and ultimately to the death of my friend Whip."

"Voko killed him?"

"Not directly. The incident at the train led to the reprisal attack by the leftists on Kilkis where Voko had his headquarters. That's when Whip was killed by the Greek sniper. Probably a member of the leftist faction."

She snuggled closer to him. "We are doing business with a very dangerous man," she said in a strangely detached way.

* * *

"It was our friend and partner the colonel," said Khoury as he walked back into the bar from the hotel phone. "He is sending someone to take us to the office of the local prefect who has drawn up the document."

"Is he going to meet us there?"

"The colonel apologizes. He is busy, and says there is no need for him to attend. The signing is strictly a formality. We begin digging tomorrow."

"Looks as if we are finally going to see what's in those boxes," said Ritter. We've had it too easy, you know, the thing was too simple to be true. This returns us to reality. It's nice of course to think what might have been if we hadn't had the pleasure of meeting the good colonel. On the other hand, two months ago, even a seventeen percent share would have seemed very good. It's all a matter of how you look at it."

"In the Caribbean," he continued, "one usually expects to pay well over fifty percent to governments, auctioneers, crews, and others. A net take of seventeen percent is impressive by Caribbean standards."

"I'm glad you're taking it so philosophically," Michelle said. "I don't know why I should feel so badly. I'm not losing anything."

Within the hour, the escort from Colonel Voko arrived. It was the lieutenant with the droopy mustache. He still reeked of garlic.

"Here's walrus face," said Ritter. "I'm surprised he hasn't asked for a share."

"Don't tempt him," said Michelle. "If Thompson is going to be upset about his seventeen percent, imagine how he would feel about, say, five percent."

They drove in silence to the office of the perfect, a large stone building that was the center of justice for the region. Entering the office, they all sensed immediately there would be trouble.

The prefect, Christofos Zakros, could only be described as disagreeably fat. His cheeks bulged from an unpleasant face that seemed to have forgotten how to smile.

Introductions were perfunctory. Zakros shook hands quickly with each of them and produced a long one-page document from a folder.

"Sign here," he said, pointing to the bottom line.

"Don't you think we ought to read it first?" asked Ritter.

"Not necessary," said Zakros. "This is the final document, drawn up in accordance with Greek law. Naturally, if you insist …"

"We insist," said Ritter.

Zakros grumbled and pushed the papers toward them. The document was in Greek.

Khoury began to translate for Ritter and Michelle. "Agreement has been reached between representatives of the Greek government and Elias Khoury and Brian Ritter—it gives our passport numbers, ages, and birthplaces, I see. The hunt for five boxes buried by the British Army in April 1941 is to be conducted on a joint basis between us and a committee of two representing the Greeks. Would you believe, the members of the committee are Colonel Georges Voko, chief of the Macedonian police, and Christofos Zakros, prefect for Kozani. It is agreed the proceeds of the find will be split between us all, the government to get a full fifty percent. *K'suchta* ..." Khoury swore in Arabic. "Look at this."

"Look at what?" said Ritter.

"I need to interpret this exactly." He read slowly and carefully, stressing each word. "It says, 'The excavation is to last not longer than forty-eight hours, unless an obvious necessity exists whereupon the committee can extend said excavation accordingly.' "

"I'm not sure we can do it in two days. You saw what it looked like," said Ritter softly, cupping his hand over his mouth to shield his words from Zakros.

"That's the point," answered Khoury quietly. "I suspect they don't think so either."

"Please sign," said Zakros sharply. "My time is short."

"Mr. Zakros," said Ritter. "We may not he able to handle the dig in only two days. We hereby request a written guarantee that the committee will automatically extend the length of the search if we request it."

"That will not be necessary. Sign now, please. I have another appointment."

"Better sign it," said Khoury. "We'll talk to Voko. He wants those boxes pretty badly."

With a disgusted shake of the head, Ritter signed. Khoury followed. There were four copies. Zakros handed them a countersigned copy, turned and abruptly left the room. He did not bother to shake hands or say good-bye.

"We'll just have to get the gold out of the ground in two days," said Ritter in a determined tone.

They returned to the car, and the droopy-mustached lieutenant drove them back to the hotel. Khoury chatted with him in Greek.

As the three walked from the car into the lobby, Khoury said, "I understand it all now."

"What's there to understand?" asked Ritter.

"Zakros is Voko's first cousin."

17

They strolled into the bar and sat down around one of the low-slung wooden tables. They all needed a drink, a moment to relax, to contemplate and decide how to cope with the latest developments. Getting any of the gold out of Greece was going to be more complicated than they originally imagined. And far more risky.

They ordered whiskeys with water and sipped slowly, each absorbed in private thoughts. Michelle reached over and briefly squeezed Ritter's hand. A sign of encouragement, affection, the gesture warmed him.

Michelle. Her blond hair needed to be combed out. She looked slightly weary. But she was beautiful. It had been a long time since he had been so taken with a woman. A long time.

They continued to sip quietly, each seeking refreshment in the silence.

The well-dressed woman in the corner watched them intensely, nervously fidgeting with her handbag. She was a handsome woman, with strong features clearly under attack by middle age and a deep inner sadness she wore like a veil of mourning. After several anxious minutes she stood up, hesitated, and walked over to them.

Ritter could sense the woman standing over him behind his chair. He turned and looked up over his shoulder at her.

"Hello, Brian," she said softly. "I thought it might be you." She nervously glanced at the scar on his temple.

He looked at her intently. The dark, tormented eyes, vaguely familiar, spoke of tragedy and profound grief. Deep shadows under her eyes had aged her face beyond its years, but the basic lines of the face had not disappeared. She was still attractive. She had just missed being beautiful. "Melanie?" His voice cracked.

She nodded. "You haven't changed much," she said, trying to interject a light note into her voice. She bit the inside of her lip.

Khoury and Michelle looked around. Ritter stumbled for words, trying to recover some sense of composure. "Melanie," he said, getting to his feet. "Melanie ..." He couldn't get the sound of disbelief out of his voice. "I, uh, I want you to meet my friends."

Melanie looked over at the younger woman. "Hello," she said, offering her hand and an awkward smile.

Michelle responded with a cautious smile of her own.

"Please sit down. Join us," said Ritter, gradually recovering from the initial shock.

"If you'll excuse me," said Khoury, "I've got to go upstairs."

"Me too," said Michelle hastily. She was tom between her curiosity and the realization that the woman and Ritter needed to speak privately.

Melanie offered a grateful glance. She didn't attempt to protest their departure.

"Something to drink?" asked Ritter.

She shook her head as she sat down.

A long, difficult pause. So much to be said. Where to begin?

"I, uh …" They both spoke at once, interrupting each Other. Awkward laughs.

"As you were saying …" said Ritter.

"No, please go ahead," she replied.

"When we took off, the Germans were shooting at us. I thought they captured you … or worse."

"I was captured," she said. "They held me for several weeks. This is where I got this." She pulled up the sleeve of her dress and showed him an ugly scar. "There are others."

"Melanie …"

"No, there is nothing you can say. Or could have done. They held me for three weeks before I was rescued."

"Andropolous?"

"Voko," she said quietly.

"Voko?"

"Yes, I am his wife." Her voice had dropped to a whisper.

The words squeezed the breath out of him. "You … that's how you heard …"

"Yes, my husband mentioned an American who had been here during the war. He doesn't know much about you, but he mentioned the scar." She bit the inside of her lip.

Ritter touched his temple where the German bullet had grazed him thirty-two years earlier as he lunged to save Melanie's life. "Permanent souvenir." He smiled cautiously.

"I waited for you as long as I could," she said. "After Voko freed me from the Germans, he insisted I marry him. I didn't want to, but he was in a position to ruin my father. You can't imagine what that means. My family insisted. I … I had no choice." Her eyes were suddenly red and watery. "I'm sorry, I didn't want it to be like this. You are married?"

"No. Never got around to it."

"The girl?"

"A friend."

"You know where the gold is?"

"I think so. We are going to dig it up with your husband."

He leaned toward her. The cross around his neck dangled out.

Melanie stared. "You're still wearing it."

"I wasn't sure—"

She interrupted, her face turned down so he couldn't see the tears. "I must go. I should not be seen here with you. So many years have passed, so many things have changed. Please be careful…. He is not to be trusted."

Ritter's own eyes blurred as he watched her walk away.

* * *

"She's lovely," said Michelle carefully. Ritter obviously had been strongly affected by the unexpected appearance of the woman.

He sank into the chair in the corner of their room, fingering the silver cross he always wore around his neck. "I thought she was dead." he said.

Michelle remained silent.

"Bullets were hitting the plane as I jumped on. We had to get up fast. I could see them closing in on her. There had been plenty of stories about the Germans not taking prisoners among the partisans. After the attack on the train, I was certain …"

"Are you planning to see her again?" Michelle asked.

"It's impossible."

"Impossible?"

"She's Voko's wife."

Michelle gasped.

"I'm not sure Voko would react kindly to the reappearance of her wartime lover." Ritter paused, looking at Michelle, turning the cross over and over in his fingers. "I'm just part of her past. I have no right to suddenly become part of her life now."

18

Colonel Georges Voko was in a good mood. For the first time in over two weeks his hemorrhoids were not bothering him. A letter in the morning's mail from headquarters in Athens commended him on the efficient apprehension of a jewel thief who had fled north from the islands after relieving several rich tourists of their valuables. And it was the warmest day of spring so far, sunny, bright, and promising, a perfect day to dig up a fortune.

Or even better, not to.

The Colonel had assembled a convoy of seven cars and a truck to transport the digging force of eighteen men to the hunt site, a remote mountainside off one of the minor feeder roads. He had to admit, it had been extremely thoughtful of the British to leave the gold in his district. He had always liked the British, and now he was feeling even more kindly disposed toward them. It would be a shame, of course, if they weren't able to find the money within the two-day limit, but alas, that was life. Once the government officially declared the search over, the gold would still be there for private hunters to dig up. Perhaps even an off-duty police colonel.

And if by accident they did find the gold, Zakros assured him the three had not taken notice of the clause "in accordance with Greek law." It was illegal to transport gold out of Greece except in the form of limited personal jewelrey, thus the foreigners would be able to dispose of their fifty percent only with the help of the colonel. Either way, it would work out very well.

Khoury, Ritter, and the girl were subdued during the drive from the hotel. Perhaps it had all been too obvious. But what could they do about it? Nothing. It was the colonel's game, and he was making up the rules. Nevertheless, he reassured them by telling them that with the large group of men, there would be no question of not completing the dig in the given time.

"It is just that I am very busy," the colonel explained. He was sitting in the back of the car with Michelle and Khoury. Ritter sat in the front with the driver. "I am responsible for law and order in this entire region. I just can't devote more time to this. But I have brought sufficient men. We could dig up the entire mountain in two days, not to mention a small cave blown shut with a hand grenade."

Ritter ignored the obvious exaggeration and turned to face those in the back. "It is more manpower than we originally counted on, Colonel," he conceded. "Maybe it will be enough."

The American was an interesting sort. Obviously a man of the outdoors. It would be hard to guess his age if Voko didn't already know it. Ritter had kept himself in extraordinarily good shape, a fact the colonel noted with a touch of envy mixed with guilt. He had an easygoing manner about him, but also traces of insolence. Under other circumstances he might be a pleasant luncheon or drinking companion. He suspected Ritter, like himself, had a knack with women. One could always tell.

Voko was thus both intrigued and bothered by the revelation that Ritter had been in northern Greece during the war. At the time of the attack on the train, an American and an Englishman were killed. There had been another American who almost immediately afterward was picked up by the British. Someone Voko had never met. Could this be Ritter? It was widely rumored at the time that the American had saved Melanie's life and had an affair with her. She certainly had behaved strangely when he mentioned the man's name. He wanted to know more about this.

Khoury, the Lebanese-Greek, sat on the opposite side of the car, saying nothing. He was a smart one. No question of that. And obviously upset at having his share trimmed from its original thirty-three percent. If only he realized the truth, thought Voko, he would be delighted with getting seventeen percent. But for the moment, it was good for him to grumpily believe he was going to get away with only a lesser amount.

"We have all the digging tools we need," said the colonel. "We'll have the boxes out of the ground perhaps by the end of the day." He smiled his most diplomatic and appealing smile. His teeth were sharp white against his swarthy coloring. The smile was always a hit with the ladies.

Almost always. He looked at the girl next to him, smiling mechanically when she had to, making little secret of her feelings. An arrogant look sharpened her eyes. Challenging, one could say. She was a crafty one. Resourceful. With strong passions. That was the kind he liked. He would love to have her for a night. He would teach her a few tricks she had never imagined in her wildest fantasies, certainly things she would never learn from the American. His thoughts drifted briefly to the last attractive female prisoner he had. At first she spit on him defiantly. Two hours later she was on her knees begging him to do anything he wanted, begging him to let her please him. A very satisfying evening. Her mutilated body was found by peasants miles away a few days later. The official report said she had been attacked by a wild animal while walking along the road, and her death was attributed to natural causes. Case neatly closed.

Khoury directed the driver in Greek as they led the convoy to the digging site. Shortly after nine-thirty A.M. they were looking up at the caves on the mountain about 150 yards above them.

"Somewhere up there," said Ritter, pointing.

"I don't see anything that looks like it has been blown shut with explosives," said the colonel.

"From here, I don't either," said Ritter. "But just think, it's been thirty-four years. Let's get up there and have a closer look."

Led by Ritter, the party scrambled up the hillside to the base of the layers of rock that formed the caves. Some were just small openings, little more than stone shelters. Other holes obviously led to more substantial caves. But many areas where rocks had piled up from slides or other causes offered no openings. Even with all the men it was going to be tough to cover the entire area in only two days.

"I recommend we break the men into teams of two. Elias and I will form one team," said Ritter. "With Michelle. We'll just pick out the most likely-looking sites and start digging."

The clank of picks and shovels soon rang out over the normal stillness of the valley. For the next three hours the party worked steadily, Michelle with a shovel alongside Khoury and Ritter. It was a site chosen by Ritter that looked particularly hopeful. The colonel stayed below near the cars, talking on his car radio and watching intently. No one expected him to take part in the actual digging.

"Now I know why I like diving so much more than this," wheezed Ritter. He had stripped off his shirt, and small rivers ran off his sturdy body. It was the first heavy physical work he had done in weeks, and he could feel his muscles straining. But he needed it. He was too old to permit his body to fall out of shape. After a certain age it became too difficult to get back into form, the temptations of a soft life were too much to resist. Khoury was breathing heavily. He certainly was feeling the effort. He would be stiff by nightfall, Ritter knew. Not used to this kind of heavy stuff. Michelle was in surprisingly good shape, helped undoubtedly by her relative youth. She worked steadily alongside them, never complaining. Ritter thought he detected a sense of competitiveness on Khoury's part as he struggled to show he could not be outworked by a female, even a much younger one. Some of the men began to drift toward the convoy. "Looks like it's about time for lunch," said Ritter.

"Not a minute too soon," huffed Khoury, dropping his pick. Ritter and Michelle put down their own tools, and, they all made their way down the hill to the vehicles.

"You have been working hard," said the colonel. "How does it look?"

"It's early, Colonel. We're just getting warmed up. It's tougher to dig through that rock than I thought. And none of us is any younger than we used to be."

"With the possible exception of Miss Simonet." The colonel carefully leered at her. The expression did not go unnoticed. "Well, come and have some lunch," he said. "We've got rations in the truck."

Most of the men were already lined up for a feeding of cheese, bread, olives, and fresh hummus, but stepped aside for the colonel and his three companions. No question of who's in charge here, Ritter thought.

Someone produced several bottles of white retsina. They sat at a table and four chairs put up by one of the men. Michelle held up her hand to show a blister to Ritter and the others.

"You need something for that," said the colonel sympathetically. He snapped his fingers, and an aide ran forward to take an order. In a few minutes the man returned with a first-aid kit and tape for the offending palm.

"Anyone else?" asked the colonel jovially as he cut off strips of tape for Michelle.

Somewhat sheepishly both Khoury and Ritter put out their hands to display blisters, which were then taped by Michelle.

"The results of what you Americans like to call good honest work, heh, gentlemen?" needled the colonel. "You do not seem so used to it."

"It's a bit out of my bag, I admit, Colonel," said Ritter. "But I can use the excercise. I was getting a bit soft researching my book."

"It is also not my usual style," allowed Khoury. "But for so noble a cause…"

They laughed. All for different reasons.

"By the way, Mr. Ritter, when did you say you were here in northern Greece?" said Voko conversationally.

"Pardon, Colonel?" A stalling question. A moment to gather his wits.

"You said you were here during the war. When was that?"

"Oh. September 1943."

"Don't think we met."

"No, I don't believe I had the pleasure."

"You weren't by any chance at Kilkis during the attack on the train when the American and English officers were killed?"

"I was with them. I was flown out with the papers we captured. Wasn't exactly the time for social calls, Colonel."

"It was rumored you found a surprising amount of time for socializing, Mr. Ritter." A visible cutting edge in his voice.

Careful. Careful, Ritter thought, not clear what he knows. Or how he feels about it. "Idle stories, Colonel. Most of the time I was laid up with a head wound. I left the morning after the raid."

"Unfortunate about your comrades. They were among so many victims of Communist duplicity and treason."

In less than an hour they finished lunch and returned to the mountainside. Ritter, Khoury, and Michelle were working a face that appeared to have been covered years before by a rock slide, a likely-looking spot. Chipping at the large rocks demanded enormous energy and strength. The benefits of the restful lunch break evaporated quickly.

At one point Ritter strolled along to inspect what the others were doing. The men had dug a number of holes and escavated several caves. But they had found nothing resembling the boxes. One group uncovered some animal bones. Another found some pottery shards dating back perhaps several hundred years. As the sun began to sink behind the mountains, the work crews drifted back to the vehicles. The day's search was over.

Ritter, Khoury, and Michelle dragged themselves down to the cars. It had been an exhausting and fruitless day.

"Nothing, heh?" said the colonel a bit too cheerfully. "Well, tomorrow is another day. You and my men covered much of the hillside today. Tomorrow there should be no difficulty in covering the rest and finding the boxes."

They crawled into the car and began the long drive back to the hotel. Khoury and Ritter exchanged places and Michelle fell asleep on Ritter's shoulder.

"I apologize that I will not be able to ask you to join me for dinner," said the colonel as they arrived. "Unfortunately, I have another obligation. I hope you will excuse me."

"It's all right," said Ritter. "I'm not sure we would be such good company anyway. I think we'll all turn in early."

The colonel flashed his usual smile, glanced at Michelle, and with a trace of a bow bid them good night.

"Hot-bath time," said Ritter. "But maybe we ought to have a drink first."

"Not me," said Khoury. "I just want to sleep. I'll have dinner in my room." He was obviously exhausted.

"While you're having that drink," said Michelle to Ritter, "I'll run the water. That's one thing I like about this place. They have bathtubs big enough for two."

* * *

"The colonel apologizes, but he is tied up this morning. He will join you later," the driver said.

Ritter, Michelle, and Khoury looked at each other but said nothing. They climbed stiffly into the car sent by Voko, strongly conscious of the beating their bodies had taken the previous day. They arrived at the dig site about nine-thirty. The others were already there, moving up the mountainside to begin digging in the caves. It was another warm morning, and some of the men quickly shed their shirts to take advantage of the spring sun.

"Still a bit too cool for me to copy that," said Khoury as Ritter again pulled off his shirt.

"Me too," said Michelle.

The digging began. At about eleven, they saw the colonel's official-looking black Mercedes; Voko waved to them from below but did not come up.

"Executive hours," said Michelle.

"Rank has its privileges," said Ritter. Khoury glared down at the colonel but said nothing.

To their left, one of the men began to shout. He had found something. The three scrambled over to the digger, who was quickly surrounded by other members of the work party. He was holding up several rusted clips of .303 rifle ammunition, possibly from British Enfields.

"British," shouted the man, holding it up for all to see. "We've found something."

Voko came running up the hill. He was breathing heavily and obviously excited when he reached them.

"What is this?" he shouted.

"British rifle clips, Colonel. It certainly means the English were here," said the man.

"This could be a definite clue," said Ritter. "This is an out-of-the-way area, certainly not the kind of place where the English spent a lot of time. It's possible that when they buried the boxes, these clips were left behind."

"I agree, Mr. Ritter. We'll concentrate the digging here. Does this look like it could have been the place?"

Ritter took a few steps for a broader look. "Could be, Colonel. It's not too high up. The area is a bit overgrown, and that's not a bad sign. An explosion thirty-four years ago could have disrupted the earth enough to have encouraged plant growth. Also, thirty-four winters of snow and rain and normal erosion, one can't expect a place to look exactly as it did when they buried the gold."

"Probably not," agreed the colonel. "All right, men," he shouted in Greek, "let's start digging."

An editorial "let's," thought Khoury.

Ritter, Khoury, and Michelle joined the excavation work at the new site. But the next hour they worked steadily, digging into the mountain, but shovelful after shovelful of earth and stone turned up nothing further.

A whistle blew. Lunch break. The men quickly made their way down to the truck for their rations.

"Maybe we're too low or too far off to one side, Colonel," said Ritter as he, Michele, and Khoury joined Voko at the table set up for them.

"It is hard to say," said the colonel. "But finding the clips is very encouraging." He had them on the table before him. They were badly rusted and caked with dirt. "If only they could talk," said Voko wistfully. "It could save a lot of work."

"Too bad you can't apply your usual methods, heh, Colonel?" said Ritter lightly.

The colonel decided to accept the comment as a joke. He smiled and opened a bottle of retsina, pouring for all. "To a successful hunt," he said, raising his glass and looking at Ritter. He would settle with the American later.

They finished their meal and turned wearily back to work. Voko drove off, apologizing once more for his heavy schedule.

"Do you think there's something here?" Michelle asked.

"Let's find out," said Ritter.

For the rest of the afternoon they helped excavate the area around the spot where the clips were found. As the sun began to dip behind the mountains, they had found nothing more.

"There go our two days," said Ritter, staring into the approaching sunset. "Now what?"

"We will see tomorrow," said Khoury. "It looks like the committee will have no choice but to let us continue this dig."

"That should prove most interesting," said Ritter.

"The colonel's move," said Michelle. "I don't think we should do anything until he's played his hand."

They returned to the cars and were driven back to the hotel. It was well after dark when they arrived.

"Drinks are on me," said Ritter.

"An offer we can't refuse," said Michelle.

"Yes, Brian," answered Khoury, "a double anything would be most welcome for these tired bones."

They made their way to the bar and ordered a round of drinks, which quickly disappeared. As they were ordering seconds, a waiter walked up to them. "Mr. Khoury? Someone to see you."

They looked around as the colonel's aide, the droopy-mustached lieutenant approached.

"Would you come with me?" the man commanded stiffly. Shrugging they followed.

"Please sit here," he ordered, motioning them to couches in an out-of-the-way corner of the lobby. The colonel has instructed me to ask you to sign this." He produced a legal--looking document from his pocket. It was typed in Greek. "You all must sign."

Khoury unfolded the paper. "Here it is.

"It says that on May 4 and 5 of this year," he began translating, "the three of us, in accordance with the agreement we signed in the prefect's office, carried out the search and excavation at the site. It says that on our direction, an area about two-hundred meters long and thirty meters high was thoroughly searched. No treasure was found and work was terminated."

"Sounds like the party is over," said Ritter.

"What does this mean?" said Khoury angrily, shaking the document in the lieutenant's face.

"I have my orders. You must sign," said the man.

"You tell the colonel we are complying under extreme protest," said Khoury.

"I will relay the message. Please sign now." He thrust a pen into Khoury's hand. With an obvious gesture of futility and anger, Khoury took the pen and signed the document. He handed the pen to Ritter, who calmly signed. And then Michelle.

The lieutenant picked up the paper and carefully folded it before slipping it into his pocket. "You are hereby officially requested to leave this hotel no later than an hour after dawn tomorrow. You must be out of the country in twenty-four hours. Failure to comply with these orders could lead to your arrest and a charge of conspiracy."

"Conspiracy to what?" demanded Khoury.

"I have nothing more to say. You have heard the order. I must leave now." The lieutenant stood up and left.

The three looked at each other grimly.

"Let's go up to a room and talk there. It will be more private," said Ritter. They walked up the stairs to Khoury's room. As they closed the door, their expressions of anger and dismay dissolved into uneasy smiles.

"Just what we thought," said Ritter.

"Shh," said Khoury. He walked over to the radio and turned it on loud. "It is safer this way."

"So the colonel has us out of the way and now will go back and dig up the treasure all by himself," said Ritter.

"Hmmm, lucky," said Michelle.

Ritter laughed. "I wonder how long it will take him to realize we led him to the wrong site?"

"I can imagine him digging for days and not finding anything. Maybe he'll never catch on," Michelle laughed. The idea of the colonel sweating over something not there tickled her.

"Yes, it's a funny joke," said Khoury more seriously. "But our problems are just beginning. Now we know for certain Voko was trying to cheat us out of the gold. But what do we do now? The order to leave the country is serious. Maybe no one will get the gold now."

19

"*Rousfeti*" said Khoury bitterly. He spat out the word.

"Sounds like an embarrassing social disease," Michelle grimaced.

"It is," continued Khoury rubbing his thumb against his teeth to clean them. "Voko and his cousin Zakros. Voko undoubtedly arranged to get him his position. It's what Europeans or Americans would call nepotism or cronyism. It's an important part of the Greek social and political system that has rotted the national fabric. They say a man is lucky who has an uncle in Koroni. That's where the national gendarmarie headquarters used to be. It means if you have a relative with the police, you can get things fixed. In this case, it's the other way around. Voko is in a strong position through his cousin to play not only prosecutor but judge. That gives him very firm control over this area. He can get away with practically anything. He's protected by the courts. In fact, he's probably more powerful in his own way than any local politician."

"Sounds a bit overwhelming," said Ritter.

"The Greeks like it that way. The prime minister, for instance, made his brother a key aide in his office. The average Greek distrusts the government and the bureaucracy. He likes to feel he knows somebody somewhere or, even better, has a relative in a position to get things done for him. No one trusts the government to do its job fairly and efficiently without favoritism."

"Getting to the point," said Ritter, "we need someone who outranks Voko."

"Exactly."

"We obviously aren't going to find him here."

"But we can't get to Athens from here under these conditions," interjected Michelle.

"I don't think so either," agreed Khoury. "You can bet that bastard Voko will have us watched until he is sure we are safely out of the way, out of the country in fact. He would never permit us to reach Athens to seek help."

"So what do we do?" said Ritter. "I'm really tired. My legs ache, a sign I'm really beat."

"Me too," Khoury sighed, raising a stiff arm and rubbing it. "I guess we'll have to make contact with Athens from London. That means leaving the country now and making contact at the ambassadorial level. We still have a copy of the agreement we signed with Zakros. That will be of great interest I am sure to the central government in Athens. They have been cheated out of a share of a major treasure by a greedy and undoubtedly corrupt local warlord. If we can get a real sharing agreement with the central government, with firm guarantees for our safety and with time to properly find the gold and dig it up, then we can come back and get it. It means delay and a lot less than we originally counted on. But it's still a good amount of money."

"Looks like the only way," said Ritter, yawning. "It's been a good try, but just not meant to be. I always thought the whole thing was too good to be true. On the other hand, we probably were less than a meter or two from it.... Shit."

"You mean you two are going to give up, just like that?" demanded Michelle.

"Any other ideas? We aren't exactly holding all the cards here. A high-suited deuce would outbid us at this point."

"There must be something," she continued. "You're a treasure hunter, Brian. Think of something. Just because that crook is a cop is no reason to let him get away with what he's doing. That money is yours. And Elias' and Thompson's. That pork chop doesn't deserve a milligram."

"He sure doesn't, baby. In the Caribbean it's what we call claim jumping. But we don't have the muscle. The only card we hold is we know where the gold is. He doesn't. And doesn't know it yet."

"Yet," said Khoury with fresh sharpness in his voice. "What time is it?"

"Almost eleven P.M."

"Let's examine it. If we started driving now, we could reach the site in an hour. On these roads at this time of night, we would stand a fair chance of getting to the site without being followed. How long do you think it would take us to dig it up?"

"You mean ...?" said Ritter.

"It would be a long shot," admitted Khoury.

"A mad dash to the site. Hope we can break the tail. Dig it up and dash for the border," said Ritter, putting the idea into words. The presentation didn't flatter it.

"It only took them a short time to blow the cave shut. It shouldn't take all that long to dig it open," pressed Khoury.

"What if we couldn't find it right away? You know what it was like scrambling around yesterday and today. We might run into the same business for real."

"Look, Brian, it's the only thing I can think of that would restore our shares from zero back to the original thirty-three percent. The site is off the road. If we didn't find it or have it out of the ground by then, we could hide the camper in the streambed and wait until dark. And then resume digging," said Khoury.

"It's a chance, Brian. Better than giving up," urged Michelle. "Better than doing nothing."

"It's a long shot that compares roughly with winning the Irish Sweepstakes top prize with a single ticket the first time you bet. Worse than that, it's also dangerous. I don't want to sound too practical and old-maidish, but what if we aren't able to shake off whoever the dear colonel has hanging around to keep an eye on us?"

Khoury sat in a chair in the corner of the room. He had turned the chair around and was leaning with his arms over the back. With a glance he acknowledged the question, but made no move to answer.

"Or, Elias, what if they followed us and we thought we had lost them? In the dark on these roads that we aren't familiar with, it could easily happen. That would just be leading Voko to the real site. Is that what we want to do? For all we know, he's waiting outside for us to try something like that. Maybe he would even let us get all the way to the site without tipping his hand."

Khoury remained motionless, saying nothing.

"Yes, maybe that's what he wants us to do. But even if we gave them the slip, and got there without being followed, I'm frankly not sure we could find the right spot so easily. It would be hard enough during daylight. In the dark without proper lights, it would be like looking for a diamond in a ton of ice. I've been on too many hunts to think we could find it just like that. Particularly after the past two days. And the condition we're in. Even if we were lucky and could get right to it, what makes you think we would be strong enough to dig it out quickly and then carry those five heavy boxes to the van? But even if we got it out of the ground and into the camper okay, how in the hell would we drive undetected out of this district? The minute the camper disappears, Voko will suspect something. If he doesn't know where we are and can't quickly find us, he'll throw up day-and-night roadblocks all over northern Greece. If he has any helicopters, he'll put them up. Every cop and volunteer he can muster would be looking for us. What would be our chances of escaping such a manhunt? None. But even if we did, our names and faces would be on watchlists at every border point. We'd never get out of the country. The result would be just turning the gold over to him. Is that what you want?"

Khoury was still motionless. He had realized the problems all along. Now that Ritter had defined them so clearly, there was no further use kidding himself or them. Even Michelle was now quiet.

They were defeated. "The bastard," said Khoury. "May the fleas of a thousand camels infest the crotch of his firstborn." An old Arabic curse in a moment of need.

"The bar is still open," said Ritter. "Let's go get drunk."

"Hold it," said Khoury as they moved toward the door. "We do have a final card to play."

"Cut the crap, Elias. Stop kidding yourself. It's over. Admit it. Let's get down to the bar before they close. No sense in making the day a total loss." Ritter grabbed Michelle by the arm and began to walk out again.

"Goddammit!" shouted Khoury. "I said wait."

"Look, Elias, you're not running the show," barked Ritter irritably. "It's over now."

"It's not over. We still have one option. I should have thought of it sooner."

Ritter hesitated. Khoury was serious. "I'm tired, Elias. What is it?"

"Dimitri Metaxas."

"Who's that? What's he got to do with this?"

"Nothing yet."

"Does he outrank Voko? Or his cousin?"

"No, but he might be able to help us." Khoury's thoughts were churning. "I've done business with Metaxas. He owes me a large favor. It is so large he is not in a position to refuse any reasonable request from me."

"Sounds like you saved his life," Ritter said.

"I did." He didn't offer to elaborate.

"Where is this angel of mercy? How can he help us?"

"He is here in Greece, in Macedonia. I saw him the other day in Thessalonica. He was on his way to spend a week with his father and mother. He is only about one-hundred kilometers away. He could easily get here before dawn." Khoury paused.

"Go on," said Ritter unmoved.

"If he could help us convince Voko that we had left the area, we might be able to set up a dig undisturbed at the real site and get away with it. The advantage we still hold is that—"

"Voko doesn't know what we know," interrupted Ritter, beginning to get the idea.

"That's it. Metaxas has many relatives and friends. We could turn the Greek *rousfeti* around to work for us. They could hide us for a few days while Voko cools off. Perhaps we could work undetected at night and sleep during the day. Metaxas could tell the locals we were looking for artifacts. A lot of people come to Greece for that. They pay off a farmer who looks the other way, and anything they find they keep. No questions asked. It's illegal, of course, forbidden by the antiquities law. But the village people usually can be tempted by the money, and they never really comprehend the value of the stuff that's dug up other than the cash it brings in. For them, it's just another crop. I've even heard of villagers salting their backyards to encourage such diggings."

"So we'll dig for old pottery, and if we happen to find five boxes containing a million pounds worth of gold, nobody will know the difference or really care, right?"

"That's the idea. All we have to do is locate Dimitri and get him here before dawn."

Khoury got up and left the room, walking down to the front desk. A sleepy-looking man with a dull look in his eyes stood behind the desk. "Yes, sir?" he said as Khoury approached.

"Like to settle our bill, please."

The man went to a box of cards and shuffled through them, finally pulling out Khoury's charges. "You're with Mr. Ritter and the lady?"

"That's right."

"You also paying their bill?"

Khoury nodded.

"You aren't leaving now?"

"Tomorrow morning. We want to get an early start. Thought we would pay now. You know, speed things up."

"Yes, sir."

The man shuffled the bills around some more and finally rang them up on an adding machine. He showed the result to Khoury. "Cash, check, or credit card?"

"American Express." He handed the man his card.

The man shuffled the bills some more and made out the credit-card chit. "Enjoyed your stay, sir?" he asked, handing the chit to Khoury to be signed.

"One of the most interesting holidays I've ever had," said Khoury.

"You're not Greek?"

"My mother."

"It's been good having you with us, sir."

"Thank you. Like to use the phone."

"Local call?"

"Yes, in the region. I should be able to direct-dial."

"Yes, sir. Just pick up the phone in the booth and dial nine, followed by the number you want."

"Thanks." Khoury walked over to the booth and dialed the number Dimitri Metaxas had given him. It was the number of his father's house in Veria, 117 kilometers east on the road to Thessalonica. The phone rang for several minutes before someone finally answered.

When Khoury was finished, he put down the receiver and slowly walked up the stairs to Ritter's and Michelle's room.

He knocked and walked in. They looked at him expectantly.

"Well?" said Ritter.

Khoury sagged down in the chair. Suddenly his back hurt. His legs and arms ached. He felt like crying, something he had not done since he was a child.

"He left the house this evening. His mother thinks he may have gone into Thessalonica. It's possible he won't be back for a couple of days."

20

Early in life Ritter learned one of those rare and valuable things that never can be taught. It was not clear when or how he learned it. Most probably he never unlearned it. For it is a marvelous facility that every small child has, but few are able to carry it with them into adulthood. This is the enviable ability to clear one's mind of worldly concerns each night and sleep. Unlike others who sought refuge from their cares in drink or drugs or other self-destructive diversions, Ritter always had been able to sleep off his worries and problems. He found sleep a balm, a nourisher, a mending process that indeed knitted together his unraveled sleeves of care. It meant each day could begin fresh after nature's soothing second course.

Hearing the crushing news from Khoury, Ritter and Michelle quietly said goodnight as he glumly got up and went to his own room. After an affectionate but weary exchange of words, they fell asleep in each other's arms. Michelle, bothered by their loss, dozed restlessly. Ritter, as usual, celebrated the death of a bad and disturbing day with a deep and untroubled sleep.

It didn't last the night.

About an hour before dawn Michelle was awakened by a soft tapping at their door.

"Who is it?" she called. Ritter stirred slightly.

"Elias."

"Just a minute," she said. Michelle, as always, was sleeping in the nude. Up in a flash, she slipped on the shirt and jeans she had worn the previous day, went to the door, and opened it cautiously.

"He's here," said Khoury, pushing his way past her into the room. "Quick, get him up." He pointed an impatient finger toward Ritter.

"Who's here?" she asked sleepily.

"Metaxas."

The name and its implications jolted her like an electric shock.

"Brian, wake up." She stepped over to the bed and shook him roughly.

"Huh?" he mumbled groggily.

"Get up. Elias' friend is here."

Ritter rubbed his face, yawned, and looked over to see Khoury standing in the doorway.

"We haven't got much time, Brian. Get dressed. Come to my room." Khoury slipped quietly out of the door.

Ritter's mind cleared quickly. He jumped up, hitting the floor with a thud, harder than he intended. He slipped on his shirt, jeans, and shoes and they hurried to Khoury's room. They didn't bother to knock.

Khoury was frantically throwing clothes into a suitcase, speaking in Greek to a man sitting in a chair in the corner opposite the door. As Ritter and Michelle entered the room, Khoury swung his arms toward the corner. "Meet Dimitri Metaxas."

He was a good-looking man in his mid-thirties with a strong, broad face and a steely smile. His thick black hair was like a mane on an expensive race horse. Ritter would learn later that Dimitri Metaxas had been linked for some ten years to the grubby, shadowy world of espionage and terrorism. It was believed that among other assignments he once worked for the Israeli intelligence organization Mossad, posing as an arms dealer in Lebanon to gain information on the needs and capabilities of the PLO.

Metaxas stood up slowly to shake hands with Ritter and Michelle.

"He knows the basic problem," said Khoury. "He's going to help us."

Metaxas spoke English with some difficulty. But he was able to make himself understood. "Voko has two men parked in a car at the end of the driveway. They can see the hotel entrance pretty well, but not the side door. They also have a poor view of the parking lot, particularly in the darkness."

"What about the hotel itself?" asked Ritter.

"There is only the desk clerk. He is still asleep. But we must move quickly," said Metaxas.

"Dimitri will need the cap you've been wearing, Michelle," said Khoury. "He has two men downstairs who came with him. One of them is his brother. They will drive the van out. One of them will wear the cap. They can slip unseen into the van in the dark and take off. The lights of the camper will blind Voko's men as it goes past. They will think it is the three of us, with one of us in the back, out of sight."

"And we'll just wait in the parking lot until Voko's goons take off following the van?" said Ritter.

"That's it."

"But at some point they'll be able to see that it's not us in the van," protested Michelle.

"That's one of the risks," said Khoury. "But Voko's men don't know exactly what we look like. They can be deceived up to a point. Metaxas' brother will try to lose the tail as soon as he can. He will make sure, however, the van is seen along the road on the way south. He'll take it as far south as Larissa and then give them the slip again. Voko will be worried, but hopefully he will think we are at least out of the immediate area and trying to reach Athens. Until he realizes what's happened, that should give us enough time to find the boxes. In the meantime, a cousin of Metaxas' will paint the camper, give it a new license plate and registration, and we'll pick it up in a few days in Trikala and be on our way."

"Nice to have friends," said Ritter. He was impressed.

"Let's get going," said Khoury. "We only have thirty minutes or so before dawn."

Ritter and Michelle returned hastily to their room, gathered their belongings together, and met Khoury and Metaxas in the hall as they quietly moved downstairs. Two men were seated in the lobby. No sign of the desk clerk. One of the men silently pointed toward a couch at the end of the lobby. It was making a restful snoring sound.

Suddenly a car crunched over the gravel in the driveway.

"A woman," whispered the man nearest the door.

It was Melanie. Ritter moved toward her, putting his finger to his lips and pointing toward the couch. Melanie nodded her understanding.

"What are you doing here?" he asked softly.

"I've come to warn you," she said. "Voko is planning to kill you. They have set up some sort of ambush. Those men in the driveway are his."

"We figured that," said Ritter. "But how do you know?"

Melanie self-consciously rubbed her cheek with the tips of her fingers, providing an artificial pause as she attempted to gain control over the words pushing their way out.

"Voko is a vain man. Pompous. I know him well. Too well. He can't avoid talking about his exploits. He bragged about trapping the foreigners." Her voice dropped to a whisper. "Brian, I hate him. And he hates me…. Yes, I am married to him, but there is no marriage. No children. Nothing. It is a trap. So many years …" She clamped her trembling lower lip between her teeth. "You saved my life once. I want to help you now. Maybe I am saving yours." She looked over at Michelle and then back at Ritter. "Go, now. Hurry."

Ritter drew her close, wrapping his strong arms around her, kissing her cheek. She shuddered in his grasp.

"He won't get us, Melanie," Ritter said soothingly. "Certainly not as easily as you got me the rainy night I jumped out of that airplane." He smiled warmly, looking directly into her dark, uncertain eyes. She managed a cautious smile in reply, unable to stem the increased moisture in them.

"Yes," she whispered. "I thought I had caught a German agent. Instead … I caught you. But, only for a little while." She looked again at Michelle. "She is lovely. I wish you much happiness. Go now, there is not much time." She pushed herself away from him. "The sooner you leave, the better."

Michelle handed her cap to one of the men as Ritter passed the camper keys to the other. The two men slipped quietly out the side door. With a last longing glance at Ritter, Melanie turned and followed them.

Within a few seconds they heard the four cylinder camper engine turn over. With a sewing-machine roar it sped out of the parking lot down the drive and onto the highway. Another engine coughed into life, and with a squeal of tires it hurried after. Finally they heard Melanie's car come to life, and crunching across the gravel it headed off.

The four of them walked out into the darkness. Metaxas motioned them toward a black four-door Mercedes. He and Khoury got in front. "The girl should stay down," he instructed. Three men had driven in. It would not do to have four persons driving away.

Ritter and Michelle climbed in the back. Michelle lay down on the seat. They were all quiet, thinking of Melanie—and Voko.

"Your arrival was a very pleasant surprise," Ritter said when they were some miles from Kozani. He was leaning forward to speak to Metaxas. "Frankly, we had written you off."

"We were on our way to Thessalonica," Metaxis said. "But as we drove through town, we saw an old friend. He asked us to have a drink. We did. By the time it ended, it was too late to go on, so we went home. My mother had thought to leave a note. An urgent call from Mr. Khoury. Needs help. I woke her up. She said you had called from the hotel in Kozani and asked that I come as soon as possible. A matter of life and death. I came as soon as I could."

"We're grateful," said Michelle.

"Elias says you're looking for something near the village of Mouzakion, not far from the Mitata Pass. The brother of my cousin's wife lives there. He has a small farm where we have stored certain items in the past when we did not wish the authorities to know about them. The head man of the village is also known to us and is no friend of Voko's. We will hide there a few days while they paint your camper. That should give you enough time to find what you are looking for."

"Artifacts," said Khoury easily. "Mr. Ritter is an antique dealer from New York. Miss Simonet is a scholar. They specialize in Mediterranean and Greek antiquities. They have learned that near the village are hidden some documents and artifacts relating to the Turkish conquest of Greece. They were left there in the late 1940's by a group of archeologists and scholars who had a run-in with the local Communists. They hid the material to avoid it falling into Communists hands. As you can imagine, there is strong competition between museums and private collectors for this sort of material. It is feared Colonel Voko might be in contact with unscrupulous private dealers who would bid up the price, ensuring it will end up in private hands and not in a museum for all to share."

"Why do you want to take it out of the country?"

Political reasons. Our sponsor wants to make a gift to the Greek government that will end any chance of the material falling into a private collection. Of course, it will also help his public standing and political position. You understand."

"Of course," said Metaxas.

The small mountain village of Mouzakion was shown on only the most detailed maps. It had no official charter or status and was so remote that few persons outside the immediate area had heard of it. There was a question of whether it even should be called a village. It was really little more than an insignificant collection of houses and farms inhabited by fewer than eighty people, giving it more sheep than human occupants. Its whitewashed dwellings and barns nestled in the crook of a mountain ridge not far below the Mitata Pass. The peaks of the dark mountains loomed above, alternately sheltering and threatening the village.

It was just after dawn when Metaxas drove into Mouzakion. White wood smoke drifted lazily out of chimneys, indicating the people were already stirring, but no one was out as they moved slowly through and pulled into the farm of Metaxas' relative, Andreas Manglis.

Hearing the car outside, Andreas stepped out into the crisp morning air and invited the party in. Metaxas embraced and kissed him before making the introductions.

Like most Macedonian mountain men, Andreas was lean and hard. His heavy, frowning eyebrows and high-bridged nose provided a fierce shelter for his wary and reserved eyes. But his welcome was, if not effusive, genuinely warm. Immediately his hearty-looking wife, Chloe, came forward to ask who would have coffee. Her hair was lighter than his and still in a state of early-morning unkemptness. She was a pretty woman, in her middle twenty's with a delicate jawbone and nostrils setting off her smooth cheeks, blue-gray eyes, and glowing skin. In her left arm she carried their thirteen-month-old son. These were simple, salt-of-the-earth people and their dwelling reflected as much about their personalities and life-styles as did their rough wool peasant garb.

A cheery fire crackled briskly in the blackened hearth, obviously the center of family life during the long, hard winters and cool early-spring months. The visitors were immediately greeted by an agreeable and pungent aroma of wood smoke, milk, tobacco, and goat hair. It was the same scent Ritter had known years ago, during his week with Melanie. A semi-circular arch appeared to support the large old wooden beams above them and the roughly plastered ceiling. The furniture consisted of several stools, a wooden table, and a loom with which the woman spun cloth. On the wall opposite the fireplace hung three small icons and several faded brown-and-white photographs of fierce-looking turbaned ancestors swathed in bandoliers and holding menacing-looking rifles. One of the men also had a large pistol in his belt. Two nineteenth-century-vintage rifles hung on the wall near the pictures.

"They are hiding from Voko," said Metaxas.

Andreas spat into the fire. "I spit on Voko," he said in Greek. Khoury translated the encouraging remark for Ritter and Michelle. As they took places around the warming fire on the black-and-red wool carpets, Andreas threw a new log onto it and his wife brought cups of thick, hot coffee.

Andreas spat again, somewhat theatrically. "Voko is a Kravarite." Obviously not a compliment.

"I'll explain," said Khoury after translating. "Kravara is a region of Greece notorious for having produced generations of gypsylike beggars, theives, wanderers, rascals, and other no-goods. It has always been a poor region with little rain and few crops. The people had to find ways to feed themselves. The area got its evil reputation because some of the more desperate and unscrupulous beggars deliberately twisted the arms or legs of young children, permanently deforming them so they could increase their earnings as they wandered through Greece. Over the years 'Kravarite' has become a derogatory term for liar or charlatan. Which applies to Voko? You can take your choice."

The woman brought plates of cheese and bread. "Manuri," she said.

"Goat cheese," translated Khoury. "A local specialty."

Ritter and Michelle began eating in silence while the conversation swirled around them in Greek. He'd wanted a change, thought Ritter. Who could have imagined he'd end up sitting on the floor before the hearth of a Greek shepherd eating goat cheese at seven in the morning, trying to keep out of the clutches of a less-than-reputable police colonel? Unreal.

Khoury turned to them. "We've explained the antiquities problem," he said, "and how it relates to Voko. Andreas was properly incensed. He is anxious to help. He is sure the headman will be also. It has been agreed that we will work at night and that only the people in this house and the headman will know what is going on. If the other villagers hear anything about our presence, as is possible, they will be told we are digging for artifacts in exchange for a payment to the village. It is common practice here. The woman will make a place for us in the back room. I'm afraid we'll have to spend much of the daylight hours there. We will begin work tonight as soon as it's dark. Once we've found what we've come for, Metaxas will take us to the camper."

"What about the digging tools?" said Ritter. "They're all in the camper."

"Andreas is going to lend us each a *skeparnia*. It's an all purpose Greek tool with a curved blade they use for hacking or cutting. The Greeks have been using them since biblical times, so I'm sure they'll be all right. In English, you would call one an ade."

"I'll be going now," said Metaxas. "I'll return tonight to help where I can."

"See you then," said Ritter. Michelle nodded, and Khoury walked with him to the door.

"Chloe has laid out some makeshift beds," Khoury said as he walked back. "We might as well get some rest. It's not a good idea to hang around in this room too late in the morning. A nosy neighbor could drop in and want to know who the strangers are and what they are up to."

"Ah, the Mouzakion Hilton," Ritter said as they entered the dusty storeroom that had been made up for them. Andreas' wife had placed blankets on the floor over sheep and goatskins. Not a luxurious accommodation, but warm, dry, and, for the moment, secure. "Reminds me of some of the places I stayed in years ago in South America."

"Reminds me of places I've tried to avoid staying in," sniffed Khoury. "But under the circumstances, I won't bother with a complaint to the management."

"Not at these rates," said Michelle. "We'll have to send a recommendation to one of the guidebooks. By the way, how did you think up the story about the artifacts?"

"It would have been unwise to tell even Metaxas the truth. It could slip out or cause troubles we don't need. Surely we've had enough problems."

"More than enough," said Ritter.

21

Ritter, Khoury, and Michelle found the skins and blankets Andreas' wife had provided comfortable enough. As usual, Ritter had no trouble sleeping. The other two dozed. They were awakened early in the afternoon by Chloe who brought them a snack of warm mutton and the inevitable goat cheese and bread. The bread was hard, but surprisingly tasty.

"It's paximadia," said Khoury. "It's been baked twice. The second baking makes it hard and thus acts as a kind of preservative. The shepherds take it with them when they are in the mountains with their flocks and aren't able to come in for a week or more for fresh bread."

The meal was interrupted by the arrival of Leonides Pangolis, the self-inflated village headman. His sharp, sculptured features were typical of the mountain men. So was his obviously wary attitude toward them.

"He welcomes us," said Khoury, translating as they shook hands all around. "He says he hopes we will have a comfortable stay and successful hunt. He would not want the items we are seeking to fall into the hands of Colonel Voko, who, he confides, is corrupt beyond reason. He explains the police are, of course, expected to get a little something extra for the dangerous and often disagreeable tasks they perform for society. But he says Voko has been unreasonably greedy."

"That's our boy," quipped Michelle.

"He doesn't say so," continued Khoury, "but there is the implication he has had some personal run-in with the colonel that was not to his liking. But I also sense he is afraid of Voko. They all are."

"Tell him we appreciate his hospitality, for which the Greek people are world-famous," said Ritter, summoning all his diplomatic experience. "We find his village very beautiful. We thank him deeply for his help and his hospitality."

The headman allowed a pleased smile as the words were translated.

"Mr. Pangolis thanks you for your kind words," said Khoury, continuing his role as translator. "Any assistance he can provide will be an honor."

With a further exchange of superlatives and pledges of cooperation and friendship, the conversation ended and Pangolis withdrew, leaving them in the storeroom.

"Very nervous," said Khoury. "They'll all be glad when we're gone."

"I have the feeling they don't fully believe our story," said Ritter. "But they don't really care. Mainly they don't want any trouble. We could mean problems for them."

"It means we don't have a lot of time," agreed Khoury. "Their hospitality is genuine enough for the moment. But we can't stretch it. We've got to find those boxes soon."

"I'm all for it," said Ritter.

For the rest of the afternoon they napped fitfully and talked. Khoury borrowed a backgammon board from their host and began to teach Ritter and Michelle the game.

Metaxas arrived just as it was getting dark. "My brother managed to lose the tail," he said. "The word is that Voko has begun a hunt for the camper around Larissa. We will arrange for a sighting to reach him later from Lamia, farther south. This will divert his attention even more from this place and give us breathing room. If he thinks you are headed for Athens, it might shake him up a bit and keep him off balance long enough for you to complete your work here undisturbed."

"Guess we ought to start moving," said Ritter. They pulled on their sweaters and jackets, and after accepting a packed lunch from Chloe, set out for the site.

It had been agreed they would walk to avoid arousing the attention of any villagers who might notice unusual vehicle sounds and start asking questions.

The site was almost an hour's hike from the village, but the effort on the dark mountain road warmed them against the chill that had set in. A three-quarter moon on a clear night helped light the way. Ritter, Khoury, and Metaxas carried adz-like *skeparnias* over their shoulders. Michelle carried a small shovel borrowed from the Manglis family. Andreas had volunteered to come along, but it was agreed it would be better if he remained at home to maintain a show of normal family life.

They walked up the road until they came to the dry streambed turnoff and followed it to the caves. It was uncanny how similar these caves were to the ones where they had taken Voko. Using flashlights, Ritter and Khoury examined again the Waddell sketch, checking it against the caves.

"There," said Ritter. "Notice where he placed the X on the fifth layer. There is a line of rock running along here. It seems to correspond." He pointed the light.

Khoury looked at the sketch and the spot with his own light. "As good a place to start as any," he agreed.

Bells jangled in the background. "Goats," said Metaxas. "After you spend enough time up here, you don't hear them anymore."

Ritter and Khoury began attacking the hillside with their *skeparnias*. A good tool, thought Ritter, well balanced, strong without being too heavy. Equally good as a pick or small shovel. For over an hour he and Khoury chopped away at the rocks, gradually forcing their way into the hillside.

Both men rapidly revived previously painful blisters. Their strong hopes and expectations, however, drove them on. It was not until they took their first break, that they realized they were in pain. Michelle produced some tape she had held over from the previous dig and patched their hands. Khoury had used up more of his limited strength than he realized, and Metaxas took over for him, swinging hard against the rock.

The steady chipping echoed in the hills. At first the loud sounds startled them, making them fearful someone would hear. But Metaxas assured them there was no one about. The people of the village were several miles away and asleep. There would be no one else out here this time of night.

Shortly after midnight they took a break for a snack of goat cheese and the hard bread.

"Never tasted better," said Ritter bravely.

When they returned to the dig, they realized their pace had slowed considerably. The initial excitement of the project had worn off and the drudgery of the moment began to weigh on them.

Shortly after three a.m. Ritter felt his *skeparnia* slice through the rock to an opening. "Got it," he said.

"What?" Michelle and Khoury both spoke the same anxious question.

"I'm through to something, an opening."

They all joined in frantically pulling away rocks and earth. It was a cave, a small one hidden behind the rock face, obviously closed by a rockslide years before.

"We're through," shouted Ritter. "Give me a light." He poked his head into the opening they had made and shone his light around. It was a small cave. He could see the back wall less than twenty feet inside. He shone the light around several times. There was nothing.

"Empty," he said, unable to hide the disappointment in his voice.

"Let me have a look," said Khoury.

Ritter sat down. It would be dawn shortly. "I think that's enough for tonight," he said.

After everyone had a chance to see that the cave was indeed empty, they began the long walk back to Mouzakion. At least it was downhill.

There was little conversation.

Ritter was beginning to doubt again whether the gold was really there. What if it had been dug up by the Germans or some local Greeks long ago? There would be no record of it. It would be long gone. Maybe they were just endangering themselves and others for nothing.

* * *

Normally, Leonides Pangolis was not a nervous man. After all, he was a man of nature, a shepherd and farmer who had spent his life quietly in the mountains, free from the destructive pressures of modern civilization. His income from herding and his small *magazi* was not great. But neither were his needs. True, there had been trouble during the time of the Communists, but that was over now. These days his greatest worries were the weather and the grape crop. But this business with the strangers was different.

He arrived at the house late in the afternoon, just after Ritter, Khoury, and Michelle had awakened. Doffing his woolen cap as he entered the room, he flickered his eyes from side to side, surveying the room. Nervously he fingered a set of worry beads. Chloe brought coffee for him.

Khoury and Ritter rose to shake hands. They resumed their places on the warm animal skins on the floor. Pangolis sat down with them.

"How is your work?" he asked. Khoury translated.

Ritter turned over his hands to show a full set of raw, ugly blisters. Khoury and Michelle joined the pantomime. Smiles. Big joke.

Pangolis spoke, His words tumbled out hastily, often crowded together. One didn't need to understand Greek to detect his feelings of uncertainty. Khoury continued to translate. "He says it is obvious we have been working hard. He asks if we are finished."

Ritter shrugged and shook his head negatively. "Maybe tonight," he said.

The headman rubbed his hands together as he answered through Khoury. "He emphasizes he appreciates the work we are doing. He hopes we can quickly end our labors before Voko or other authorities hear about what is going on. Normally, he says, an artifact dig never lasts more than a night or so. But he is happy to extend the hospitality of the village for another night."

"We are deeply appreciative," said Ritter.

There were more flattering and gracious words from both sides before the headman withdrew.

"The mayor thinks we are intruding," said Ritter.

"Voko frightens him to death," said Khoury. "He will be glad when we're gone."

"He's not the only one," said Ritter, holding up his blistered hands again. "We'll have to tape up before we go out tonight."

A gradually growing torrential drumming on the roof indicated their sore hands and backs would not be their only torment.

"*Merde*," said Michelle, standing up to look out the window and confirm their worst suspicions.

Metaxas arrived shortly after dark. He had heard about Voko's search for the camper.

"Things have cooled," he said. "Voko has requested the authorities in the south to look out for you, but I suspect he is just glad to have you out of his hair. To be on the safe side, we are arranging for a 'sighting' tomorrow morning in Athens."

Khoury nodded. "It is late. We must go."

The walk was long, the rain steady and cold. After nearly an hour's march, they reached the dig site, already tired and thoroughly miserable. Khoury kept thinking of the warm, enticing beaches, the comfortable casinos, the pleasant cafés of the Riviera. Why did he ever allow himself to get involved in this? Michelle was also thinking about France, the sunny fields of Normandy. It would be warm in Vierville now. The food would be good and the wine wonderfully drinkable, better than this resin-flavored bile they were being subjected to. Ritter's mind was on water too; he didn't mind the stuff as long as he was completely submerged in it with a pair of aqualungs strapped on his back. But this was ridiculous. He needed to have his head examined for letting Thompson talk him out of the warm Bahamas.

Ritter and Khoury looked up at the rock face. The place they had chosen the previous night was exhausted. Two other spots possibly fit Waddell's sketch. After a brief discussion, they agreed to work both at once. Ritter and Michelle would take one, Khoury and Metaxas the other. Without further discussion, they began hacking.

Hampered by the rain, mud, blisters, sore backs, and the chilling loneliness of the moment as well as the nagging sensation that maybe there was nothing behind the rocks after all, they found the work progressing far more slowly than the previous night. Their enthusiasm had badly fallen off. Cold and rain had a way of drying up the adrenaline, thought Ritter. He had been through similar letdowns in other hunts. The only solution was to keep working.

Around one A.M. they huddled in a nearby cave for a quick and unsatisfying snack of soggy bread, olives, the inevitable goat cheese, and retsina wine. The break did not last long. Ritter was afraid muscles would grow cold and even stiffer than they were, making it difficult to continue.

"Don't work too fast," he cautioned. "Just keep at it steadily. Don't slow down to the point where you get cold."

As dawn approached, they were all near exhaustion. They began the long trek back to the village feeling very near defeat.

"Maybe it's not there after all," said Khoury, voicing what they all felt. "I am about ready to give in. I'm not sure I can take another night of this. I'm just not up to it."

Ritter shrugged. It would be a mistake to answer. To argue. They were all dead tired. Their morale was shot. The exhaustion-surrender phenomenon was all too familiar. It never helped to fight it when people were this tired. They all needed to get into dry clothes and have something warm to drink. To sleep. Tomorrow would be time enough to decide.

Khoury woke first. He had never known his body to be so sore. He looked at his hands, each finger and the palms taped because of the blisters. His body told him enough. It was time to call it off. But they couldn't quit yet. They might be only a shovelful away from nearly two million dollars. One didn't give up so easily on something like that. On the other hand, maybe the whole thing was someone's cruel joke. Or maybe the gold had been dug up by somebody else years ago.

Ritter opened his eyes. "Morning," he said, looking over at Khoury.

Khoury nodded, a neutral gesture.

"Two million dollars for your thoughts," said Ritter.

"If it's there. Or if we can find it." Khoury grunted.

Awakened by their voices, Metaxas staggered in, still rubbing the sleep from his eyes. Michelle was stirring.

A commotion in the front room. Andreas appeared to inform them Pangolis had arrived. The headman, fingering his worry beads as nervously as ever, walked in without waiting to be invited. He attempted a shallow smile. It did not hide his thoughts. "So your work is finished?" he said expectantly.

"Not exactly," answered Ritter, again speaking through Khoury, who acted as interpreter.

"Your work has lasted long enough. There will be questions. Already there are whispers in the village. Voko might hear. It is very dangerous for us."

"We need one more night," emphasized Ritter.

"I cannot permit it," answered Pangolis, his voice rising to the edge of hysteria. His face hardened. The polite formalities of the conversation had all but disappeared. "You must leave now. I order it."

"Sounds like he means it," whispered Ritter. "How about a donation?"

Metaxas interrupted in Greek. He understood immediately Ritter's suggestion. "I also have friends, Mr. Pangolis, who want to see this project carried out successfully. You must give them another night. As a token of good faith they would like to give you a present."

Pangolis sulked. The worry beads snaked through his fingers.

Metaxas spoke quietly to Khoury and Ritter in English. "I have mentioned my own friends. An indirect threat he understands. But he still could be dangerous. Even a cornered mouse will bite. So as I believe you were suggesting, I also have offered him a gift. A face-saving device. Can you afford three-thousand drachmas?"

"Done," said Ritter. Khoury nodded his approval.

"For your understanding and patience," said Metaxas in Greek, "they would like to make a gift to the village of three-thousand drachmas. Naturally, the gift would be presented to you as the headman."

Pangolis scowled. He did not want to show it, but the mention of so much money stimulated his hereditary instincts. "One last night. That is all. I already have risked too much for these foreigners. Besides, they are rich. Tell them to make it eight-thousand."

"He wants eight-thousand."

"Make it four-thousand," said Khoury.

Metaxas turned back to Pangolis. "They appreciate your understanding and sacrifice and would like to present the village with four-thousand drachmas. They would like to present more, but it is all they can afford."

"We are risking much."

"It is a generous offer."

"Only one night," said Pangolis. "That is my last word. After that, I will have to call the authorities myself. We are obliged to report suspicious activities of foreigners."

"One night," agreed Metaxas. He turned back to Ritter and Khoury. "Your last night of digging will cost you four-thousand."

"I never thought I would live long enough to have to beg an illiterate shepherd to accept four-thousand drachmas to agree to let me torture my body digging in a mountainside that doesn't belong to him for something I'm not sure is there. Okay, if that's the best we can do."

"We may be paying him for nothing," said Khoury. "If we haven't found anything by now…"

"At least it's not raining as hard as it was yesterday," said Michelle searching for something encouraging to say. She was looking out of the window at the gray skies. A light drizzle was falling.

"Our kind of weather," said Ritter. "We should be getting used to it."

Khoury snorted. His enthusiasm had vanished.

* * *

They paired off as they had the night before, attacking the two possible spots in the rock formation. Although they were all sore and stiff, they seemed less so than the night before. Only the blisters were worse. Their hands looked like the hands of professional football linemen toward the end of the season, with barely their fingertips showing from under the layers of tape. But the tape did not ease the hurt, the pain that came with each swing of the *skeparnia*. It was agony. Several times Ritter felt like saying "Fuck it. Let's go." If any one of them pulled out, the others certainly would follow.

Ritter looked around. Michelle could barely raise her shovel over her head. The feeble chops she was making against the rock and mud were having only a marginal effect. Khoury and Metaxas were working about fifty yards down from them. Metaxas was carrying the load. Khoury looked thoroughly beat. His unenthusiastic swings were almost as weak as Michelle's. Yet he continued in zombielike fashion, going through the motions, driven by previously unknown reserves.

Sometime after midnight, Ritter called a halt and they sought shelter in the cave where they had eaten the previous night. Again, the wine warmed them, but the food was tasteless. Their taste buds had stopped functioning.

"This is our last effort," said Ritter. "We know it's here. This is the last chance. Everything we've got, one more time."

No one answered. Even Ritter didn't really believe it. They looked out at the cold drizzle, shivered, and moved stiffly back to work.

Thunk. Thunk. Thunk. The tedious unencouraging digging continued. This is the last, Ritter kept saying to himself. Why did I ever let that idiot …? *Clink*. At first he didn't believe he'd heard it. It wasn't his *skeparnia*. It was Michelle's shovel. He looked at her. She raised her face. She was looking quizzically at him and then at the shovel. A look of confused expectation. The *clink*. The sound that every treasure hunter, amateur or professional, young or old, rich or poor, dreams of, lives for. The *clink* of metal against metal. Ritter didn't move. He nodded encouragingly at Michelle. Try again. Khoury and Metaxas still had noticed nothing. They were struggling with their own problems in the wet predawn darkness.

Michelle raised her shovel and hit again. *Clink*. It was louder. No doubt. She had hit metal.

Khoury was looking over. He had heard it too. As though a starter's pistol had been fired, they suddenly all clustered around the spot, their tools frantically digging and scraping. An olive-colored metal box began to take shape. Ritter fell to his knees, scraping mud and rocks away with his taped hands. Metaxas flashed a light. It was a box, a large gray metal chest. The white, mud-smeared, stencil-painted letters said "Property of H.M. Forces."

Ritter and a newly revived Khoury leaned down to grab a rough rope handle. They pulled. The chest didn't budge. It was heavy. Loaded with something heavy—and valuable.

"Looks like a box of artifacts to me," said Ritter, grinning as he stood up to grab Michelle in his arms. She hugged him tightly. There were handshakes and kisses all around. Even Khoury was smiling.

"There ought to be four more. Let's get moving. It's late," Ritter said soberly. "Too early to celebrate. We're going to need a truck to get this out of here."

Without hesitation, Metaxas began moving down the hill in the direction of the village.

They dug steadily for another forty-five minutes, clearing the other four chests out of the earth. All five were heavy, heavier than they had imagined. It was wonderful. The value of the contents was measured by weight.

"Let's try to drag them down to the streambed before Metaxas gets here," said Ritter. "Once the vehicle arrives, we don't want to waste any time."

The three of them, using the remainder of their strength, the remainder of their adrenaline, struggled to drag the chests down the hill. Ritter wondered how in hell Waddell and the major had ever managed to haul the chests up to the caves.

As they dragged the fourth chest down the hill, they could hear the sound of Metaxas' small van moving slowly up the streambed. In another hour they would be on their way south with the treasure safely in hand.

Nearly two million dollars in gold. All theirs. It was an exhilarating moment. The exhaustion that had gripped them only an hour ago had miraculously vanished. It was a wonderful high. Better than any drug could ever produce. They could see the van moving up the streambed now.

Behind the steering wheel, Metaxas was smiling broadly. He still didn't know what the chest contained, but he instinctively knew it wasn't artifacts. He was figuring a generous reward. They couldn't have done it without him.

He pulled up beside the first chest.

"One more to bring down, and we'll load them on," said Ritter. Metaxas walked back up the hill with him. For the last time, thought Ritter. It's one hillside I won't miss. Grunting and straining they struggled to haul the last chest down to the van and began the loading job.

Clunk. The first box hit the back of the van. It was really heavy. Over 150 pounds. As Ritter, Metaxas, and Khoury stooped to get the second one, they heard a metallic but frighteningly familiar voice float over them. Ritter's stomach leaped into his throat. Khoury began fighting off an attack of nausea.

"You have done very well, my friends," said Colonel Georges Voko. He was speaking through a portable loudspeaker just above them. They looked around. Dawn was breaking. In the dim light they could see Voko and another man, slightly hunched over, walking down the hill from a convenient watching point. The other man was holding what appeared to be an automatic rifle. Even at a distance it looked deadly. A third person walked along with them. It was Melanie.

"You've shown remarkable initiative," the colonel was saying as he moved closer. "Now we shall see what this is all about."

22

Even years later, Ritter could not speak of that awful moment.

The arrogant Voko, smiling sleekly, making his way steadily down the hillside. Beside him, the walrus-mustached lieutenant brandishing a meanacing-looking Swiss-made SG510, the best selective-fire automatic rifle made in Europe, capable of a cyclic rate of fire of over five-hundred rounds per minute. A single short burst would slice them to ribbons.

Stumbling ahead of the two men was Melanie. Her face was swollen and badly bruised, as though she had been beaten. One arm hung stiffly at her side.

"I am indeed grateful," said Voko as he reached them. He could not control the soupy sarcasm in his voice. "You have saved me a great deal of work and time. How shall I ever be able to reward you? Perhaps you'd like to spend a last few minutes with this traitorous bitch." He roughly shoved Melanie toward Ritter.

"A woman who betrays her husband deserves no mercy," Voko said. "Oh, she's a clever one, but you already know that, eh, Mr.

Ritter? Fights, too, when she's provoked. I had to … well, persuade her to tell me the truth.

"My men spotted her at the hotel when the camper left. I figured the rumors about her wartime associations were true after all. Then, with the help of the reluctant but sensible Pangolis, I was able to put it all together."

Voko looked up at the hillside where they had brought out the gold. "You've even dug out a convenient spot for us to leave your bodies. Very accommodating."

Melanie touched the bruises on her face, and spat at her husband. He swung violently, striking her hard in the face. Ritter moved instinctively toward her but was checked by the threatening movement of the lieutenant's automatic rifle.

"Don't do anything stupid, Mr. Ritter." Voko laughed. "You've been stupid enough. My dear wife tried to stop us, but …" He shrugged. "Now, let's get the rest of the boxes loaded onto the van you were so thoughtful to provide."

The lieutenant made another threatening gesture with the rifle. Ritter and Khoury leaned down and with Metaxas' help put another chest into the van. After they had placed the third and fourth box in, Voko's curiosity spilled over.

"Before the last one," he said, "let's see what this gold looks like." The chest was sealed, and would have to be forced open. The lieutenant stepped back to cover them as Metaxas picked up the *skeparnia* and hacked open the lock. He raised the lid. The chest was filled with neatly stacked gold bars, untarnished by thirty-four years in the ground. The colonel looked down greedily. Beautiful! He was rich. The lieutenant stepped forward wide-eyed to see for himself. More money than anything he had ever dreamed possible.

A sudden blur of motion, a deadly swishing sound. The lieutenant's attention had wandered just enough for Khoury to grab the *skeparnia* leaning against the van and fling it desperately at him. The blade sliced into the side of the man's skull. A bewildered look flashed onto his face. It lasted the rest of his life.

Voko reacted sharply, pulling the 9-mm Swedish m/40 automatic from his holster, but he already understood he had been stupidly careless. From the side, he could sense Melanie lunging at him. He swung the pistol and fired directly into her chest. The instinctive action cost him a precious and all important moment as Melanie staggered and fell against him. Ritter was already on the ground with the SG510, rolling onto his back and firing at virtually point-blank range a two-second-long burst of seventeen murderous rounds, blowing out the colonel's gaseous midsection. He couldn't even manage a last gulp. His remains sank into the mud beside Melanie.

The silence that followed was disturbed only by their heavy, relieved breathing and the jangle of goats' bells in the distance. Ritter sprang to Melanie. Her eyes flickered in recognition and went blank.

Michelle moved beside Ritter, putting her arm around him. Khoury stared fascinated at his handiwork. He had never felt more alive.

Ritter tried to wipe away some of the cold, clinging earth. His hands were shaking badly. This kind of violence wasn't part of him.

"Didn't know you could handle one of those," said Khoury, a touch of admiration in his voice.

"Neither did I." Ritter struggled to keep his voice steady. He felt as if he might shake apart. "It's been a while since I fired anything more serious than a spear gun. I was just hoping it wasn't on safety."

Michelle held him close, trying to steady him. She was having trouble getting her own breath. It had been much too close. "I'm sorry about Melanie," she said.

Ritter nodded, not daring to speak.

"We've got to get these bodies hidden," said Metaxas. "If they find them here, there will be trouble for the village."

"Back up," said Ritter. "This place was good enough to conceal the gold for thirty-four years. Should be good enough for at least another thirty four."

"There is another factor in our favor," added Khoury shrewdly. "The fact that Voko only had the lieutenant and his wife with him indicates strongly he was acting unofficially. Perhaps he planned a two-way split of some kind with the lieutenant. If so, then officially no one knew he was here. Which means he may not be missed for a while. Or if he is, there should be no reason to suspect foul play. Certainly nothing that could point the finger at us."

"What about Zakros? He might have known," said Michelle.

"It's possible," said Ritter. "We've got to hurry."

Ritter reached down, took Melanie's body in his arms, and carried it up the hill to the cave. They let him go up alone. He placed the body down gently and covered it with his jacket. Reaching into his shirt, he pulled the silver cross from around his neck and placed it into her hand, closing her fingers over it.

He walked down the hill, quietly thinking of the fresh young girl he had loved years ago. She had deserved better. Wordlessly he helped drag the other two corpses up the hill and dumped them into the cave away from Melanie's body. "Better you than us," said Ritter as they tossed what was left of Voko into the excavation.

It only occurred to him later the colonel's pistol was missing.

They spent another fifteen minutes piling rocks and mud over the corpses, then returned to the van. Exhaustion slowly began to overtake them.

"We won't have to stop in the village," said Metaxas, slinging the automatic rifle into the truck next to himself. "I've brought your clothes with me. I don't think we want to see Pangolis after what has happened. You can change out of these wet muddy clothes and we'll head straight for Trikala, where your camper will be waiting."

For the next four hours they drove in weary, self-conscious silence. Michelle fell asleep in the back on Ritter's shoulder. Ritter dozed fitfully. He was having trouble clearing his mind of Melanie and Voko. There was no choice, he kept telling himself. It was obviously either Voko or himself. He kept seeing Voko fire the pistol into Melanie and her fall against him. Voko was the first person he'd ever knowingly killed. Perhaps during all the shooting in Greece he might have nicked a few Greeks or Germans. And maybe later in Italy he might have shot a few Germans. But that was different. This had been very close and very personal. The growing look of horror on Voko's face as he realized he wouldn't be able to stop Ritter from blasting him away had lasted less than a second. But Ritter's memory cells already had frozen it into a mask he would always carry with him. A souvenir he could do without. He knew he should feel exhilarated about the gold. But even with the change of clothes, he was uncomfortable and tired. Voko haunted him. Melanie's death wounded him. It would take time, time to free himself. But he couldn't get distracted now. They were anything but home safe.

Khoury's arms, back and legs ached. His hands, like everybody else's, were sore and blistered. But he had to admit he had rarely felt better. He had loved the look of astonishment on the lieutenant's face as the *skeparnia* crashed into the side of his head. These stupid Greeks. Who did that cretin policeman and the slimy Voko think they were dealing with? Elias Khoury hadn't survived all these years to be finished off by a couple of country cops. Ritter had been a pleasant surprise. The American was in excellent shape. And fast, damned fast for a man of nearly fifty. But he had noticed Ritter's hands shaking afterward. Wasn't used to the real rough stuff. Well, what did he think this was, a Sunday outing? For the kind of treasure they had in the back, they had to be ready for anything. And anybody. And then there was Metaxas. Now he knew they weren't after artifacts. He had seen the gold. And he had the rifle. They would have to be careful. But Metaxas, despite his experience and reputation, was weak. Khoury knew that from Paris. No, Metaxas wouldn't be any trouble.

Artifacts, my ass, thought Metaxas. There was gold in those chests. An emperor's fortune. With a proper share, he could buy himself a yacht and spend the rest of his life leisurely taking rich tourists around the islands—rich tourists who would bring beautiful women and pay fat fees. It was all there in the back of the van. The rifle rested reassuringly against his leg. It still had some bullets in it, enough bullets to make him rich, very rich. Metaxas didn't care about the Americans. The man was all right. He had eliminated Voko. And the girl was very nice. She had a lovely ass and a nice balcony. He would like to get his hands on those. But there would be no time. This was the greatest chance of his life. Yes. Such a chance came only once to a man. Only Khoury was a nagging problem. Two times Khoury had saved his life. It was a matter of honor. He couldn't rob such a man.

Metaxas continued to think about it as the van passed through small villages on the way to Larissa. It was a lovely spring day. Young green leaves were emerging on the trees as they wound their way out of the mountains. Spring flowers in gay yellows, purples, and whites were poking their way out of the rocky earth. Khoury didn't seem all that close to the Americans, Metaxas thought. Perhaps Khoury would consider a split. Yes, that would be fair. An even split with the man who saved his life. Metaxas looked in the rearview mirror. Ritter and the girl were sleeping. They were tired. Unsuspecting. When they got to Trikala, he would speak with Khoury. They would have to move fast. No one would miss the Americans. He and Khoury could make an easy split of the gold. There was more than enough for two. He looked in the mirror again. The Americans were definitely asleep. Neither spoke Greek. Still, it would be better to wait.

They pulled into Trikala shortly after noon. The first lambs of the season had been born the night before, and the village was buzzing with the excitement. To celebrate, the local farmers had flocked into the cafés to mark the event with ouzo and coffee, as they marked almost every day of their lives. The camper had been left at the home of a Metaxas cousin who lived in a characteristic stone house on the eastern edge of town. Behind the house was a large garage where the cousin ran a part-time auto-repair shop. There were two fulltime garages in town, and Metaxas' cousin, who farmed as a regular occupation, used the garage to earn extra money.

The cousin was not around when they arrived, so they drove directly inside. The smell of fresh lacquer filled the reconverted barn. Their camper, formerly green, was now an undistinguished tan. The license plate had also changed. A fairly professional job, Ritter thought.

"You may wish to inspect your vehicle," Metaxas said, motioning Ritter toward the camper. One side had not been done well—patches of green were still showing conspicuously through. There had been no time to sand off the green or put on a primer.

The paint-spray equipment was still beside the camper. "Do you mind?" said Ritter. He walked over, turned on the compressor, and picked up the spray gun. A little touch-up won't hurt.

"Nice job," said Khoury to Metaxas in Greek. They stood together, watching Ritter spray the badly finished side and speaking over the noise of the compressor. "What do we owe you?"

"Those are not artifacts in those chests," Metaxas said carefully.

"What do you mean?" said Khoury. He was not surprised by the remark. The fencing had begun.

"I opened the chest. I saw what was in it. Without me, you would not have it."

"That is true," admitted Khoury, stalling. In a negotiation like this, he didn't want to make the mistake of being the first to offer terms.

"After what happened, it seems a shame that it must be shared with the Americans."

Ahhh, thought Khoury. He's going for a biggie. "They are my partners. Ritter saved our lives this morning."

"Also true," admitted Metaxas. "But these chests are very valuable. With the Americans around, you are headed for a three-way split after you settle with me. A straight two-way split would be much more profitable for you."

"That too is true," agreed Khoury. "But it is not so easy to break up a partnership sealed in blood. And it could be difficult to dispose of… the evidence."

"It could be arranged easily enough. No one in Greece knows they are here but us. No one knows about the boxes except those of us in this workshop."

"What do you propose?"

"We will take them for a ride into the mountains in their camper. Along the way they shall disappear."

"I don't think Ritter would be very agreeable."

"I have Voko's rifle. The Americans can't do much against that."

"What if I don't agree? What if I offer you only part of one of the chests?"

Metaxas was opening the door of his van, reaching for the rifle. "I might have to consider no cut at all. All for one. But you have saved my life. Two times. I would prefer to divide with you fairly."

"You've got a point," said Khoury as he watched Metaxas pull the SG510 out of the van. "After all, I suppose, business is business. One doesn't want to get too emotional about these things."

Ritter turned from his work to see Metaxas pull the rifle out of the van and point it at him. "What's this?"

"There's been a change," said Metaxas. His hands were trembling slightly. He kept thinking about the yacht.

"There's been no change," said Ritter firmly. "We're going out of here with our boxes."

"You are no longer in a position to make such a statement," said Metaxas.

"I'm afraid he's right," said Khoury. "We have a new, how do you Americans say, ballgame."

Ritter put down the spray gun and stepped forward. "Now, just a minute."

Metaxas made a menacing gesture with the rifle. "Don't do anything rash, Mr. Ritter. You already have shown us what this thing can do. You and the girl will begin transferring the chests from my van to your camper. Then we are going for a ride."

Metaxas stepped aside and motioned Ritter and Michelle to begin moving the boxes. He didn't notice Khoury picking up the spray gun from the floor. The compressor sputtered in the background. Metaxas was still watching Ritter and Michelle when Khoury moved carefully beside him, holding the spray gun by his side.

"As soon as they are finished with this, we will be on our way, eh, partner?"

Metaxas never heard a reply. His last sensation was a burning pain in his eyes and a panicky choking feeling of heavy fluid flooding his nose and mouth. He dropped the gun and frantically tried to shield his face. Khoury moved forward aggressively, knocking one hand back, continuing at close range to spray the heavy tan lacquer into Metaxas' nose and gasping mouth. His knees buckled. Khoury followed him down, keeping the deadly spray going. Metaxas was unable to get his breath, the paint already in his lungs. The supply of oxygen to his bloodstream was cut off. It was over. There would never be a yacht for Dimitri Metaxas.

With a sickening helpless gurgle his life ended.

"You know," said Ritter, "for a minute there, you had us worried."

"I never argue with an automatic rifle," said Khoury.

23

Michelle moved unsteadily to a corner of the garage and quietly vomited. There was little in her stomach, but she was no longer in control of her rebelling system. She had felt weak since the awful incident in the mountains, but the sight of Metaxas choking to death, drowning in paint, had been too much. She heaved again.

Ritter walked over, wrapped his arm around her trembling shoulders, and wiped her face with a handkerchief.

"Come on, kid. Get a grip on yourself. It's not over yet."

"I'm sorry, Brian. I'm just… well, I'm not used to…"

"Who is?" He didn't mention it, but he also had a queasy feeling deep in his stomach and his knees were a little weak.

Khoury, breathing heavily, stared somewhat proudly at his latest kill. It was admittedly messy. But he was pleasantly surprised at how he was able to take such a detached view of the whole affair. After all, Metaxas could have wrecked everything. That was the basic point the fool hadn't understood. The gold was of limited value in Greece. Its full value could be realized only in Switzerland, where it could be converted anonymously and easily into unrestricted hard currency, without bother, without notice. That would be impossible in Greece. So much gold would attract too much attention. Everybody would want a cut—or worse, everything. The gold would end up a liability, a huge gold elephant. Metaxas just hadn't understood that. It was too bad. Khoury had actually liked him.

Ritter was still holding Michelle. He walked over to the van and pulled out a jacket to place over her shoulders. She sat down in the camper to catch her breath, to try to recover her strength.

"We've got to get moving," said Khoury. "We can't stay here any longer."

Ritter nodded. "Let's transfer the chests."

Khoury walked to the van, and he and Ritter began lugging the heavy boxes to the camper. "We'll have to take the body and dump it along the way," said Khoury. If we leave it here, it will be quickly found. Metaxas' cousin probably painted the camper himself and certainly knows the new license number. We've got to leave here without a trace of trouble."

"I hope this is the next-to-last time we have to move these damned things," said Ritter as he and Khoury strained to shift the boxes from one vehicle to the other.

They found an oily ground cloth at one end of the garage, wrapped Metaxas' body in it, and placed it in the camper with the chests. They transferred the luggage and were ready.

"What about all the paint?" asked Michelle. They looked down. The outline of the upper part of Metaxas' body had been painted grotesquely on the floor. Ritter picked up the spray gun and pulled the trigger. Empty. A can of motor oil was sitting against the wall. He poured the oil over the paint, smearing the form beyond recognition.

"Let's go," said Khoury. "I'll drive."

Ritter opened the large garage doors and climbed into the front seat next to Khoury while Michelle got in the back with the chests and Metaxas' body. Khoury edged the camper out of the building; a glance toward the street indicated their problems weren't over.

"That's all we need," said Ritter as they stared helplessly at the shabby pickup truck pulling into the driveway, blocking their exit.

Metaxas' cousin," said Khoury. "Only two more minutes and we would have been clear." He slowly edged the camper down the driveway to the point where Metaxas' kinsman pulled in.

Khoury leaned out of the window and shouted. "Thanks, friend. We're on our way."

Two men and a girl. Probably the foreigners. "Where's Dimitri?" shouted the man.

"I'm Khoury. This is Ritter and Miss Simonet. Dimitri said he couldn't wait, left about five minutes ago with a friend in another car. His van is back there by the garage. Said he'd come back for it later." He jerked his hand in the direction of the garage.

Metaxas' van was clearly in view. The man scowled. "Didn't say anything to me about it."

"You just missed him," said Khoury. "He said he'd call you tonight or tomorrow morning. Said he had urgent business up north." The look on the man's face eased.

"Nice job on the camper," continued Khoury. "This color looks a hell of a lot better than the original green." A cautious smile. He knew the original color of the camper. "Also a good job on the new plates and the papers. You're a real professional."

The man smiled with pride. It was good to have one's work appreciated.

"We'd like to stay for coffee," added Khoury. "But we've got to get to Athens. Important government people waiting for us."

Metaxas' cousin understood. He and Dimitri had helped them get away from Voko, and now they would be able to make it to Athens and go over Voko's head to get their business settled. Dimitri had not been entirely clear on what it was all about, but the cousin knew it had something to do with the widely hated Voko. He was glad to be of help. "Have a good trip," he shouted. He backed the pickup out of the driveway to let them pass.

Khoury pulled into the street and halted momentarily beside the man. "Sorry about the spilled paint in the garage." he said. "Dimitri can explain." The man shrugged, waved, and watched them drive off. Nice folks. And, as Dimitri had told him, trusted friends.

It was early afternoon as they sped westward out of Trikala. They all looked tired and haggard. The strain of the past three days showed clearly on their faces. Both Khoury and Ritter badly needed a shave. Michelle's hair was stringy and unkempt. Her lips were parched and her face felt drained. She was afraid to look in a mirror. Ritter realized they were all going to need sleep soon. In addition, they had had nothing to eat since their snack shortly after midnight. Ritter was thinking how delicious a good old American McDonald's hamburger would taste. He was looking forward to never having to eat goat cheese again.

Michelle's stomach had still not entirely settled. She was brooding about the body wrapped in the ground cloth beside her. She had never had to dispose of a body before. The matter was beginning to worry her. How did one go about it? They couldn't just toss it out of the camper as they drove. The corpse would have to be hidden so it wouldn't attract attention for at least a few days—and preferably never. They wouldn't want to get caught in any kind of extradition problem. Not with the Greeks. She knew the men were also looking for a suitable place, but the drive through the valley from Trikala to Kalamabaka, where they would again climb into the mountains, offered no opportunities.

Khoury's thoughts had temporarily wandered elsewhere. He was thinking how good it was going to be to have money again, to be financially fluid. To have dinners at the George V and not have to fret about the cost. To drop a few thousand at the casino and not have to worry about it the next morning. To have the social power that money creates. Yes, it was going to be good to be rich again.

"We've got to dump him as soon as we can find a spot," said Ritter. He was looking at the map. "If we hurry, we can make the last ferry from Igoumenitsa to Corfu. That means we can catch the ferry to Brindisi too, and be safely out of Greece an hour before midnight. It's still early in the season, so we should have no trouble getting cabins. We can rest and freshen up on board. God knows, we all need it."

He turned to the back and winked encouragingly at Michelle. "How you feeling, beautiful?"

"Ugh," she replied, sticking out her tongue in disgust at the whole mess.

Khoury drifted back into the conversation. "I've been thinking about Zakros, Voko's cousin," he said.

"Zakros?"

"I have the feeling they were in the thing together all along. Obviously, Voko was not acting in an official capacity this morning. But there's a chance Zakros was involved and may now be wondering where his beloved cousin is. He may have even sent a search party. If Zakros reacts too quickly, there could still be trouble."

"Ah, come on, Elias," Ritter chided. "You've seen too many movies."

* * *

Christofos Zakros rubbed his enormous stomach, lifted his right leg slightly, and passed wind. He had just finished a generous lunch and was thinking about his customary afternoon nap. He had eaten even more than usual and now he needed a drink of soda water. He belched. And perhaps another ouzo.

He was waiting for a call from Voko. The colonel had called last night to say the watch on the foreigners was going well. He expected to have some results soon. Clever, that Voko. Always had been, since they were kids. As he had predicted from the beginning, a squeeze on the foreigners would force their hand and cause them to point the way to the real treasure site. Voko hadn't been fooled. He was too shrewd to fall for such an obvious trick. He suspected all along the foreigners were trying to make a fool out of him. But the only way to see their cards, as he explained, was to let them play out their hand. Once the gold was uncovered, Voko would know how to handle them, quietly and privately. And they would split the gold. But now it was getting late. In the past two days Voko had called by this time to report they were digging. It was unlike Voko not to keep in touch. Zakros picked up the phone and dialed.

* * *

As Michelle had realized, disposing of a body was not as easy as one would have thought. Particularly when one was pressed for time and worried about the body being found. That's what bothered Khoury. He had been too tired and distracted to think clearly about it before, but he realized now that if Metaxas' body was found and his family was able to add it all up, his death would point to Khoury. They would track Khoury for the rest of his life. The gold would be useless if he couldn't enjoy it in peace. On the other hand, if the body was never found, he could always stick to his cover story and blame the disappearance on Voko. Metaxas' family hated Voko and would believe anything against him. But Metaxas' corpse suffocated in paint, would point undeniably to Khoury. He would spend the rest of his life looking over his shoulder. They would have to do a good job of hiding the body. It would be best if they could do it at night, sticking it in a cave where it might not be found for years, where the remains could not be easily indentified, where there could be plausible denial. But on the other hand, they had to hurry. They had to make the Brindisi ferry tonight.

"We can't just dump it down a ravine or gorge. There are too many people wandering over these mountains. It would be found in no time. We've got to find something better," Khoury worried aloud. They had just passed through Kalamabaka and were climbing back into the mountains. The road was steep and winding. The temptation to throw the body over one of the steep cliffs in a deserted area was great. With each mile their options narrowed. There was no way they could risk driving onto the ferry with the body still in the back.

As they searched for a logical spot, the camper started to move more and more slowly.

"If we spend much time at this speed, we'll miss the ferry," said Ritter.

"Goddammit, don't you think I know it?" snapped Khoury. "But we just can't toss it any place."

"How about down there?" said Michelle. The mountainside sloped steeply away from the road toward a stream about 250 yards below. The forest was thick with pines and rocks. "We can cover it with rocks."

Ritter looked at the map. They had just passed through the small village of Orthovouni. The next town wasn't for over twelve miles. Orthovouni was some two miles behind them.

"Probably as good a spot as any," said Ritter.

"Okay," grumbled Khoury. "Let's try it." He pulled the camper off onto the narrow shoulder. They looked around. No signs of civilization. A truck passed on the other side of the road, heading toward Trikala. Traffic was steady on the road, but there was no evidence of any human activity in the area off the road itself.

They stepped out of the camper and stretched their arms and legs. After another brief look around, they quickly opened the back and pulled the body out. It was heavier than they had remembered.

"Just slide it down," said Khoury. "We'll take it about halfway and try to cover it there."

Michelle stayed with the camper while they slid down the hill with the body. About 150 yards below the road, they reached an almost level spot thickly covered with fir trees. "In here," said Khoury. "We'll cover him with these rocks." He and Ritter piled rocks and branches over the wrapped body. The mound was not particularly conspicuous. It would not be hard to find if someone was searching for it, but a casual hiker would never notice it. As they scrambled back up the hill, they reassured each other there was little if any chance of anyone accidentally coming upon the corpse. By the time anyone would, it would be so badly decomposed, there would be no chance of making a proper identification.

Khoury was feeling considerably relieved as they climbed in the camper and drove off. Michelle was delighted she no longer had to share the back with a corpse. She asked Khoury to open the sun roof. The spring sunshine was lovely, the fresh mountain air invigorating. If she had looked up through the roof at the proper angle, however, she might have seen Alexis Kalergos, a local shepherd, pulling up his trousers on the hillside above them on the other side of the road. Enjoying his daily constitutional, he had casually watched the whole thing. He was wondering what kind of garbage they had dumped.

* * *

Christofos Zakros was concerned. No one knew where Voko was. No answer at home. His wife had also vanished. This was highly unusual. He had not checked with his office since the night before. It was now late in the afternoon. The nagging thought was growing within him that perhaps something was wrong. Voko's office said Lieutenant Doriacles had also not reported for duty. The lieutenant's wife said she had not seen him since the day before, when he told her he was off on a special assignment. He had given her no details. He never did. Zakros realized he was the only person who knew what Voko and Doriacles were up to. After all, it was an unofficial act. That was the whole point, to keep it private. Was it possible something had happened to them? Zakros hated to show his hand. Perhaps Voko and Doriacles were busy disposing of the bodies of the foreigners and simply had no time to check in. If he said something too soon, he might spoil it. On the other hand, if something had gone wrong, there would be no time to lose. He would have to act fast. He was not sure what to do. He consulted his watch. Almost dinnertime. He finally decided. He would wait until after dinner. If he still hadn't heard from Voko by then, he would start making some checks. He was trying to remember. What was the name of the village Voko said the foreigners were hiding in?

* * *

The last ferry of the day left Igoumenitsa for Corfu just before eight P.M. It was a typical local car ferry with a long low deck in front for vehicles and a retractable ramp for driving them on and off. At the rear were the engines, bridge, and passenger accommodations. A small snack bar served coffee, spirits, sandwiches, and other light food. It was not the best food they had tasted, but it was the first solid nourishment they had consumed in nearly twenty hours, and the cold lamb sandwiches were wolfed down hungrily. Ritter enjoyed a frosty beer with his sandwich. The snack bar was placed so they could keep a watchful eye on the camper as they ate, to make sure no one decided to take an unauthorizd peek at the boxes in the back.

"You both could do with a shave," said Michelle. She reached out and rubbed Ritter's face affectionately.

Ritter sipped deeply on the beer. "We'll try to freshen up a bit before we go through customs," he said. "If we look too grubby, we might attract attention. Normally, there is no customs inspection for tourists at Corfu. That's what we want—to look like three happy tourists who've had a good time spending their money in Greece. We want to be waved through like everybody else. No special treatment, please."

Khoury was staring at the camper at the end of the ferry. It was all there. And they were getting close. No mistakes now, they were almost home. "Just three average tourists," he added. "With the usual souvenirs."

The ferry shuddered as it pulled into the quay at Corfu. The three got into the camper and drove off the ramp and into the city. It was a few minutes past nine-thirty p.m. They would have just enough time to drive onto the Brindisi ferry.

The town of Corfu was a busy, picturesque port of call for steamers plying between Brindisi and Piraeus, the port city of Athens. It was still early in the year, and the legions of sun seekers who in a few months would flock over the city's imposing sixteenth-century Venetian fortress were still in their living rooms worrying their travel agents. The modern harbor extended along the northwest edge of the city from the Adriatic steamer berths where they planned to catch the Brindisi ferry. The drive along the quay from the Igoumenitsa ferry berth below the fortress was quiet. They passed the Corfu customs headquarters at the base of the fortress.

"There it is," said Khoury.

"There what is?" asked Ritter.

"Customs. Let's hope they are having a dull day and will continue to have one."

"I have never wished anyone a more routine, quiet day in my life," said Michelle. She was combing her hair and working on her face. The rich, enticing scent of French perfume filled the camper.

"Christ, what's that?" said Ritter.

"A little diversionary scent," answered Michelle. "All us tourists wear it."

Khoury glanced in the rearview mirror. Michelle was changing into a fresh blouse. Her bra was briefly in view.

"Watch where you're going," she said, noticing his backward glances.

He smiled. It was a shame such a lovely thing had been wasted on Ritter for the entire trip. Ahead was the steamer ticket office, and beyond that, passport control and customs. Khoury tensed. This was it.

They pulled up to the office. It was already dark, but the brilliant port lights illuminated the scene in artificial sunshine. As they stopped to buy the tickets, Michelle got out of the camper and made a show of stretching her elegant arms and legs. The movements showed off her fine, trim body. In the artificial light she looked fresh and sexy, with no hint of the troubles of the past few days. Yes, there were tickets and space. Two cabins? No problem. They were lucky it was so early in the season. In just a month or so, reservations would be needed far in advance to get a cabin, much less two. The ticket taker looked at the men and at Michelle stretching herself like an expensive cat under the arc lights. He tried to guess which man she would be sharing the cabin with. He bet himself it was the sandy-haired American.

Michelle climbed back into the camper and they edged up to passport control. Khoury handed over their passports, with Michelle's and Ritter's American documents on top. They never bothered Americans. The immigration officer looked at them, taking a satisfying second look at Michelle. She winked at him. He smiled. "Enjoy your stay?"

"We just loved Greece," she said from the back. "Most beautiful country I've ever seen."

The man beamed with pride. He never got tired of hearing the tourists tell him how lovely his native country was. He stamped their passports and waved them through. The next moment was the big one. Customs. Khoury edged the camper up to a customs officer. He held the passports out the window; again the American papers were on top. The man signaled them to stop. He accepted the passports and examined them carefully.

"Anything to declare?"

"No," said Khoury. The man wiggled his nose. That was some perfume. He peered inside the dark camper. Michelle looked forward, smiling demurely at him.

The man returned the smile, handed the passports back, and waved them through. It was ten o'clock. In an hour they would be on the high seas, safely out of Greece and on their way to Italy.

* * *

The phone rang. It was one of Voko's deputies, the nondescript Lieutenant Koufala.

"We have spoken with Pangolis, the headman."

"Well?"

"He admits the three foreigners stayed in Mouzakion, but he insists they left with a man named Metaxas late yesterday evening. We have talked to a distant relative of Metaxas. They stayed at his house. He started talking when we took his wife into custody. He says they were looking for something in the hills outside of the village, artifacts. He said it was a dig for some historic goods that involved politicians in Athens. Claims he doesn't know who."

Artifacts, thought Zakros. Of course. Not a bad cover story. The kind of thing the simple villagers would believe. But the mention of the Athens politician was something new. He wasn't sure how that figured in. "But they didn't see Colonel Voko?"

"No, they swore they hadn't. It is always hard to say with these peasants, but I doubt if they did see the colonel."

"I assume you are searching the area?"

"We have a number of men out looking. But it is a large place. They could have been digging anywhere."

"Anything else?"

"Nothing really. We've received a preliminary report from the constabulary at Kalamabaka. It's sketchy; a local shepherd claims to have seen two men and a girl in a camper with Greek license plates pull a body out of the vehicle and conceal it on a hillside beyond the village of Orthovouni."

"Has the body been identified?"

"Not yet. Those local idiots just sent a vehicle for the corpse."

Voko? Zakros thought. Two men and a girl. It was possible. Along the Kalamabaka road. That meant they might be heading for the coast. For Corfu. With the gold. He looked at his watch. It was nearly eleven o'clock.

* * *

The luxury ferry *Carissa*, put into service in 1963, had a gross tonnage of 5,500 and carried in great comfort, according to the shipping company's prospectus, six-hundred passengers and sixty cars. Smart modern lounges and an excellent dining room as well as a swimming pool, an open-air bar, and comfortable cabins made it a pleasant way to cross the Adriatic.

After parking and locking the camper in the vehicle hold, they made their way to their cabins.

Ritter and Michelle spent nearly thirty minutes scrubbing each other in the shower, delighting in the luxury of making love under a stream of endless hot water. Their bodies were still sore from the dig, but the hot soak and the lovemaking relaxed them both. As Michelle rubbed her hair dry, Ritter shaved.

"I'd almost forgotten how good hot water feels on sore muscles," said Michelle.

"I'd almost forgotten how good hot water feels on some not-so-sore muscles," replied Ritter. "And then there are some things one never forgets."

"So I noticed." She smiled, forming a kiss on her lips.

"You're obviously feeling better."

"Hot water does wonders for me."

"Only hot water?"

She smiled again. She also was feeling better. "Let's get dressed. Elias will be waiting. Besides, my appetite is coming back with a vengeance. I'm really hungry."

"We'll certainly know what to give you the next time you have an upset stomach."

Khoury was already at the bar when they reached the main deck. He had also freshened up, and with a clean shirt and a jacket and slacks, he was again the Khoury of old, very much at ease in luxury surroundings. They had a quick drink together and went to the dining room.

"Pardon me if I forgo the goat cheese," said Ritter, "but I think a beefsteak will look pretty good to me. In fact, I think I could eat two. With a mixed salad and some good French wine."

"What, no retsina?" teased Khoury.

"Only for her," said Ritter, nodding at Michelle.

They all laughed. The dinner was excellent. The lights were dim, and soft dance music drifted softly out of the sound system. The harsh reality of the past few days began to recede.

"One more hurdle," said Khoury. "But it shouldn't be any real trouble. We will declare every bit of what we have. After all, there is no law against bringing gold into Italy. With the declaration form we get, there will be no problem in taking it out on the other end. In eighteen hours the gold should be safely in Switzerland."

"Amen," said Ritter. "I'll drink to that."

"I'll buy," said Khoury expansively. "What are you having?" A waiter stepped forward and collected the dessert plates. "We've got to have a good-night drink."

"Not me," said Michelle. "I'm tired. If you gentlemen will excuse me, I'm going to the cabin. It's already after midnight, and we'll be docking in less than six hours. I need a bit of beauty sleep."

"Go ahead," said Ritter. "We'll just have a quick one. I'll be along in a few minutes."

"Good night, Michelle," said Khoury. "See you in a few hours."

Michelle smiled, nodded, and headed for the cabin.

"Lovely girl," said Khoury as she walked off. "You're a lucky man."

"We couldn't have done it without her," said Ritter. "She came in handy several times."

"She did indeed," agreed Khoury. "I'm sorry now I opposed her coming. It worked out fine."

They each had a quick cognac. "Spin around the deck before retiring?" said Khoury.

"Why not?"

They paid and stepped out onto the main promenade deck. The night was cool and bracing, slightly overcast. There was no moon. Only a few stars peeked through the clouds. The deck was deserted. They strolled along for a few minutes, enjoying the fresh sea air. Ritter stopped and peered over the side at the white foam churned up by the large ship. The loud rushing sound as the ship cut through the water was a reassuring one, taking them farther and farther from Greece with each moment. Ritter looked out across the sea. Too dark to see anything. There were no lights. He turned back. Suddenly, it was obvious what had happened to Voko's Swedish-made m/40 automatic. Khoury was pointing it at him.

"What's this?" said Ritter.

"The end of our partnership, I'm afraid," said Khoury. "As they say, it's been fun, but it's time to part. As a final gesture of goodwill, however, I'm giving you a choice. You can dive over the side and swim for it, or we do it my way."

"Not much of a choice."

"Up to you."

"What about Michelle?"

"She's expecting you. She'll open the door with no problem. Then she will have the same choice through the cabin porthole. Maybe you can make it together." He didn't believe it.

"She said she didn't trust you. I should have believed her."

"Too late now. I'll count to five. When I reach five, you'll either be swimming or it's shark-bait time. One … two… three…"

Michelle's hand hammered professionally across the side of Khoury's neck. The blow stunned him. Before he could recover, she reached under him between his legs, and summoning all her strength, flipped him over the side. "I couldn't sleep," she said.

"I think he said he could swim," Ritter said.

"I really hope so," she replied.

"Really?"

"Yeah." She sighed. "He's got the keys to the camper in his pocket."

24

"Well, for fuck's sake, wake him up," bellowed Zakros. His vast stomach quivered as he shouted into the phone.

"But it's very unusual," said the uncertain voice on the other end of the line. After all, it was just after five in the morning. Waking up the captain at this hour was not the sort of thing the men lined up for.

"This call is officially made on behalf of Colonel Georges Voko," threatened Zakros. "If the captain hasn't called me back within five minutes, you'll be lucky if you get to spend the rest of your career on the Bulgarian border."

"Yes, sir," trembled the voice.

Zakros slammed down the phone. He didn't have the authority to order police personnel around, but he was becoming increasingly apprehensive, alarmed that something bad really had happened to Voko. He had to find out. For without Voko, without the implied power of the gun behind him, his own position as prefect was in jeopardy. He had made many enemies over the years. He knew it was only because of Voko's enormous power that he retained his position and own power. Without Voko he was vulnerable. In fact, without Voko, his life could even be in danger.

Voko had now been out of touch some thirty-six hours. There was no question something had happened. Zakros' fears were momentarily eased when he learned that the body found at Orthovouni was not the colonel's. The man had been identified by local police as one Dimitri Metaxas. The files revealed he was actively involved with the Cypriot EOKA-B movement and had been connected with a number of other gray activities. The police report showed he died of suffocation by paint. Large amounts clogged his nose and mouth, blocking the passage to his lungs. A brutal murder.

Zakros had no doubt the body had been dumped by Khoury, Ritter, and the woman and they were headed for Italy with the gold. After more telephone checks, he located the Igoumenitsa ferryboat operator, who confirmed that he had carried an American, a Greek, and a good-looking woman to Corfu on the last run of the evening. No, he hadn't noticed anything suspicious about them—except maybe for the smell of fresh lacquer on the camper. Otherwise, all he could say was that they looked a bit more tired and dirty than most tourists, except for hippies of course.

Finally, just before five a.m., Zakros got through to immigration at Corfu. The sleepy-voiced duty officer said that Khoury, Ritter and Miss Simonet had sailed for Brindisi aboard the *Carissa* at 2300. It was due to dock in less than an hour.

Not much time. The Italian police were only a call away, but it was not that simple. Thus far, Zakros realized, the evidence against the foreigners was only circumstantial. The shepherd who saw the body dumped was unable to provide any real descriptions or make any sort of identification other than to say he thought he saw three persons, probably two men and a woman. He couldn't remember the color of the vehicle; gray or brown—maybe. This alone was not enough to hold them, particularly outside Zakros' immediate area. He still needed something to connect them directly with Metaxas. But they certainly held the key to Voko and, of course, the gold. He had to find a way to hold them, to get them returned to Greece.

Metaxas' family was finally traced to Veria. They said they hadn't seen him in nearly three days. They suggested a check at Trikala, where Dimitri often visited with his cousin. He had mentioned something a few days ago about visiting this relative.

Zakros was now waiting for the police captain at Trikala to call him. Dammit. Why was that imbecile taking so long? In half an hour the boat would dock and they would slip out of his grasp forever. So would the gold.

The phone finally rang. A very grumpy voice. "This is Makri. What is it?"

Zakros, again invoking the name of Voko, explained they needed a quick check with Metaxas' cousin to see if he had seen Dimitri in the past day. He described Metaxas' death. It was very important. He hinted state security might be involved. The captain promised to check and call back.

The minutes shot by. It was already six o'clock. Time was running out. A feeling of panic swelled in his enormous belly. For a change Zakros was not hungry.

He grabbed the phone as it rang again.

"Makri here."

"Well?" Zakros demanded.

"We talked with Metaxas' cousin. Said he hasn't seen Metaxas in a week. Wondered why we were asking. Was obviously evading the question. I told him about the discovery of Metaxas' body. When

I mentioned the paint, he suddenly went into hysterics. Started screaming about three foreigners. What color was the paint on Metaxas' face?"

"Let me check." Zakros looked at his notes to be sure. "Tan."

"That's it."

Zakros quickly rang off. He had them. Metaxas' cousin could tie it all together. He called the international operator. It was official and most urgent. He must speak with Italian immigration police at Brindisi. It was already twenty minutes after six. God, he had them, if they hadn't already slipped through.

The boat's car park was sealed off to all passengers until fifteen minutes before docking at Brindisi. As soon as the doors to the hold opened, Ritter and Michelle dashed to the camper. Using a wire coat hanger, Ritter tried to jigger open the door by forcing it through the edge of the window, trying to pull open the inside door handle. Khoury had mentioned something about hiding an extra key somewhere inside the camper. If they could just open the door without attracting any attention, they could search for it. But the last thing they needed was a lot of friendly, curious Greek seamen climbing over the camper helping them, perhaps even thinking to inquire where their companion was. Or asking what was in the boxes. Ritter's brow sweated as he struggled with the coat hanger. Car thieves never had any trouble.

A young ship's officer walked over to them. "A problem?"

"Locked the keys in the camper." Ritter provided his most embarrassed what-an-ass-I-am grin.

"Happens more often than you would think," assured the young man. "Just a minute. I'll get some help."

"No... it's ... Please don't go to any trouble."

"No bother," said the man. "This has happened before. We're ready for it."

Ritter was still fishing with the coat hanger and considering breaking the glass when the young officer returned. A small crowd gathered to watch. One woman was peering in the back window of the vehicle. Thankfully, a drawn curtain blocked her view of the boxes. The boat was slowing noticeably; they would be docking shortly. The officer had a large ring of keys. He tried one. Didn't work. Nor did a second. Or a third. Or a fourth. He inserted a fifth. The button on the inside of the door popped up.

"Oh, thank you," gushed Michelle. The expression of gratitude in her voice was genuine.

"My duty, miss." He saluted and walked off. The crowd moved off to their own vehicles.

"Now, Khoury's extra key," muttered Ritter. They scrambled inside and began searching.. The big boat shuddered to a halt. The large doors at the end swung open. Cars in front of them and behind them switched on their ignitions, anxious to get away. The cars in front of them roared off. The man behind, an Italian, beeped. Michelle was on the floor of the camper searching under the dashboard. Ritter leaned out and shrugged. A universal gesture—camper won't start. The young officer was walking back toward them. The cars behind beeped impatiently. If they couldn't... "Found it," shouted Michelle. Joy. Under the floor mat.

"It's okay, officer. I dropped the key. Thanks very much for your help." Ritter waved, started the camper, and they drove out to face Italian customs.

Inspector Giovanni Bussino had just reported for duty. He really shouldn't have come to work at all. Not only was it his day off, but his wife was suffering from an infected foot and having trouble getting around the house looking after their hyperactive two-year-old son. But two members of the staff were sick and two others were on vacation. Someone had to cover the shift. Bussino scratched his pudgy face and looked in the cracked mirror as he washed his hands in the bathroom. *Porca miseria.* What conditions they had to work in. A real dump. Just look at the place. Filthy. People in private business didn't have to work under these conditions. Just civil servants. It wasn't fair.

He raised his head at the sound of cars. The ferry from Greece had docked. The first cars were rolling off with the usual tourists and business people. Brindisi customs was among the quieter posts. They kept a sharp eye out for American and European youths smuggling drugs in from Greece, businessmen who tried to cross with excessive amounts of cigarettes and liquor or untaxed goods, and truckers. Occasionally they could look forward to the seizure of a good supply of pornography. The magazines had great resell value on the black market, and Bussino was rather proud of his own growing collection. Generally, however, there was not much. But it was a job. The pay was steady and the pension would be adequate. Above all, with the payoffs from businessmen who wanted to avoid customs duties, he had been able to nearly pay for his farm overlooking the sea at Taranto on the instep of the heel. In fifteen years he could look forward to quiet retirement in relative comfort.

Bussino yawned. It was nearly a quarter after six. He still hadn't adjusted to getting up so early in the morning. Even after all these years, he hated to draw the early-morning shift. Even the sleepy overnights were better.

Bussino straightened his olive-colored uniform, patted his trim mustache in an approving way, and winked at himself. As he stepped out of the bathroom, a junior inspector called.

"Signore Bussino. Come quickly. Something special."

Madonna. Probably some kids trying to sneak marijuana in a knapsack. He hated to see them go off to jail, but it was his duty. "What is it this time?"

"Two Americans, signore. They have a special declaration to make."

He walked out to the vehicle-inspection shed. A sandy-haired man who looked like an American and a pretty woman who didn't were standing by a camper with Greek plates.

"May I help you?" asked Inspector Bussino. He made a small courteous bow in Michelle's direction.

"We would like to declare some gold," said Ritter matter-of-factly.

"Certainly, signore. How much is it?" Bussino expected to be shown a box of coins or perhaps a few small bars. It was not illegal to bring gold into Italy as long as it was properly declared and registered.

"It will have to be counted and weighed so there will be no mistake," said Ritter.

"Where it is, Signore?"

"Here." Ritter opened the back of the camper and pointed to five fairly large metal boxes.

Inspector Bussino stifled a gasp as Ritter opened the chests, *Madonna.* Millions and millions in lire in gold bars and coins. More money than he had ever seen. A treasure for a pope. For a moment he was speechless.

Ritter stood patiently as the inspector gawked at the gold trying to retain his composure.

"Yes, well … We'll have to move the boxes into the office for the counting," said the inspector finally. He snapped his fingers and a junior officer hastened over. "Help the signore move these into my office," he said in Italian.

One by one, Ritter, the young inspector, and Michelle lugged the heavy boxes into the office. Bussino, his Italian sense of manhood and chivalry offended by the sight of Michelle doing such heavy work, attempted to stop her. "No, no, signora," he pleaded. "We'll get someone else to help."

"Thank you, signore," she said. "I can do it. I insist." Bussino was not offended enough to step in and help himself. He nodded in a respectful way. The boxes were moved.

Bussino fumbled through one of the file cabinets searching for the proper forms, which he located after a good deal of paper throwing, cursing, and accusations aimed at his staff about their filing procedures.

The count began. It was hard to estimate, but Bussino guessed there might be as much as two billion lire worth of gold before him. Staggering. Halfway through the count of the second box, the phone rang. The aide helping with the count answered. "For you signore. Greek police."

Giovanni Bussino was not a particularly intelligent man, but he was no fool either. It was obvious the Americans had brought the gold out of Greece illegally. It had to be so, because it was a violation of Greek law to take large amounts of gold bullion or coins out of the country. It was not clear how the man had acquired it, but technically that did not concern him. It was not against the law to bring the gold *into* Italy, and unless there was some official charge or complaint from the Greeks, he was not in a position to refuse to register gold.

Thus the call from Greece did not surprise him. One just didn't leave a country with that kind of treasure without someone saying something about it. The caller, in accented English, identified himself as a prefect somewhere in Macedonia. Christofos Zakros, he said, calling on behalf of the Macedonian Gendarmarie. He wanted to alert the Italian authorities to the expected arrival of two Americans—a man and a woman—and a Lebanese. They were travelling in a tan Volkswagen camper with Greek registration. It was possible they were carrying boxes that belonged to the Greek government. They were wanted on suspicion of murder.

Bussino excused himself and stepped into another office to complete the call.

Ritter tried to continue the count, pretending he had no idea of what was going on. He maintained a deadpan expression as a herd of elephants stampeded across the pit of his stomach. He glanced at Michelle. She smiled reassuringly and continued the count as the aide registered and double-checked each bar.

In the next office, Bussino picked up the phone. "Who are these people?" he asked.

"The American is called Ritter," said Zakros. "The woman's name is Simonet. The other man is Khoury. They should be on the ferry from Corfu."

"What is the charge against them?"

"Murder of a Greek national."

"A serious charge, signore. Do you have a warrant for their arrest?"

"Uhh, no, not yet. But we are working on one."

"What is this about boxes?"

"The boxes contain, ah, items that belong to the Greek people."

"Items?"

"Yes, uh, some gold artifacts and other antiquities that belong to Greece. They have great cultural and historical value."

Yes, thought Bussino. Great historical value indeed. Bussino's mind turned over as fast as it would go. He was no human computer, but the picture was clear enough. There was no Lebanese, but these were definitely the people the Greek was seeking. He claimed they were wanted for murder but did not yet have an official warrant. That meant there was not yet a formal charge. But if the Americans were detained now, the Greeks would have no trouble coming up with one. And if they were detained, the boxes would have to be returned to Greece with the Americans. Returning the boxes to Greece was not exactly what Giovanni Bussino had in mind.

"Just a momento, signore, let me check. Many vehicles have already passed through from the boat. It docked a bit early." Bussino put down the phone and wandered out of the room to the inspection shed. He glanced around, waited a proper interval, then returned to the phone.

"Hello, signore. There was no sign of any Lebanese, but two Americans went through about fifteen minutes ago. They drove out via the green alley, meaning they had no declaration to make. They were routinely waved through, as are most tourists."

Missed them. Zakros cursed his bad luck. "Can you catch them?" he asked anxiously. His feelings showed in his voice.

"I am afraid it would be nearly impossible, signore. We have no facility for that here. This is a simple customs post. Now they are past, you will have to place such a request through Rome."

Delay. The deadliest form of denial. Zakros sensed it, but could do nothing about it. He could try to contact Rome through normal Interpol channels, but it would take time, and because it was clearly beyond his authority, would involve officials in Athens. It was all over.

In frustration and rage, Zakros hung up. He did not hear Bussino's parting comment. "I'm sorry I cannot help you, signore."

Bussino would see the gold count was speeded up and finished as quickly as possible. Then he would see his copy of the registration form never made it into the files. The aide involved in the count, properly looked after, would forget there had ever been such an incident, and he would not discuss it with the others. Bussino picked the phone up. He had to reach his brother Mario as soon as possible.

* * *

"You see, the Italians are not as bureaucratic as you feared," said Michelle. "The man could not have been any nicer or more efficient."

"I know," said Ritter. "It bothers me."

"You mean the call from Greece?"

"That too."

"You thought maybe it was the police or that pig Zakros?"

"I was *scared* for a minute. I'm still not sure. The customs guy seemed much friendlier, much more accommodating after the phone call. As though there was a connection."

"You could be right. But is it possible he just respected so much wealth? Or maybe he was a typical, friendly, warm-hearted Italian?"

"Not a customs inspector. Not anywhere in the world."

"Well, let's not worry about it. One more border to cross and it's all behind us. The worst is already past." She waved the customs form and put it back in her handbag. "Our ticket to Switzerland and home."

"It is beautiful," admitted Ritter. "Almost as beautiful as your bottom."

"That's the Brian I love."

It slipped out before she realized it. She hadn't meant to say it. But it was out.

Ritter reached one hand over and placed it high up on her thigh. A loving squeeze. "I didn't think you were the type to fall for an aging treasure hunter with an uncertain future."

"I'm not that concerned about your future. But I've always had a thing about aging treasure hunters. I just never got around to telling you."

"How can I be sure you're just not another treasure-hunter groupie?"

"What groupie did you ever know that didn't mind spending her nights digging in the cold rain and sharing sleeping accommodations with a sneaky Greek-Lebanese?"

He moved his hand the rest of the way up her thigh and gave another squeeze.

They had been cruising along the autostrada toward Naples for over an hour when he first noticed the red Fiat behind them. The car suddenly appeared from nowhere, obviously having approached at high speed and then positioned itself about a quarter of a mile behind them. The Fiat had remained in that position for almost forty-five minutes. The camper was doing fifty-five miles an hour. No Italian with a sporty red Fiat drove only fifty-five on the autostrada.

"I think we've got company," he said finally.

"Hmmm?"

"A car behind us. Red Fiat I think they're following us."

"Maybe a car full of treasure-hunter groupies," she said, twisting her head around. She stared through the back window for a few minutes. "But I never heard of boy groupies for a guy like you."

"Exactly."

"Pals of the customs man?"

"Maybe. We'll stop at the next gas station and tank up. See what happens. If they are following us, I doubt they'll try anything there."

The stop produced the result Ritter expected. The Red Fiat pulled into the rest area and lingered while they filled the tank. Four men inside appeared to take no notice of them. One got out and went through the motions of relieving himself by the side of the rest area. Under other circumstances, Ritter and Michelle would never have given them a second glance. As Ritter pulled back onto the autostrada, the Fiat resumed its position about a quarter of a mile behind them.

"No question," said Ritter. "Just waiting for the right chance. Perhaps for dark, or hoping we'll stop where they can get a crack at us."

"Maybe we could lose them off the autostrada," said Michelle. "We obviously can't outrun them in this thing."

Ritter grunted affirmatively. After some discussion and a look at the map, they decided to go off the autostrada into one of the adjacent towns and try to lose the Fiat in urban traffic. The town was not overly large, but it seemed it would be large enough for their purposes. Then they could find a less obvious route north and lose the Fiat forever.

Ritter quickly discovered it wasn't that easy. The driver of the Fiat was aggressive and skillful. His car was also much faster and more maneuverable in traffic. After nearly twenty five hectic minutes of cat-and-mouse through the town, it was clear to Ritter he wouldn't be able to shake them off so easily. The Fiat driver ran red lights when he had to, once ran up onto the sidewalk, and generally stayed close behind. By now, the chase was obvious to both parties. Each knew the other knew. Ritter guided the camper out of town and onto a road that led to the surrounding hills. The Fiat dropped back, waiting for the false move that would provide the shot for the hunters.

The red car maintained its distance as they wound their way upward. The road was narrow, as Ritter hoped. The shoulders were uncertain, inadequate. The dropoffs on the sides were becoming steeper and more perilous.

"Let's try it now," Ritter jammed the accelerator to the floor and raced the camper down a small hill as fast as he could, building up speed, tearing into a turn, and then dashing up the next rise, obviously making an attempt to lose the Fiat. The other driver reacted predictably. No camper could outrun a Fiat driven by Mario Bussino on these roads. He would show them.

The more powerful Fiat closed the gap quickly, roaring up behind the camper. Ritter swerved into the middle of the road to block them from overtaking—a clear challenge. One of the men was waving a pistol; they were probably all armed. Michelle rolled back the sun roof. The Fiat tried again to overtake them, but this time Ritter made only a minor attempt to block the pass. The Fiat roared up alongside. A single point-blank shot from the man seated next to the driver would be enough to stop Ritter and the camper.

The men in the Fiat didn't notice Michelle creeping through the sun roof. The red car was running flat out in second gear now, directly alongside. A pistol aimed at Ritter thrust through the window.

Michelle hurled the heavy jack in her hand. It crashed through the Fiat's windshield, smashing the glass and Mario Bussino's forehead. His hands flew off the steering wheel, clutching his shattered face. The Fiat swerved unsteadily, bounced against the camper, and then careened off, pitching over the other side of the road into the valley below.

"Jesus," said Ritter, rubbing his hand over his head, pushing the sweat away from his forehead. Michelle dropped back down into the camper. She said nothing. There was nothing to say.

Shortly after midnight, Ritter and Michelle crossed safely and without incident into Switzerland. Glancing at their American passports, the sleepy Italian customs officer on duty, anxious to get back into his warm shack, waved them through. He showed no interest in the camper. Ironically, they didn't need the gold-declaration form. A more alert Swiss officer checked their passport pictures against their faces, and they were in.

Suddenly the exhaustion of the past week caught up to them. Michelle brushed away moisture collecting in her eyes. Ritter ached in every bone. The road to Geneva was covered in relative silence. It was early Sunday morning when they rolled into Geneva and checked into their hotel. The place had an underground garage where they could park the camper in relative safety until the banks opened Monday morning.

The window curtains were tightly pulled shut so no one could peer into the vehicle. They locked it, double-checked all the locks, and headed up to their room overlooking Lake Geneva.

Little needed to be said. As he kicked off his shoes, Ritter reached into a small refrigerator bar in the room and liberated a bottle of champagne. The pop of the cork was very much a victory sound, an expression of celebration and success. He poured them each a glass. It was a good moment.

Michelle raised the glass to her face, letting the bubbles spray refreshingly onto her upper lip and nose. They had done it.

"To the last dig of my life," said Ritter. "And all future dives."

"To the end of the retsina days," she responded. They laughed and drank, first the champagne, then each other. For the first time since leaving Thessalonica, they fell into each other's arms in comfort and joy. The pressure was off, the reward in their hands, eyes, mouths and hearts. There was nothing to do until the banks opened Monday morning but enjoy themselves and each other and sleep.

* * *

Ritter blinked and opened his eyes. His arm flapped expectantly across the bed. The other side was empty. He sat up. The room was dark, but the bright edges around the curtains indicated it was daylight. Ritter yawned, stretched his arms and torso, and forced himself out of bed. He pulled open the curtains and looked out over the lake to the snow-capped mountains beyond. It was going to be a beautiful Monday morning. He had rarely felt so refreshed.

"Michelle," he called. Probably in the bathroom. There was no answer. He walked over to the bathroom door and knocked. "Hey, beautiful, come out of there. Let somebody else use it." No answer. He pushed open the door. She was not there.

Probably gone for a walk or to get a paper. That was when he saw the note propped on the mirror.

He picked it up and read, numbly:

"Brian, I'm sorry, but the boxes do not belong to you. They were a secret Lend-Lease allocation meant for Greek partisans. The government sent me to find them. And so I did. I hadn't counted on finding you. Please try to forgive me. M."

Cursing silently, Ritter quickly pulled on a pair of jeans, a shirt, and shoes and rushed to the elevators. An eternity later the doors slid apart in the garage, revealing the obvious. The camper was gone.

25

Michelle slipped silently into the carpeted hallway. She glanced back a last time at Ritter, curled up peacefully, innocently, contentedly in the double bed. She closed the door softly. Ritter would not wake for another few hours at least. They'd never prepared her for this. During the long months of training at Camp Perry, no one had adequately warned her about getting personally involved.

She rode quietly down in the elevator, tears sliding unprofessionally off her cheeks, thinking back to her recruitment almost ten years ago. The man had been a friend of her father's years before. At least he had claimed to be a friend. That had been enough to convince her to accept a dinner invitation.

The man talked about her father, what a fine, patriotic person he had been. How he voluntarily had given up a secure noncombat executive job with a safe defense clearance to join the fight against the Germans.

He talked about the dangers to the world, the growing Communist threat, the continuing challenge to the West, to democratic insitutions and freedoms. Her father had accepted and died for the same challenge. Two decades later the fight was far from over. The fight for freedom would never end. She was needed to help.

At first, Michelle hadn't quite understood. But as the man continued to talk, she slowly realized what he was offering, what he was asking. He didn't say exactly whom he represented, but it was increasingly obvious.

The idea of working for the Central Intelligence Agency excited her. Kennedy was dead, but the nation more than ever needed the enthusiastic participation of its youth. Her marriage had just broken up. She needed something to fill the vacuum. The prospect of a career with the CIA was appealing.

Following the harrowing months of training in Virginia, they decided she should resume her studies in France. She was in a perfect position to keep tabs on the leftist student groups increasingly infiltrated by militant Communists threatening France's and thus Europe's basic stability.

Life in the university community was challenging. The leftists wanted to bring down France's entire political and economic structure. She felt they offered nothing but hollow slogans as a replacement. She was proud of her small role in trying to thwart them.

During a student crisis, it became clear she had fallen under suspicion of one of the more radical and dangerous groups she had infiltrated. It was decided to transfer her for her own safety to London. Her assignment was similar—to infiltrate the leftist university groups.

During a quiet period, the station chief asked her to try her hand at finding a lead on the First Armored Brigade gold. It was one of the

London station's unfinished projects, low on the list of priorities. But it *was* a quiet period. Her boss asked her to take a week or two and poke around, see what she could find. Maybe they could at least get it off the books. That was when she ran into Ritter in the library. The rest of it had fallen into her lap before she realized what was happening. The chief told her to follow along, try to bring back the gold to a point where the agency could retrieve it.

She knew she would have to seduce Ritter to make the trip. It was an enjoyable task. But she never counted on falling in love. She had believed she was too professional.

The big lovable trusting oaf. He'd waited his whole life for a strike like this, and now she was pulling it out from under him. Of course, the gold wasn't his to begin with. In one of the first of many secret deals under the Lend-Lease Act, President Franklin Roosevelt had arranged for it to be flown secretly to Greece to be used by the hard-pressed British to pay their Greek allies and to set up partisan groups to resist the Germans, particularly in the case of an invasion which everyone knew would come. The British never had a chance to use the gold the way it was intended. In a top-secret report that eventually reached Washington, the British had reported its loss.

Michelle watched the lights blink as the elevator sank slowly into the bowels of the hotel. Why should the gold be returned to the government now? They didn't need it. It was financial peanuts where budgets were counted in billions. It was strictly a paperwork exercise, clearing up a still-open file at the request of a faceless Washington bureaucrat. If she hadn't met Ritter, he and Khoury would have gone to Greece without her and the agency would never have heard about it. By right, the gold belonged to whoever found it.

The elevator door slid open. She stepped out into the neon-lit concrete garage. There was the camper, undisturbed.

She reached inside the vehicle, which still smelled faintly of lacquer. Everything was in order. Yes, the gold really was Ritter's. After all, he had found it. He had recovered it. That was the universal law of treasure hunters. But she was under orders. The success of this assignment would look good in her record. It would help her career.

Perhaps they could take it together to the embassy. Ritter would get a hefty finder's fee. They would pay him a third, maybe half. Yes, to hell with it. Back upstairs and explain everything. She was in love with him. And he felt the same way about her. She knew it. If she took off with the gold now, he would be out of her life forever. She had to talk to him. She just couldn't run out like this. No. It wasn't worth it. Life could be very long.

She turned to hurry upstairs, before he woke, before he saw the damning note.

"Just a moment, my dear." A voice came from behind the car in the shadows next to the camper. She hardly knew the man, but she realized immediately who it was. She looked around at the sad mousy face with wire-rim glasses.

J. Alfred Thompson stepped cautiously forward. The pistol, a Webley & Scott .45 partially concealed under a newspaper, was pointed directly at her.

"Just going up to get Brian," she said, vainly trying to bluff. "He said we weren't meeting you until ten o'clock."

"As you can see, I've come a bit early. It was good of Brian to call from Italy. A most conscientious partner. But I'm afraid I can't wait until ten. In fact, my dear, it almost looked there for a moment as if you yourself were considering dissolving your relationship with Brian and me. Indeed, that time has come, I fear. But it must be under slightly different circumstances than you were planning. The banks will be open in a few hours, and I want to make an early deposit in one of those wonderful, untraceable secret numbered accounts. Now, let's get in."

Michelle glared at Thompson. The old fox. If the arthritis Brian had mentioned was bothering him now, he certainly was not letting it show. The Webley looked very menacing. His hand was steady. She might be able to disarm him, but the odds were not good. He was aging and his reflexes would be slow, but he had a clear, easy shot at her. The .45 was powerful. One shot would do it. It would be best at this point to open the camper, wait for a chance to get the old bastard. Slowly and deliberately she pulled the keys from her pocket and opened the door. Thompson motioned her to the driver's side. He followed, still pointing the pistol at her.

"You take it from here, my dear. I'll let you know where we're going as we drive along."

Thompson concealed the Webley under the newspaper as they paid the parking fee and drove out of the garage.

"We'll go for a little drive into the country," he said calmly. "It's just until the banks open, you understand. Perhaps we can find a nice quiet spot, out of the way. We can rest and wait. Yes, a very quiet spot. I don't want to have to trouble you with all that boring old banking business."

* * *

Merde! Rudolf Margion had rarely been so angry. He had been with the company nineteen years and the boss had just given the pleasant lake route to a man who had been with the company only twelve years. By right of seniority, Margion felt the highly desired lake run should be his. It was a shorter run and there were fewer stations. The job was much easier than the Geneva-suburb route he was stuck with that took him every day through heavy city traffic and the dangerous hard-to-drive, twisting rural roads. He was sick of it. After all these years, they should have given him the lake run. He would talk to the union. Launch a protest. Maybe a strike. That would do it. That would bring them to their knees. That was the only kind of reasoning the bastards understood. Damn. The more he thought about it, the more furious he became.

Margion was still cursing his luck and his boss when he carelessly ran through the red light. From the side, the camper seemed to leap through the intersection into his path. Whoever was driving obviously wasn't looking. Too late he leaned on his horn, simultaneously trying to brake and swerve the big rig out of the way. But he was going too fast.

26

Three steps at a time, Ritter assaulted the concrete stairs to the ground level breathlessly confronting the heavy-eyed ticket collector who controlled access to the hotel garage.

"Tan camper," he demanded. "You see it leave?"

The man poked an index finger into his right ear, drilling for wax. "Good-looking woman and an old man?"

Old man? Christ. Thompson. Ritter nodded weakly.

"Just left," said the man, gazing curiously at the tip of his finger, casually examining his find. "About five minutes ago. Headed up that way, toward the mountains." He nodded his head in that direction.

Ritter swirled, dashing to the taxi rank.

"Where to, sir?" asked the driver as Ritter jumped into the cream Opel.

"Straight ahead. Fast," barked Ritter. "And hurry."

"Somewhere in particular?" inquired the driver.

"Looking for a tan Volks camper," urged Ritter. "Just left the hotel garage."

The driver shrugged and goosed the Opel, speeding up slightly. Ritter was seated behind him, anxiously scanned the road.

God, this was insane. Thompson and Michelle had crossed him. It didn't make sense. He never imagined she would bug out on him. They had been through too much together. But that was just it. You could never tell about women. He would have been ready to spend the rest of his life with her. To settle down, maybe even start a family.

He exhaled deeply. He couldn't get over her leaving him. The gold must have mattered far more to her than he realized. Gold. Fucking gold. It did strange things to people. Unpredictable things. He'd seen it a lot of time in the Caribbean.

And Thompson. The shrewd old bastard. Arthritis. Shit.

"Faster," urged Ritter.

"There's a speed limit in the city, sir," protested the driver gently. Behind them a siren screamed. Ritter glanced back. A frantically blinking blue light was closing fast on the cab.

"Ach," grumbled the driver. "You see!" he shrieked, accusation in his voice. He slowed the taxi.

The police car swept past them, the two uniformed men not giving the taxi a second glance.

"Not after us!" shouted Ritter as he intensely peered ahead. "Follow them! Hurry!"

The road eased through a gentle S curve, the last turn revealing the awful reason for the police activity. A devastating crash in an intersection ahead. Vehicles were burning, blocking the street, the brilliant fire sending up a thick column of dense black oil smoke.

Flames engulfed both wrecked vehicles. One was obviously large, like an oil or gasoline truck. The other was -- oh, God, the camper.

Ritter leaped out of the taxi, sprinting toward the fire. Anyone in either vehicle had certainly perished. Roasted.

A policeman roughly grabbed Ritter by the arm. "Move back," he ordered sternly. "You can't go there. It's too dangerous. That's a gas tanker. It could blow again." More sirens. Fire engines rushing.

Ritter stared helplessly. It was all over. Finished. All dead. The two British officers. Poor incompetent Waddell. Voko and his walrus-faced assistant. Greedy Mataxas. The opportunist Italians. Perfidious Khoury. Melanie. And now Thompson and Michelle. All for some lousy gold bars. He was the only survivor.

Suddenly, a voice speaking to him. It couldn't be . . .

"Brian…Brian…" Stunned, Ritter swirled around. Gasping for breath, he took a step forward. With blood on her face, Michelle limped toward him. This couldn't be possible. No one could have survived the crash. But somehow, she had.

Michelle grabbed Ritter, wrapped her arms around him. She fiercely held him in a way that suggested she would never let go.

"I'm so sorry. A terrible mistake. I'm so sorry." Her body was shaking. "Thompson," she sobbed. "H…he had no intention of sharing the gold. He intended to kill me once we got away from civilization. I jumped out of the camper when we slowed at the turn. The camper kept on going into the intersection."

27

As he had stared at the burning wreckage, it was obvious the gold was gone.

There was no way to recover it. The van had been purchased by Khoury. Ritter had no legal connection to it. In fact, there was no obvious connection of any kind. It was impossible for him to make any claim for the anonymous smoldering, melted metal on the street in front of him. Also, there would be awkward questions about the charred body with the gun found in the incinerated van. For all they had been through, now there was an overwhelming sense of loss. Heartbreak. Ritter's gold was not to be. It would become the unclaimed property of the Swiss gnomes.

They had dragged themselves back to the hotel, Michelle limping badly. She refused to see a doctor. Tearfully, she explained what had happened. Her sobs were almost uncontrollable as she talked about the note. Torn between a sense of duty and her feelings for Ritter, she had momentarily made a dreadful choice. She was blocked by

Thompson from going back up to the room to destroy the note. In turn, Ritter could only feel relief. He had not lost her. He held her tightly until she finally calmed. A near disaster had been avoided.

They spent the rest of the day struggling with an immense sense of depression and exhaustion, both fiscal and mental. They could only appreciate they were alive and with each other. Ritter was now contemplating what he would do next. What about Michelle? Her CIA connection had shocked him. How could he have missed that? But he also was impressed. She was a serious human being. And something he never thought he would find. Someone to spend his life with.

Rummaging through his bag to check his passport, he recognized something he had not thought about. He suddenly shouted. "Michelle, look. Look at this!"

Dozing on the bed, Michelle opened her eyes and raised her head. Ritter was waving a piece of paper he had pulled from the bag.

She glanced at him. In a drowsy voice, she asked, "What's that?"

"Look what's here. The key to the gold."

She looked puzzled. She didn't understand. In her mind, the treasure was gone. What was this about?

Ritter was now jumping around, waving the paper. "How could I have forgotten this? How bloody stupid!"

Michelle sat up and, swinging her legs around, was sitting on the edge of the bed.

He handed it to her. She looked at the paper. With an explosive yelp, she leapt to her feet. They both started laughing, uncontrollably, tears flowing on both their faces. They hugged, consumed in an exhilarating emotional moment. They looked at the paper again. Yes, how could they have forgotten?

It was the customs declaration from Brindisi that perfectly accounted for the amount of gold that would be found in the wreckage. It had Ritter's name and passport number on it as well as the license plate number of the van. There would also be the remains of one of the boxes with the British Army markings. And now he would have a powerful arm of the U.S. government as a partner. They also wanted the gold.

* * *

Michelle and Ritter stepped out into the bright May sunlight. It was a beautiful spring morning in Washington. Summer was almost upon them. The comforting smell of fresh flowers enhanced the moment. The scent of cherry blossoms, already forgotten, had been replaced by rhododendrons and dogwoods. The lovely sounds of chirping mockingbirds were mixed with distant traffic noises and a plane that had just lifted off from Dulles International Airport.

After several weeks of meetings with various officials and government people, their lives had changed forever.

Indeed, there had been tough questions about the identity of the burned body in the van with the gun. But with the assistance of the man from the U.S. consulate, everything had been smoothed over. The CIA had ways of explaining away dead bodies.

Ritter and Michelle had then left Geneva, flying to Washington, where Michelle resigned from the Company.

"I never thought I would ever visit the CIA," said Ritter. "And I certainly never thought I would be partnered with them."

He glanced back at the impressive building before they headed to their car.

"They bargained pretty hard, but I'm glad for a 25 per cent cut. Actually, it's a greater percentage than I've gotten in a lot of other hunts. And it was close to the original one third we had been working for. So I can't complain."

"Brian, he was just a bureaucrat doing his job," said Michelle. "It was an open file that needed to be closed. And it was time for me to resign and get on with my life." She chuckled. "With you."

Nothing stirred Brian Ritter more than Michelle's laughter. It was a marvelous, joyful, often mischievous sound that affected him in a way that nothing else could. He found himself staring at her. Her limp was almost gone. How had this happened? A visit to a library at the right moment. That's all it took.

Days later, they were in the Florida Keys, where her sister lived in a large oceanfront property. The salty breeze caressed their bodies, relaxing their souls. But it didn't take long for Nelson to show up, trying to draw Ritter into another treasure hunt.

"They say it's one of the most valuable seventeenth century wrecks ever. And it's located just off Key West. My friend Mel says he knows more or less where it is. He can help us find it. And there would be no digging on a cold, rainy, and inhospitable rocky mountain in the dark. What do you say?"

Ritter smiled. Michelle shrugged. Another day, another treasure? What could possibly go wrong?

About the Author

Frank Hawkins was a clandestine intelligence agent for the DIA during the Cold War, operating out of the shadowy Bremerhaven Station running agents into Eastern Europe. Subsequently he became a foreign and war correspondent for The Associated Press in South Asia, East Asia, Europe and the Middle East where he headed up all AP operations in the Arab countries as well as Iran and Cyprus from his post in Beirut. In the 1980's, he was a senior officer at Knight-Ridder, then one of the largest newspaper companies in the world. Hawkins also had a stint as president of a small Hong Kong conglomerate and went on to successfully start his own consulting companies while living in the Florida Keys. He is the author of the highly rated *"The Zurich Printout"* and co-author of *"$ea Weed,"* which we wrote together with his daughter Liv. He and his wife Inge live adjacent to the Everglades in a space shared with an alligator they call Fred.

www.ingramcontent.com/pod-product-compliance
Lightning Source LLC
LaVergne TN
LVHW011442170325
806119LV00030B/277